PRETTY ON THE OUTSIDE

PRETTY ON THE OUTSIDE

Young, Loaded, and Fabulous

KATE KINGSLEY

Simon Pulse
New York London Toronto Sydney

This book is a work of fiction. Any references
to historical events, real people, or real locales are used fictitiously.
Other names, characters, places, and incidents are the product
of the author's imagination, and any resemblance to actual events
or locales or persons, living or dead, is entirely coincidental.

SIMON PULSE
An imprint of Simon & Schuster Children's Publishing Division
1230 Avenue of the Americas, New York, NY 10020
First Simon Pulse paperback edition April 2010
Copyright © 2008 by Brubaker & Ford, Ltd.
Originally published in Great Britain in 2008 by the Headline Publishing Group
Published by arrangement with the Headline Publishing Group
All rights reserved, including the right of reproduction
in whole or in part in any form.
SIMON PULSE and colophon are registered trademarks
of Simon & Schuster, Inc.
For information about special discounts for bulk purchases,
please contact Simon & Schuster Special Sales at 1-866-506-1949
or business@simonandschuster.com.
The Simon & Schuster Speakers Bureau can bring authors
to your live event. For more information or to book an event contact
the Simon & Schuster Speakers Bureau at 1-866-248-3049 or visit
our website at www.simonspeakers.com.
Designed by Cara E. Petrus
The text of this book was set in New Baskerville.
Manufactured in the United States of America
2 4 6 8 10 9 7 5 3 1
Library of Congress Control Number 2009927681
ISBN 978-1-4169-9399-5
ISBN 978-1-4169-9920-1 (eBook)

To Joan, Philip, Anabel,
and Dotson

CHAPTER ONE

*A*lice Rochester walked straight to the front of the line outside Emerald's, the exclusive Members Only club in Mayfair where she was meeting her boarding-school chums. People glared at her and muttered under their breath. Too bad for them. When you have a father as powerful as Richard Rochester, you don't wait around on the street.

"Hi there, Graham," Alice purred, flashing her most charming smile.

"Evening, Miss Rochester," the doorman said, touching his blue cap and lifting open the club's heavy velvet curtain for her. Alice brushed past, trailing a cloud of jasmine perfume. Victory, as usual. Bouncers, taxi drivers, the ladies who served lunch in the school dining room—she could always get everyone to do what she wanted.

Inside, Emerald's was dim and steamy, lit only by glowing panels of pink and green and blue light. London's teenage

It crowd sipped £15 Cosmopolitans from gleaming glasses at the bar, while the DJ blasted hits from the seventies and eighties—the kind of tunes Alice and her friends would get drunk and grind to later.

But Alice ignored the music for now; she wouldn't be caught dead dancing on her own. Instead, she craned her neck toward the back of the room. There her crew was. She could just make them out through the darkness, lounging on low-slung couches around Seb Ogilvy's table. Dropping the Ogilvy name guaranteed that the barman would serve them, even though most of them were only sixteen. Alice spied three bottles of champagne cooling in a big silver ice bucket. There'd be more where that came from. Bring it on.

Weaving her way toward her friends, she slipped safely through a vortex of sloppily dancing men with their shirts untucked and their crotches gyrating like blenders. Bunch of jackass bankers, probably. Alice despised types like that. But it was good to be home. Holidaying in her family's St. Tropez villa was fine for a week—but a month of doing nothing but sunbathing, swimming, playing tennis, and eating French food with her parents and two brothers, Hugo and Dominic? Mind-numbing! If Alice had to stomach one more piece of Brie, she was going to be sick. Thank fuck that in the morning the Rochesters' chauffeur, Marshy, was driving her and her best friend Natalya Abbott back to St. Cecilia's School—the eighteenth-century stately pile, surrounded by rolling fields, where Alice had been a student since she was eleven years old.

"Oh my *god!*" a voice yelped. "Sweetie, you're home! I'm so happy!" Natalya Abbott flung her arms around Alice's neck, almost spilling the martini that a smitten admirer had just bought her at the bar. "Oops!" she giggled, swaying unsteadily on her platform heels.

"Darling!" Alice cried. "I missed you so much." She swept her gaze up and down her friend. Tally's white-blond hair was cascading onto her shoulders and her cheeks were flushed. Her slender, lithe figure always reminded Alice of those Toulouse-Lautrec sketches of Parisian can-can dancers—the ones Alice had bought posters of at the National Gallery last year and tacked above her dormitory bed at school. Tally wasn't tall, but like them, she moved with a wild, chaotic grace that magnetized men wherever she went. It drove Alice mad that boys were so taken in by her best friend—by the fact that she was half-Russian and so flighty she could barely tie her own shoelaces. Oh, and by the fact that she was beautiful. You didn't need to be beautiful to be successful, of course; Alice knew that better than anyone. She'd long ago accepted that her own strength was in looking striking and dressing well, and in being socially indispensable. But still, it was hard for her. No one could imagine what it was like to walk into a room with Tally and have all the boys size you up as second prize.

"Listen, babe," Tally slurred, linking arms with Alice and drawing her across the room, "I have massive gossip for you. I've just heard it from Seb. So. Funny." She hiccuped.

"Gossip? Come on, it can't be that big. Is it about—"

3

"Shhh!" Tally hissed, pressing her finger to her lips as they reached the table. There was Sonia Khan, whispering into Jasper von Holstadt's ear as he gulped champagne from a flute; next to him was George Demetrios trying to steal Seb Ogilvy's pack of cigarettes, while Seb hunched over the joint he was rolling for later on.

"Mimah's not coming, is she?" Alice asked. Mimah was Jemimah Calthorpe de Vyle-Hanswicke, their ex–best friend. She'd gone schizo last term—turned into a moody cow, to be precise—and they'd been trying to get rid of her ever since.

"Not a chance," Tally replied. "We all blanked her the last time she tried to come out. Anyway, who cares about Mimah? I've got far juicier gossip than that."

"Oh," Alice mumbled, suddenly not listening. She'd realized who else was missing from the table: Tristan. So the rumors must be true—he was still with his new girlfriend in New York. Just like him to ditch everyone and turn up a day late for school. Tristan Murray-Middleton always did exactly what he wanted, but so charmingly that no one ever noticed he was getting away with murder. Alice missed him. A lot.

"So. Did you find out when our favorite boy's getting back?" she asked Tally, sliding in next to George Demetrios and signaling him to pour her a drink. She sounded nonchalant; she could always pull that off. Not that there was anything suspicious in her asking about Tristan; after all, he was her oldest, closest friend.

4

"Well." Tally raised her eyebrows exaggeratedly. "He'll be here later, of course." She giggled.

Alice swallowed. "What are you talking about? Isn't he still in the States with you-know-who?"

"Not exactly. There's been a change of plan"—Tally winked—"if you know what I mean."

"For fuck's sake, I haven't got a *clue* what you mean." Alice's heart was racing. Shit. *Get it together.* Her voice was ridiculously strained and squeaky, and Tally was an expert at picking up on anything weird.

Quickly downing her glass of champagne, Alice thought back for the thousandth time to that week in early July. What had it meant? Nothing? Everything? On a whim, she and Tristan had flown out to Italy together, just the two of them, to stay in Positano, the beautiful, ancient seaside town where the Rochesters owned a vast stone villa. All through the first morning, Alice had watched her friend from a lounge chair on the baking-hot patio, wondering why she'd never noticed how strong and lithe he was, how one moment he could be messing about on the side of the pool, the next be cutting through the water like a bullet. And then, when he looked up at her, shaking his wet hair, and grinned into her eyes, she thought his gaze might melt her on the spot.

That night they ate dinner in the trattoria in town, sharing bottles of local white wine and plates of fresh grilled fish that Tristan ordered in his perfect Italian. Being half-French certainly had its perks where languages were concerned. Late in the evening, a toothless accordion player serenaded them with an old love song neither of them knew. Tristan caught Alice's eye, gave her his slow, sly smile, and both of them almost died laughing. Each day following was the same: a live wire of unexplained looks until the sun went down and they finally said good night, kissed each other on both cheeks, and went to bed in separate rooms. On the last night, Alice tossed and turned till dawn, thinking she'd go crazy. Could Tristan possibly want her? Did she want him? Would either of them ever be brave enough to take the plunge?

She hadn't seen or heard from T since then. At the end of the week, he'd flown to New York to spend the rest of the summer playing golf and sailing with his cousins in the Hamptons, and he'd always been bad at staying in touch. Alice had only found out about this slut girlfriend because she'd seen the pictures on Facebook: the two of them all over each other at yacht-club dinners and beach-club parties. To make matters worse, the girl looked like a busty, blond, rich bitch. What a tacky choice.

Not that Alice cared. She was over it by now.

"Go on." She turned to Tally. "What's the scoop?" She felt warm and easy; the champagne was doing its job. But Tally grabbed her arm. Her long nails dug into Alice's skin.

"Not right now," she whispered. "Look who's here."

Alice looked. Her stomach lurched. There he was, Tristan, at the other end of the room, coming toward them through the crowd.

CHAPTER TWO

*T*ristan! Welcome back!" exclaimed Jasper von Holstadt, plucking the unlit cigarette from his mouth and thumping Tristan's shoulder. Jasper's cig was his trademark gimmick, always dangling from his lips in that "give-a-shit" way that girls went wild over.

"Jas! How've you been?" Tristan grinned, his hazel eyes sparkling. "I heard your dad caved and finally bought you that Porsche."

"Damn right he did. I lost it for a few days though. Forgot where I parked it and had to pretend to the old man that I was having it cleaned."

T laughed. He settled into an empty armchair, pulled out his vintage gold Zippo and lit up one of Seb's cigarettes.

"Yeah, go ahead. It's a free-for-all," Seb said sarcastically, snatching the pack and lighting one for himself, too.

"Come on, don't be so tight, you've probably got ten more of those hidden in your jacket." Tristan put on an official voice. "Concealed about your person." No one was allowed to smoke in Emerald's, of course, but the boys never paid attention to rules and the bouncers turned a blind eye. Just like they did with everything else that went on in the club's nooks and crannies.

"Anyway," Tristan said, shifting to the edge of his seat and giving Seb a quizzical look, "what are these rumors I've been hearing about you and Mimah Calthorpe de Vyle-Hanswicke? Did she really pay you a thousand pounds to sleep with her? That's kind of skeezy, isn't it?"

Seb took a drag of his cigarette and stared at the disco ball revolving above them. This was irritating; all people seemed to do these days was to ask him about Jemimah Calthorpe de Vyle-Hanswicke. He had no idea where the rumors had come from. All he knew was that he'd been the focus of gossip for days and it was making him very uncomfortable. Seb had always been perfectly content to be overshadowed by Tristan. He wasn't a center-of-the-group, life-and-soul-of-the-party type of guy. He was just . . . well, he wasn't even sure *who* he was anymore.

It was time to deflect the talk.

"Dunno," he ventured. "Last I heard, Mimah had become a raving lesbian."

"Are you fucking serious?" Tristan slapped the arm of his chair.

"Er, yeah. Totally. I saw her coming on to Arabella Scott at some party last week. It was hilarious."

"Arabella?" Tristan smirked, inhaling smoke. "Well, at least Mimah's got good taste. Bella's hot." He grinned slyly. "Hotter than you are, anyway."

"Dickhead!" Seb punched him in the arm. The two friends chuckled and Tristan, feeling a rush of wellbeing, contentedly surveyed the group around the table. His eyes fell on Alice, across from him. She looked good tonight. She was wearing something white and floaty, and it suited her. He wondered when they'd have a chance to talk. There was something he needed to say.

Just then, Seb and Jasper cracked up, and he turned back to find out what he'd missed.

"Mmmm, yeah, how interesting." Alice nodded to George Demetrios on her side of the table, pretending to listen as he droned on about his grandmother's houses and olive orchards in Greece. *Someone get me some drugs or I'm going to die of boredom,* she thought. Out of the corner of her eye, she watched Tristan and the others. What was making them laugh so hard? T was probably telling raunchy stories about his summer of fucking "love." All boys were the same. That was why Alice was planning to be very careful when she finally let one . . . do it to her.

She sighed. T looked so hot with his hair long and quiffy like this, and she knew very well how muscular he was under his blazer and baggy jeans. All she could think about was him grabbing her in his arms and pressing her up against a wall. That one over there, under the exit sign, would do just fine.

God, she hated him. And it was hot in here.

Tristan glanced up as Alice slipped past Tally out of her seat and hurried away, her slim hips swaying. She couldn't possibly be leaving, could she? No, her white pashmina was still on the couch. He got up abruptly and trailed her through the club.

Reaching the back entrance, Alice pushed aside the curtains and glided up the external stairway to the street. It was cool and quiet out here. Rows of Georgian and Victorian houses, their stuccoed facades painted white, shone in the streetlights like ghosts, and she leaned back against one, feeling its chilly bricks through her peasant-style blouse. By now the line had dispersed, music was pulsing up faintly from below, and in the east a stain of sunlight was just breaking through the dark.

Alice breathed in deeply. She loved these thick, late-summer nights when the dawns started early and went on forever. If the weather stayed this good, they'd be able to sneak out through the fields well into October to meet the boys in secret, halfway between St. Cecilia's and its brother school, Hasted House.

Something rattled on the iron stairway. Alice jumped. Tristan.

"Hello, stranger," he said. He sauntered up next to her, smelling of soap and cigarettes.

"Hi."

"How was France? Did Dom and Hugo piss you off as much as usual?"

"Umm. They were fine." Alice paused, studying the new gold sandals that she'd bought last week at a market stall in St. Tropez. She left one of those long, awkward silences that she knew T hated.

Tristan cleared his throat. "So, what else? What's been happening while I've been away?"

"Actually," Alice said crisply, "I wasn't expecting to see you here. I thought you'd still be in East Hampton with . . . what's-her-name. Nice of you to come back."

Tristan studied her warily. "Oh, Dylan? Yeah, she was . . . well, I mean, that was just a summer thing. Fun for a while, but . . . whatever." He trailed off. Great start. Talk about clearing the air.

"Hey, here's an idea," he tried again, jumping playfully off the curb. "Let's sneak over to Italy again at half-term, just the two of us. Or even somewhere else. I think we've got ten days off. It's funny, I can't stop thinking about how much fun we had this summer."

Alice pursed her lips, trying not to grin. This couldn't be more perfect! Not only had Tristan broken up with that American tart but here he was, basically admitting how much he'd missed her. She shrugged, as if she were utterly bored by his childish schemes.

"Mmm, that would be nice, but half-term's no good. It's

my cousin's engagement party in Rome, remember? Italian *Vogue*'s throwing that huge bash for her. You're on the guest list. I mean, I think you are."

"Of course!" T said. "I forgot—Coco's finally marrying that Italian film star of hers. Well, we'll just have to go partying in Rome instead, then."

"I suppose so. Anyway"—Alice turned away down the staircase, making sure Tristan had a view of her bare, suntanned back—"see you inside. I'm getting another drink."

In the back room of the club, the DJ had started in on his repertoire of cheese. He was playing "Hips Don't Lie" by Shakira, and Tally was gyrating provocatively, her short dress skimming her thighs. She was double-fisting martinis, and each time she moved, the drinks sloshed about.

"*Oooooh,*" lip-synced George Demetrios, raising his arms over his head like a zombie and grinding his groin into Tally's ass. Alice rolled her eyes. That song was so 2006.

"Hey, Ali." Tally stumbled across the dance floor. "There you are. I saw you go outside with Tris. So, what do you think? What are we going to do?" She shoved a cocktail into Alice's hands.

Alice stared at her. Not again. Why did Tally keep talking crap? She should really sober up.

"He told me he dumped that girl." Alice raised her voice as clearly as she could above the music. "Look, I know we didn't want him messing around with some American bitch. But it's over. Why are you making such a big deal?"

Abruptly, Tally stopped dancing. "Hold on, he didn't tell you the other thing?"

"What other thing?" Alice almost screamed. "Stop being so cryptic and spit it out!"

"Fine." Tally looked offended. "I just thought T would have said, that's all." Sinking down onto a plush sofa nearby, she patted the cushion next to her. Alice sat.

"Tristan broke up with Dylan because she lived in New York and he had to come back here," Tally explained. Her face was cracking into a sly smile.

Alice shrugged. "Yeah?"

"I said *lived*," Tally went on. "Note the tense."

Sipping from her glass, Alice narrowed her eyes.

"Just before Tristan left, he suddenly found out that Dylan was moving to London—stalking him—like, right away. And wait, here's the funniest part." Tally giggled. "Dylan's coming to St. Cecilia's! Can you believe it? Starting tomorrow, Tristan's ex-girlfriend is going to be in our class."

Alice coughed. She was choking on her martini.

CHAPTER THREE

"Advanced Level English. Room 305. Mr. Logan." Tally read the whiteboard at the front of the classroom. Mr. Logan? Who the hell was he? She frowned at her crumpled school schedule while trying to catch her breath. Fantastic. It was her first morning as a junior, and she was already confused and in chaos. At least it was a beautiful day. The windows in here were wide open, with sunlight streaming through the blinds and fat, lazy flies buzzing in and out over the sills. And there was Alice, right on time as usual, settled in by the wall and saving her one of the only chairs still empty.

"What a treat, we're back at school." Tally rolled her eyes, dumped her pad of paper and pile of books onto the desk and flopped down. She'd left herself barely any room to write. Whatever. It was their first lesson of the year *and* they had a new teacher. They probably wouldn't do any work.

"Hey, do you know anything about this Logan guy?" Blond

wisps of hair fell over Tally's eyes as she leaned toward Alice. "Is he a replacement for Mrs. Purcell? I heard she had a nervous breakdown. Hello?"

But Alice didn't hear. She was hunched forward, biting her tongue in concentration and printing her name carefully on a new yellow and gray school diary. The girl was so anal. She always had to be the best. At everything. Tally hoped it wasn't going to be too weird, just the two of them sharing a room together after all those years of sleeping in dorms of four or five girls. Of course she loved Alice madly, but over the summer Tally had got used to independence. She'd been staying in London with her dad and his despicable new wife (who were too busy socializing and fawning over each other to even notice she was there), and had basically had the run of their house. No curfew, no rules, no chores. Now she wasn't sure she could stand someone else in her personal space. Especially Alice, who could never resist issuing orders to anyone and everyone.

Pensively gnawing the end of her pencil, Tally slouched back in her chair. Because of the balmy weather, most girls in their class were still wearing St. Cecilia's summer uniform—a short-sleeved, yellow-and-white striped shirt tucked into a gray cotton skirt. And of course a dreaded school tie. Tally hated those ties; they made you look like some kind of second-rate office worker. A couple of losers sitting together on her row were also wearing yellow socks, yanked all the way up to their knees. Sexy. *Not.* Tally, on the other hand, had pulled on a pair of white platform sandals (without socks, obviously—she wasn't a dirty hippie) and had gathered her hair back into a messy ponytail.

From the far corner of the room echoed a mournful pinging sound. It was coming from the desk of Jemimah Calthorpe de Vyle-Hanswicke. She was flicking the tab on her can of Red Bull and glaring at the backs of Tally's and Alice's heads. What bitches, Mimah thought. They hadn't even acknowledged her presence. If this were last term, the three of them would have been sitting together just like they always had, hatching some plot to sneak into the woods for a cigarette during Break, or gossiping under their breath about the news of the day. Which, this morning, was all about Tristan's American ex-girlfriend. Rumor had it that she was coming to St. Cecilia's, but she'd failed to show up last night and no one knew why.

Anyway, Mimah told herself, maybe it was time to give up on being friends with Alice and Tally and Sonia Khan. Last term, when Mimah's father had been splashed all over the tabloids for having sex with a twenty-year-old prostitute, those three had washed their hands of her like she was dirt. Then, to make matters worse, they'd helped spread rumors that she'd paid Seb Ogilvy a thousand quid to have sex with her. Mimah clenched her fists. They knew that she'd liked Seb for ages. It was one of their clique's special secrets. Why did they have to be so mean?

She snatched up her empty Red Bull can and hurled it across the room toward the trash. Just then, footsteps sounded loudly in the corridor and the tips of two scuffed loafers appeared in the doorway, followed by a tallish, athletic-looking man wearing corduroys. *Whack!* The can bounced straight into his crotch. Mimah gasped.

"What on earth!" the man burst out, cupping his hand over his privates. "Aha!" He jogged over to where the can lay, kicked it showily into the air, and dunked it into the bin.

"I'm Mr. Logan," he pivoted round, winking at the class. "And you must be my A-level English class."

Tally and Alice shot glances at each other. Duh. It said "Advanced Level English" on the board, didn't it? This Mr. Logan character seemed like a douchebag. Plus, he couldn't be older than twenty-five, at the *most*.

"Allow me to introduce myself," he continued. He had a deep voice that demanded attention when he spoke, even though his accent was slightly, well, lower class.

"I'm passionate about literature—poetry in particular," Mr. Logan said. "I hope you all are too, since you've chosen to study the A-level English course over the next two years. Secondly, just between ourselves," he dropped his voice to a confidential low, "this is the first time I've ever set foot in a boarding school. I taught at a public school before. So I'll need you girls to help me get acquainted with the ins and outs."

Alice nudged Tally. "Ins and outs," she snickered. "What a perv!"

"Excuse me?" Mr. Logan snapped.

"Oh, nothing, sir." Alice gave a sugary smile. She knew how

to control teachers. Especially male ones. "I was just saying how much I liked your . . . belt. Sir."

"Of course you were." Mr. Logan glared. But he touched his hand to his belt buckle, wondering if he'd mistakenly worn the one shaped like a wildcat. He hadn't. "Right, what's your name?"

"Alice," Alice said, slowly uncrossing and recrossing her legs. She wasn't wearing tights. "Rochester."

"Pleasure," Mr. Logan said. "Why don't you tell me a bit about yourself, Alice."

"Ooh, I'm not sure I want to get so personal, sir."

"Keep it professional then. What A levels are you doing? What uni do you see yourself at? Even better, what's your favorite subject?"

Alice cocked her head to one side and traced a circle with her middle finger on the desk. "I'd have to say French because I'm really quite fluent. You see, my family has a villa in the South of France. We go there every summer and our maid always tells me what an excellent accent I have."

"How charming of your maid to say so," Mr. Logan beamed down. "You know, I'd probably tell you exactly the same thing—if I were on your parents' payroll. Do you think she's hoping for extra tips?"

Giggles rippled through the class. Tally laughed loudly, until she noticed Alice's red face gaping in her direction.

What? she mouthed. "Al, I'm sorry." But Alice had already turned away, her jaw trembling.

"And you?" Mr. Logan asked. He was talking to Tally and his voice was kinder now. This girl looked a little less haughty than her friend. And besides, she was gorgeous—in a pale, Slavic way. Just like Lara, the heroine of *Dr. Zhivago*, his favorite Russian novel.

"I'm Natalya," Tally said. Her voice was crisp and smooth, with just the hint of an Eastern-European accent.

"Natalya," Mr. Logan repeated, rolling the name like syrup over his tongue. "Sounds Russian. Am I correct?"

Tally nodded. "My mum's from Moscow. She still lives there."

Mr. Logan looked straight into her eyes. She noticed that his were a bewitching, piercing blue.

"Russian," he intoned, slowly rolling his *r*'s, "is an ext*rrr*emely beautiful language. And Russian people are extremely beautiful too."

Tally swallowed. Mr. Logan had deep dimples when he smiled that made his face look manly and yet soft. Feeling hot and flustered, she turned toward the window and touched her fingertips surreptitiously to her cheeks, desperately hoping they hadn't gone red.

Outside on the driveway, a car was just pulling up in front of the main school hall. The gravel crunched under its tires as it came to a halt. Curious, Tally watched the doors open and three people get out: a woman, a man, and a pretty girl about her age.

Tally squinted at the man. Did she recognize him? Wait . . .

of course! It was that sleazy game show host Victor Dalgleish, the one who'd been on *MindQuest* for a million years. Her mum loved him. And he was pretty much the first man Tally had ever had a crush on too (embarrassing as it was to admit). But what the hell was he doing at their school?

And more importantly, was that blond girl who Tally suspected she was?

CHAPTER FOUR

*H*urry up, Dylan," Piper Taylor ordered as she marched on her four-inch stilettos toward the main door of St. Cecilia's School. She didn't have time for her daughter's moods today. Not only was it disgraceful that Dylan had purposely missed her flight from New York and made them all a day late; it was also embarrassing. Piper had had to make a huge donation to the school in order to get Dylan in at such short notice, and now it looked like they were vulgar Americans who didn't give a rat's ass about punctuality.

"And when are you going to stop sulking?" she called, turning back around. "It's all you've been doing since you got to London."

"*Okay*, Mom. Give me a break." Dylan Taylor slammed the car door extra loudly. Gazing up at the grand old red-brick building where they'd just arrived, she frowned. Ivy trailed heavily down the front and sides. Big round towers with

pointed roofs rose up into the empty blue sky at either end.
Lines of blank windows gaped down at her, and Dylan's heart
sank. Was her mother serious? Was she really forcing her to
go to school in this . . . *prison*? Dylan was used to having the
whole of New York City throbbing at her feet: friends, taxis,
her family's apartment on Park Avenue.

Her first view here only confirmed what she'd always known:
she was going to hate St. Cecilia's. It looked like the kind of
place where nothing ever happened—at all.

"Dilly, come *on*," Dylan's mother snapped again. "The headmistress is waiting. Ouch!" she squealed, as the man next to
her pulled her in close and grabbed her behind. "Oh, Victor,"
she giggled, rubbing up against him.

Vomit, thought Dylan. Damn Victor Dalgleish. She still
didn't get what her mother saw in him. He might be a TV
personality, but he was also a sleazy creep. Receding hairline? Check. Oily skin? Check. Those hideous sideburns that
curled into his ears and looked like he hadn't washed them
for weeks? Check, check, check.

Besides, Dylan brooded, stomping up the path after them,
if it weren't for Victor none of them would be here in the
first place. She thought back to four months ago, when her
mother first met him at that party in New York. People had
talked about their flirtation, of course, the way they talked
about everything else—but most of their acquaintances had
just written it off as one of those social things.

Then Dylan's mother had started spending less and less time

at home. Finally, one terrible Sunday, she had announced that she was throwing in the towel on eighteen years of marriage, packing up her life, and following Victor across the Atlantic. Talk about selfish. Now she had dragged Dylan and her sister, Lauren, over with her. Made them leave everything they knew and loved and valued behind. Lauren at least was allowed to go to a day school in London, whereas their mom was making *her* come here. "You'll meet all the right people, sweetie," she'd insisted. "It's your way into *society*."

Whatever.

Dylan was walking very fast. Suddenly she tripped and lurched forward on the wide, shallow stairs at the front of the school. *Fuck*. She felt tears pricking up behind her eyes. *No*. Digging her nails into her palms, she took a deep breath, and strode on inside.

"Don't walk on the grass," instructed Miss Sharkreve. The teacher had introduced herself about five minutes before as the Junior Housemistress, and was now leading Dylan briskly through a beautiful old courtyard.

"This is Quad," she elaborated. "It's the oldest and most formal part of St Cecilia's."

"Nice," Dylan mumbled. Miss Sharkreve was kind of pretty for a teacher. She was young and voluptuous with long, wispy hair and watery blue eyes in a smooth, freckled face. "So, um, why can't I walk on the grass? Are you watering it or something?"

Miss Sharkreve wheeled round, looking shocked that anyone could be so dumb. "No! Because only *teachers* may set foot on it. It's a privilege. Otherwise the courtyard would be ruined, now wouldn't it?"

"I suppose," Dylan said. She was silent for a few seconds. "What about the cooks and janitors and stuff?"

"What about them?"

"Well, are they allowed to walk on the grass?"

"Of course not. They're not teachers. Everyone else has got to walk round the edge."

Talk about equal opportunities. Dylan stopped a minute to heave her hand luggage onto her other shoulder. This place was clearly stuck in the Victorian times and she was going to have to get to grips with the rules, fast.

They passed through a stone archway at the back of Quad, into a lush expanse of lawn dotted with trees and bushes and crisscrossed with unpaved paths. Clusters of students lay around with books spread out before them, and in one corner, a circle had gathered for a sunny morning lesson.

Miss Sharkreve strode even faster than before. "You'll find your way round soon enough," she declared. "That's the theater. Science buildings. Art block. Riding stables. Lacrosse fields. Netball courts. Tennis—"

"Netball?" Dylan interrupted, grinning widely. "Don't you mean basketball?" She giggled.

"*No.* I mean netball," Miss Sharkreve retorted. "It's a different sport altogether, *much* more skillful. None of that silly American dribbling involved. Every English schoolgirl can play it. You'll have to learn."

I can't fucking wait, Dylan thought, rolling her eyes. She sneaked glances at the students on the lawn, wondering. . . .

Butterflies fluttered in her tummy at the thought of trying to join any one of the cliquey-looking groups. She fingered the enamel Hermès cuff bracelet that her best friends in New York had given her as a going-away present just two nights ago.

"Here we are: Tudor House," Miss Sharkreve said at last, halting in front of a pretty building shaded by an oak tree. "This is where the entire junior class lives. St. Cecilia's is a very selective school, so there are only thirty-six of you in the year."

"Umm, cool," Dylan nodded. Miss Sharkreve seemed to be waiting for her to make some other comment. She scrambled around for one. "So . . . do we get en suite bathrooms?"

The teacher gave her an indignant look. "En suite bathrooms?"

"Umm, yeah."

"Of course you bloody well don't," Miss Sharkreve muttered. She didn't mind if she did swear in the face of such stupid questions. She led Dylan past a cheery living room and kitchen and up a flight of stairs, at the top of which was a hallway lined with wooden doors. Most of them were plastered with photo-collages of girls hugging each other and dancing and playing sports.

"This is your room," she said, stopping in front of one. It was already covered in pictures, even though school had only started yesterday. Most of them showed an Indian girl in front of a lavish palace that looked a bit like the Taj Mahal. "I'll leave you to get settled in."

"Thanks," Dylan said quietly. She watched the teacher's back recede down the corridor, feeling a hard bubble of emptiness expand inside her chest.

Well, here goes. She pushed open the door and stepped into the room. Immediately, a sickly stench of musk and amber invaded her nostrils. Repulsive. Whoever lived here was using *way* too much perfume. What were they trying to hide? Dylan sized the place up. The big window on the far wall had bright yellow curtains, and the light wood furniture looked new enough. She and her roommate each had a bed with drawers built in underneath, a night table and lamp, a bureau, an armchair, and a desk. There was even a sink in one corner, with a mirror nailed above it. Not exactly the Four Seasons, but still. Maybe there was something to be said for not having to live with her mother and that hideous man.

Dylan's roommate had already made herself at home. A few reed mats were tossed across the gray regulation carpet. They looked like the kind of thing you might buy when you go traveling in Cambodia or something. Bunches of necklaces, gold and beaded, hung from random hooks and nails around the walls. The bed farthest from the door—obviously the best one—was covered in a purple and gold sari-style duvet, piled with plump cushions embroidered with expensive threads.

Dylan noticed a jumble of clothes hurled across the other bed as well. Wonderful. Was that supposed to be some kind of subtle message? *Screw you if you think we're going to share.*

She sank down onto the purple bed and stared longingly at her phone. Still no text from Tristan. He must not have got her message from last night. Maybe his cell phone was broken. Wait, she'd better learn to start calling it a *mobile* phone instead. Tristan had always teased her about that in East Hampton over the summer. Suddenly it didn't seem so funny though. How was she ever going to fit in over here?

Absently, Dylan picked up a stack of photographs lying next to her hand. A little spying might give her a head start.

The top picture showed four impeccably stylish girls drinking out of steaming mugs in the Alps or somewhere like that. Dylan had never been to the Alps, but she guessed that was where it was from the wooden beams in the café and the sharp, white peaks in the background. She examined their faces. They didn't look anything like her friends back home; they seemed older for some reason. More sophisticated.

One of them looked especially intimidating: a flat-chested brunette. She wasn't exactly pretty, but was very striking. She had a figure like a model, with the kind of collarbone that juts out dramatically, and razor-sharp cheeks. Her hair was pulled back tight and all her attention was focused on pouting into the camera. But her eyes . . . There was something sort of vindictive about them, as if they concealed a poisonous snake, waiting to fly out and strike. *Watch out.*

Dylan flicked on through the pile. More pictures of the skiing trip. A load of party shots. Drinking, dancing. Boys wrestling each other in the snow, wearing nothing but boxer shorts and suspenders and socks pulled up to their knees. Dylan had thought the English were supposed to be proper and uptight, but these people looked exactly the opposite.

Wait! Suddenly, a familiar face stared out at her from the stack. It couldn't be . . . yes, it was. *Tristan!*

Her heart was galloping. Maybe things weren't going to be so terrible at St. Cecilia's, after all.

She'd obviously landed in the right place.

"He's just such a fucking bastard!" Alice exclaimed angrily to Sonia Khan as the two girls walked back to Tudor House during Break. Alice had stormed out of English as soon as the bell rang and had run to find Sonia in the science wing. She was still seething about Mr. Logan. "Why the hell didn't Tally take my side?"

Sonia nodded sympathetically and slipped her arm through her friend's. Girls were milling all around them, rushing off to get books, or heading to the cafeteria for a snack, or sneaking off for a quick cigarette in the bushes. She didn't want to look around too much in case Alice thought she wasn't paying enough attention, but she hoped people were watching them. Sonia loved it when she had visible proof of how close she and Alice Rochester were. Besides, she knew she looked so much prettier now, after Dr. Essex had stuck her under the anesthetic last month and sculpted her horrendously massive nose into a pert, curving slope.

"Well, we all know what Tally's like," she said, trying to control her voice from sounding too obviously bitchy. Alice had a good ear for things that were over-the-top. "She always fawns over older men. How old is Mr. Logan?"

"Who gives a shit?" Alice replied irritably. "The point is, she shouldn't have been taken in by him. I mean," she said, her voice suddenly turning into a feel-sorry-for-me whine, "he was so *beastly* to me. I didn't even do anything. I'm really pissed off at Tally. She should have backed me up."

Sonia was just formulating the perfect appeasing answer, when the two girls stopped short. They had reached their hallway, and the doorway to Sonia's room was wide open. There was a massive green suitcase outside.

"Ali," Sonia said, her big brown eyes widening. "Do you think that's . . ."

"Shut up," Alice whispered, snatching her arm away from Sonia's grasp. That girl could be such a moron sometimes. She wished she had Mimah around to help her strategize. Shame Mimah had been designated damaged goods.

Alice tiptoed up to the doorway of the room and peeked in.

A blond girl was lounging across that tacky duvet cover that Sonia had brought back from her trip home to India. She had huge breasts and a glowing suntan, Alice noted, glaring. But her uniform looked new and stiff, and unlike any of the cool girls, she was already wearing the winter version. She was clutching a picture in her hand, gazing into space with a stupid dreamy smile on her lips.

She's thinking about him. Alice stared for a minute, then turned to Sonia again.

"Why the fuck is she on your bed looking through your stuff?" she whispered. "Is she brain-dead?"

"Obviously," Sonia giggled, with her hand over her mouth. "I'll bet that's why T dumped her. She's a kleptomaniac!"

Both girls snickered.

"But seriously." Alice suddenly fixed her eyes on her friend and switched off her smile. "Remember what we talked about last night. You know what to do."

Sonia nodded significantly.

Footsteps clicked in the hallway behind them.

"Quick, let's go, Sharko's here," Alice said.

"Oh, Alice, Sonia—hang on a second." Miss Sharkreve's voice rang out. "Goodness," she gasped, batting her hand in front of her face like someone swatting a fly. "That's very strong perfume, isn't it?"

Dylan jerked her head around in surprise at the racket. That thin girl from the pictures! She locked eyes with Alice for a split second. The photo of Tristan fluttered to the floor between them.

"This is Dylan Taylor, girls," Sharko nattered on. "She's joining us all the way from New York. I'm counting on you to introduce her round and make her feel welcome."

Dylan saw the two girls exchange glances behind Miss Sharkreve's back. The skinny girl looked across at her, gave a slight smirk, then turned silently around and left the room.

CHAPTER FIVE

*L*essons were over for the day at Hasted House and Tristan jogged back toward the showers across the sun-soaked fields. He was feeling sweaty and happy after rugby tryouts. He wanted to be team captain again this year, and it was obvious that he'd played better than anyone else today. He breathed in the soft, warm air and the smell of freshly cut grass.

In the changing room, the boys in his year were swearing and messing around and tossing their uniforms into their bags. "Well played, Tom." Tristan nodded to his neighbor as he peeled off his shirt and clanged open his locker. He loved this familiar scene; it made him feel totally sure of his place in the world. Maybe he'd pop out for a quick smoke before dinner. Be nice to have five minutes to himself. Catch a bit of shade out in the woods. He took out his iPhone. This was the kind of mood where nothing could stress him out.

Almost.

Fuck. One new text. It was probably Dylan again. For the last couple of hours he'd managed to shove that whole mess to the back of his mind.

He looked closer. It was from Alice.

Hiya babe. Feelin like some nature. Wanna catch up 2night?

Brilliant, Tristan thought. More trouble. He stared at the phone for a second before tossing it aside and stripping off the rest of his clothes. *Nature* was their group's code word for weed. They'd been using it ever since they were fourteen, when a housemaster had confiscated Seb Ogilvy's phone, opened all his messages, and dropped their gang into a big pile of shit.

Tristan stepped into the shower and threw his head back under the hot stream. He wasn't out of breath from rugby anymore, but for some reason his heart was racing. *For fuck's sake, get a grip,* he told himself. Why was he feeling so freaked out? Alice's text was completely normal; they often met up to get high in the fields in the evenings when it was warm—usually with Tally and Jasper or Seb, true, but sometimes just the two of them. In fact, Tristan had stocked up on his weed supply in London last week for that very purpose.

So what was his problem? He pictured himself alone with Alice in the dark tonight. Sure, he was excited, but he was pretty nervous as well. What if something finally happened? What if it all went wrong? Tristan had been avoiding these questions ever since he and Alice had been in Italy together.

Thing was, it had been easier in the Hamptons when she wasn't around.

And then there was all that crap with Dylan to sort out. He hated to think what would happen at St. Cecilia's when she and Alice met.

Tristan ran a hand through his wet hair. What was that French phrase his mum always used? *Une chose à la fois.* One thing at a time. First, there was a choice to be made. He tied a towel around his waist, picked up his phone, and typed out a text.

CHAPTER SIX

The great clock outside St. Cecilia's Hall chimed eight and echoed mournfully through the empty classrooms and deserted lawns. It was prep time, which, according to school rules, meant the girls had to stay in their bedrooms for another whole hour, doing homework for tomorrow or reading books that would supposedly broaden their corrupted teenage minds.

Alice sat in front of her sleek silver laptop in the dorm she shared with Tally. Theirs was a corner bedroom, one of the best in Tudor House, and Alice had had to do a lot of bribing and wheedling to make sure their rooming ballot number had come out high enough for them to get it. That wasn't really cheating; it was more like networking, the way politicians did. Her dad would have been proud. After all, she'd had her heart set on this room since she was in sixth grade, and he always pushed her to go out and be the best.

The room was big, with three windows instead of two, and was famous throughout the school for having a large alcove set back in the wall facing the beds. She and Tally had made that nook their "entertaining area." They'd filled it with their two regulation armchairs, a brand-new white sheepskin rug, and an old wooden chest that Tally had brought from her dad's house in London. They were using the chest as a coffee table, which wasn't strictly allowed since bringing furniture from home was against the rules, but if anyone asked they'd just say it was Tally's suitcase. They'd also spent an hour that afternoon hanging Christmas lights around the edges of the alcove; not the common old bulbs that lots of St. Cecilians had, but trendy lights from the Conran Shop with red and white shades that curled delicately around them.

Facebook was open on Alice's screen. She was preparing herself for some serious stalking, her eyes narrowed and her fingers poised over the letters. Keep your friends close and your enemies closer. Whoever had made that up was probably living in the lap of luxury somewhere. Actually, they were probably dead but whatever.

Alice's fingers swooped down on the keys. *D-y-l-a-n T-a-y-l-o-r* she typed in the search box, then held her breath, praying that she'd be able to see something. Anything. Hoping that the bitch wouldn't have the privacy settings switched on.

A list of Dylan Taylors appeared. It was three pages long. But that didn't matter, seeing as most of them were boys. Alice rolled her eyes. Of course they bloody well were. What kind of name was Dylan for a girl anyway? Quickly, she honed in on her prey.

Dylan's photo was annoyingly good. It was a close-up of her at what appeared to be a black-tie dinner. Her makeup was subtle, her teeth gleamed white, her skin was smooth and creamy, her hair looked bouncy without being out of control. She'd probably posed for ages to get it just right. How lame. Alice's Facebook photo was far more spontaneous. She'd engineered it that way because your picture said a lot about your personality, and no one wanted to be friends with an uptight poser.

Tristan had taken it last New Year's, when their whole crew had gone skiing in Courchevel. She was waving a sparkler and winking cheekily at the camera. Originally, George Demetrios had been messing about next to her, making an absurd face with his eyes crossed and his cheeks puffed out, but Alice had cropped him away. She'd also Photoshopped her eyes to make them amazingly bright, and touched up her skin just a little so that a healthy pink flush suffused her cheekbones. She looked wild and free, like an enchanting winter sprite.

Dylan was in the London network. She'd obviously switched over from New York as soon as she'd moved. Alice brought up her profile. Six hundred and seventy-four friends. What a joke. So maybe Alice had a few less, but at least all of hers were *real*. Dylan's friends probably hated her anyway. Alice scrolled through the list. Yaaawn. They all looked exactly like Dylan: long shiny hair, overly friendly smiles. A bunch of despicable goody-goodies.

Several pages in, there was a pretty blond girl called Lauren Taylor, who looked about fourteen. Lauren is Dylan's sibling, read the blurb. Lauren was in the London network too. Well, at least they'd escaped having *her* at St. Cecilia's. That was the last thing they needed: two sad sisters from the Taylor family.

Time for Dylan's photos. There she was with a clique of girls and boys in school uniform; wearing a caramel-colored winter coat on a New York street corner; wearing a bikini on the beach. There was a whole load like that from this summer—Dylan playing volleyball, Dylan eating ice cream, Dylan lolling on a towel reading magazines. A terrible thought suddenly occurred to Alice: What if T had been there, just out of the frame, in all of them? Her blood ran cold at the thought. Dylan had to pay.

Suddenly, Alice saw a photo that Dylan had obviously neglected to edit out. She was wading out of a rough sea, squinting, her eye makeup smeared down her cheeks and her hair gnarled with sand and seaweed. Her brown bikini top had twisted round and one of her huge breasts had almost completely fallen out.

So tasteless to have that on Facebook. It deserved to be seen by certain people. Alice opened her iChat and typed Sonia a note.

CHAPTER SEVEN

*D*own the hall, Dylan cupped her chin in her hands and peered through her window, too tired and confused to concentrate on work. She stared at the sky as it slanted into a warm, evening yellow. Weird how the sun set so late here. In New York it would have been almost dark at this time of the evening.

Sonia's MacBook pinged on the other side of the room, followed by a flood of hysterical giggling. Sonia snuck a look at Dylan over the top of her screen.

"Hey, what's so funny?" Dylan swiveled hopefully around.

No answer. Sonia was typing furiously.

"Sonia?"

"Yeah? What?" Sonia looked annoyed, as if Dylan had interrupted her in the middle of an unprecedented creative flow.

"Uhh, just wondering what was in that message."

"What message?" Sonia inquired, raising her thin, perfectly

plucked eyebrows. "And why would I tell you about my private affairs?"

Dylan blushed. She turned back to the French grammar book she'd been studying and tried to concentrate on the subjunctive. *Que le bonheur vous sourie:* May happiness smile upon you. What crap. Tristan's mom was French, and he spoke it fluently. Dylan had thought they might take a trip to Paris together, now that she'd moved here. Over the summer, as they'd lain side by side on the beach, Tristan had told her all about the long weekends he spent there at his family's house, drinking cappuccinos in his favorite outdoor cafés and shopping for used books along the Seine. He'd said how much he wished he could show her, if only she didn't live so far away. Well, now she didn't. And they were less than three hours from Paris by Eurostar . . .

Tap tap taptaptap.

Dylan threw her head into her hands as she heard the familiar sound start up again. For fuck's sake! Sonia had been knocking her pen against her desk like that for the past hour and a half, stopping and starting and stopping and starting. It was infuriating. All day long, Dylan had been racking her brains over why her roommate was being so awful, but she just didn't get it. Unless Sonia was auditioning for a part in *Mean Girls.*

Dylan thought back over the day to lunchtime, when Miss Sharkreve had come marching into the room just as Dylan finished unpacking, with Sonia trailing after her.

"Sonia is going to take you to the dining hall," Miss Sharkreve had announced. "And she's going to make sure you feel settled in. You don't mind, do you, dear?"

Sonia had smiled saccharinely. "Actually, I was going to have some lunch here, but I'm happy to change my plans. Though Dylan probably doesn't need my help. I'm sure she'll make her own friends soon enough."

"Precisely," Miss Sharkreve said. "And you can be one of them." She disappeared through the door.

Sonia eyed Dylan coldly. "I'm going to the toilet."

"Okay, should I come with you?" Dylan jumped up. But Sonia was already gone.

Feeling like a jack-in-the-box, she sank back onto the bed. Several girls her age ran past the room, all talking over one another. Some of them looked in at her curiously. No one said hello.

Dylan twisted her cuff bracelet around on her wrist, wondering what everyone in New York was doing right now. It was five hours earlier there; they were probably just waking up, maybe meeting for coffee at the hot dog stand across the street from school.

The boarding house had gone as silent as a museum. Dylan had had enough of waiting here like an idiot. Venturing into the hallway, with its dark blue carpet and light yellow walls, she passed a bulletin board overflowing with pictures of joking, smiling girls in front of columns and ancient temples. *Athens, Spring Term*, the heading said.

That was an exotic vacation. At Dylan's old school in New York, the best place they ever traveled to was boring old Vermont for the yearly ski-trip.

Finally stumbling on the toilets, she pushed through the door. *Plip. Plip.* The only sound was coming from a leaky tap. She bent down. No sign of shoes under the stalls.

What was going on? Dylan felt dizzy. Numbly, she traced the empty hallway, hearing only the creaking of her own footsteps.

"Oy!" barked a husky, aggressive voice. A girl was standing at the top of the staircase, barring Dylan's way. She was strong-looking but attractive, with jet-black hair hacked off into a fringe. She had a tiny mole under her left eye that punctuated her face, making her look like she was constantly winking at you. Dylan recognized her from Sonia's ski-trip photos.

"You must be the famous ex."

"Ex?" Dylan echoed.

The girl didn't bother to reply, she was giving Dylan the once-over, a sour smile on her lips.

"Don't tell me," she said. "That bitch Sonia ditched you already."

Dylan shrugged noncommittally. In the photos it had looked like this girl was one of Sonia's partners in crime.

"Typical," the girl spat bitterly. Dylan felt like she was a prop in some lunatic's private soliloquy. Finally the girl held out her hand. "Mimah," she introduced herself. "You know, you're my replacement. I was meant to be sharing that room with Sonia—till she started acting like a total bitch. Follow me."

Mimah led the way across the lawn, back to Quad. Along one side, the dining hall had its own building, entered through an arched doorway. A crowd of girls was pushing and chattering loudly around it, but Mimah forced a path through them—not that she needed to. When they saw who she was, they scattered like iron filings from the wrong end of a magnet.

"Junior privilege." Mimah turned to Dylan. "We never wait in lines."

Inside, the room burst with chatter, clanging silverware, and chairs scraping across the spankingly polished floor. The vaulted ceiling was lined with warped wooden beams. Oil paintings of stern-faced former headmistresses adorned the walls. A file of girls snaked toward the kitchen, where dinner ladies in peaked yellow caps doled out portions of chicken nuggets, fries, and pizza. Mimah steered Dylan straight to the salad bar.

"Don't even bother with the cooked food," she advised, foisting a tray into Dylan's hands. "It's practically poison."

Dylan frowned at the troughs of rabbit food in front of her. Her tummy was growling. "So, what—are we supposed to eat lettuce for every meal?"

"No, don't worry. At breakfast they do sausages and eggs and baked beans on toast. That's all right. And then on good days we might get things like lasagne, or tacos, or spag bol, which aren't so hard on the old stomach."

"Spag bol?"

"You know, like spaghetti Bolognese?"

"Oh." Dylan scanned the crush of students for Sonia. There she was, at a table in the middle of the hall, picking at her watercress and grated carrots. Next to her were Alice and a stunning blonde whose hair, even though it was tangled and pinned up haphazardly, still managed to look perfect. The three of them were bending their heads toward one another, obviously discussing something. Her? As if reading Dylan's mind, Alice glanced up. Then she nudged the blond girl.

"Oh, for fuck's sake, ignore them," blurted out Mimah. "Come on, here's where I always sit. I'll fill you in on those bitches."

Beepbeep. Beepbeep. Dylan jumped. Sonia was still tapping her pen, and the sky hadn't got any darker. Her phone was lit up on her desk. She grabbed it. Maybe it would finally be Tristan.

It was. Her heart skipped a beat. She scrolled down.

Hi. Forgot you were coming this week. Things v busy. Maybe c you round. T

Dylan stared at the screen. Tears were threatening to overflow for the second time that day. She turned her face to the window again, forcing them back.

A movement caught her eye. Part of the hedge round the rear of the boarding house was trembling and shaking.

What the hell? It looked like someone was sneaking out. A slim silhouette flickered into the orchard beyond. Was it . . . ? Dylan squinted into the sunset.

Yes. It was Alice Rochester.

CHAPTER EIGHT

*A*lice's heart pounded in her throat as she half ran and half tripped over the tree roots under her feet. This walk through the woods between St. Cecilia's and Hasted House never got any less loathsome. It was like something out of a horror film. The dense leaves acted like assassins, strangling the light and whispering ominous nothings. Out of the shadows came a hooting noise. Goose pimples pricked up along Alice's arms. To her, that disembodied sound was the ultimate cry of loneliness.

Finally, the trees thinned out ahead and Alice emerged into a field. About bloody time. She sucked in deep breaths of air, watching the blades of grass flash and wave in the late sunlight. No wonder this was Tally's favorite time of day. Alice shoved back a snaking feeling of guilt when she thought of her friend. Normally she would have let on to Tally where she was running off to—in fact, normally she would have invited her along. But not tonight. Tally didn't bloody well deserve her confidence. Alice was still stinging with the memory of how Tally had laughed at her right along with the rest of them in English class. They were supposed to be allies.

Suddenly a thumping sound rushed up behind Alice and something knocked into the tender spot behind her knees. She buckled and screamed, thrashing about in the wild grass, until she found herself staring upward. Right into Tristan's grinning face.

"Ha! Got you!" He laughed down at her. He was pinning her hands to the earth. His tanned arms bulged a little in his faded blue T-shirt.

Alice's breath came fast. God, he was hot.

"Fuck you!" she squealed. She struggled feebly and pushed her chest up toward him, trying to look helpless. Guys liked that. It made them think of sex.

"Get off!" she whined. "You're too heavy."

Tristan considered her from above. Alice's olive skin and brown hair were luminous in the twilight, as if all the sunlight she'd soaked up during the day was releasing itself and making her glow. He felt protective when he saw how small and fragile her shoulders were. Stupid really, since she was actually quite tough. She could put up a damn decent fight in a tennis match, as he'd found out when she'd nearly won a set off him in Italy earlier that summer. Admittedly, he'd been feeling hungover and she'd convinced him to play. But still. It had almost been embarrassing.

Abruptly, Tristan noticed that Alice was gazing up at him. Her eyes had gone quiet. Hastily, he sprang to his feet.

"I, er, I've brought some candles and an extra sweater," he said. "You know, in case you get cold." He cleared his throat. "Anyway, the gear seems excellent. I smoked a bit before you got here."

Alice got off the ground, ignoring the fact that T hadn't helped her up, and surveyed the little spread. "Candles? A blanket? That's unusually thoughtful." She hoped her voice sounded significant. T had obviously stuffed his pockets with every snack he could lay his hands on—Snickers; chips; pretzels; and her favorite, Butterfingers—for when the munchies hit them later on. The whole thing was suspicious. He usually turned up with a can of Pringles and that was it. The fact that he'd made such an effort *had* to be a good sign.

T nudged her playfully. "I take offense at that. I'm the most thoughtful person I know."

Alice shrugged, grinning. "So, how does it feel being back?" She stretched out her long legs on the blanket and crossed her ankles in front of her. Maybe it was a dangerous question—T might mention Dylan's sudden distasteful appearance—but she had to start the conversation somehow. Tristan didn't catch her eye. Instead, he took out a packet of papers and a plastic bag of weed. Ever since he was a freshman he'd been famous for rolling perfect joints; back then, the older boys at school would gather round, egging him on, and watching his light-moving fingers to see if they could pick up any tips. T had got a lot of free weed that way, and he'd made a lot of friends.

"S'pose it's not bad," he answered at last, nodding noncommittally. "Cool to see the crew again. Seb's quite chilled out—it'll be good fun sharing a room with him. And Jas is just down the hall."

Fine, Alice thought, so he wasn't taking her bait. Well, she wouldn't force it. Not yet.

"That reminds me, tell me about Seb." She leaned in. T was always good for some gossip from the boys' side. "Has he let on anything about what happened between him and Mimah? Did they really . . . ?" She left a suggestive pause.

Tristan stared at her. "Really what?"

"You know. Do it."

Tristan laughed, flashing his straight white teeth. Little crinkles appeared around his eyes. "*You know . . . do it.*" He mimicked her insinuating whisper. "You're ridiculous. I don't know—probably. Mimah clearly always liked Seb. But he's being a bit cagey about it. What does Mimah say?"

Alice screwed her face up. "Who the hell knows? I don't want to get anywhere near her. She's such a freak now. Quite frankly," she continued, turning her hand over and examining her fingernails, "I always found her annoying—even when we were meant to be friends."

Tristan rolled his eyes. "Oh, come on, no you didn't. You're just jumping on the bandwagon. Mimah used to be wicked. She was loads of fun. I reckon all that scandal with her dad last term just sent her over the edge."

"Whatever. Like father like daughter." Alice raised her right eyebrow in her trademark scornful expression. "Her dad's a corrupt judge who's been prosecuted for sleeping with prostitutes. She's a screw-up who pays confused boys to have sex with her. What's the difference?"

"If you say so," Tristan retorted. Alice stared at his mouth as he licked the seam of his finished spliff to seal it, then slid it between his lips. She wasn't sure how much longer she could bear this.

"Anyway." Tris slowly exhaled a thick cloud of smoke. "How's St. C's? What's up with Tally? You sounded a bit off with her earlier."

"Oh, well, you know I adore Tally," Alice began, "but I got so pissed off. She made me look like an utter fool in front of this horrid new English teacher. She's such an attention seeker."

Alice stopped. God, she sounded nasty. Why couldn't she just get over it? She rarely bitched outright to T about her best friend. He had this funny loyalty thing about Tally. He was always defending her to people. Anyway, besides that, Alice and Tally were soulmates, partners in crime. Until Tally had come to St. Cecilia's three years ago, Alice had never met anyone so magnetic and sophisticated and so up for adventure. Until then, her posse had been mostly Mimah and Sonia. They'd had a good time, of course—a better time than anyone else in their goody-goody school—but Alice used to get so tired of them, the way they constantly sucked up to her. She could see right through their little mind games and competitions with each other. Whereas Tally—Tally was way above any of that crap.

"The thing is," Alice continued carefully, plucking a few stalks of grass out of the ground and weaving them between her fingers, "it's just that I worry about Tally." She stole a glance at Tristan. He'd knitted his eyebrows together. "She seems so messed-up sometimes. I mean, her mum lives halfway across the world and criticizes her all the time, and her dad's a total cokehead who basically can't be bothered with her. I dunno . . . I couldn't handle it. D'you know what I mean?"

Tristan shrugged and passed her the spliff. "Sure. But I reckon Tally's all right. She's got a way of winning people over—not just us, I mean adults, too. She can charm people more easily than anyone else I know." Alice frowned; Tristan wasn't supposed to disagree with her. "I've always thought she was trying to make up for having a bit of a difficult family," he said. "She needs everyone to accept her." He lolled his head back with an exaggerated groan. "Oh shit, that weed clearly went to my head. I'm talking crap."

Alice sighed. *No,* she thought, *you're not.* She shredded her handful of grass. Why hadn't any of this stuff about Tally occurred to her before? Tristan was so fucking thoughtful and clever when he tried. It reminded her of when they were much, much younger and they'd all play "It" or badminton or some silly made-up game with a million rules in one of their families' gardens. It was always Tristan who was the peace-maker. He mediated their fights. He sniffed out the cheats and exiled them. He dictated who'd be on which team. And then T was always the first to get bored with whatever they were playing, and wander off across the lawn to talk to the grown-ups while they chatted and sipped their after-lunch port or coffee.

Anyway. Time to get to the bottom of things. Especially now the weed was kicking in. Alice could feel the icy coldness behind her eyes. A sure sign.

"How was East Hampton?" she asked.

Tristan sighed. "Fine. Being with my dad's a bit of a stress. He's always dropping hints about my future in Parliament and how hard I should be working, and getting into bloody Oxford."

"Poor you, babe." Alice nodded sympathetically. "He's always known how to pile on the pressure." It was true. Tristan's father, Lord Cecil Murray-Middleton, was deter-mined that his only child should follow him into politics. Alice suspected it was his masterplan for Tristan to be elected Prime Minister someday. Not a bad goal actually. The more famous and powerful you could be, the better. But it wasn't going to happen—not if T had anything to do with it. He had other plans. Like moving to Paris, where his mum was from. He'd live in a garret and subsist on cigarettes and red wine while he painted the view from his window over and over in different colors. Or became a cutting-edge architect. Or a documentary filmmaker. His latest was some absurd idea that he could sail his tiny boat round the world and not go to university at all. Idiotic, Alice thought. She was determined to go to New College, Oxford, like her father, and planned to persuade T to do the same.

But now wasn't the time to talk about all that. She had other things on her mind.

"I wasn't asking about your dad though." Alice leaned back on her hands with a strange rush of confidence. "Isn't there anything else going on? I just feel like we have more to catch up on." She leveled her stare straight at Tristan.

He dropped his eyes. "Really?" He took a deep toke on their joint. "Like what?"

"Oh, I don't know. Like the fact that your summer girlfriend just turned up at my school, and is now in my boarding house, sharing a room with my best friend?"

Alice stopped herself. She hadn't meant to sound so vehement.

"Look, Al," T began in a stilted voice, "Dylan isn't my girlfriend anymore. Like I told you, it's over. I don't know what you suspect, but she's not here because of me."

Alice curled her lip. *Why would I suspect that?* it seemed to say. But Tristan had started now and he was determined to get it out.

"We had a good time together," he carried on, absently picking some threads out of a hole in his jeans. "But when I left I thought it was finished. I *wanted* it to be finished. She's only here because her mum ran off with Victor Dalgleish." Tristan cleared his throat. "Maybe she thinks we'll get back together, but . . . I'm . . ."

He trailed off and stole a glance over at Alice. This felt like perilous territory. Maybe he should shut up before he said something irreversible. Before he changed things forever.

Or maybe he should just close his eyes and jump.

"You don't have to explain," Alice mumbled stiffly. "It's nothing to do with me. Why should I care?"

Tristan looked hurt. "Oh, I thought . . ."

"What?"

"Nothing. Just, I'm sorry I didn't tell you the other night at Emerald's that Dylan was moving here. I thought you seemed upset and—"

"Whatever, I'm fine."

They sank into an awkward silence. Tristan stared up at the sky. It was dark and inscrutable. Shit, girls were so moody— what had he done wrong?

He heard a noise come from Alice. She was shaking. Crying? He looked closer. No, laughing.

"What's so funny?" he asked. She'd better not be making fun of him.

Alice was giggling so hard she couldn't answer.

53

"V-V-Victor," she finally gasped. "Victor Dalgleish! What the f-fuck? How could anyone fall in love with him? He . . ." She caught her breath. "He looks like roadkill!" Her giggle sounded funny and high-pitched. It was infectious. Tristan cracked up.

"Shit, you're right. Those hideous furry sideburns. He's like a fucked-up squirrel."

They both subsided, helpless with laughter. Finally, Alice lay panting, her stomach muscles aching. She smelled the damp grass and soil and the sweet, faint remnants of weed. Tristan was spread out next to her, his arm almost touching hers. She heard him trying to catch his breath.

Neither of them spoke for a long time. In the end it was Tristan who broke the silence.

"Moon's so big tonight," he said softly. "It's almost full."

"Beautiful," Alice whispered. But she wasn't looking. She was watching his chest rise and fall.

He shifted his head on the blanket. "Your hair's all shiny," he murmured. He took up a lock at the side of her face and she felt him run it through his fingers. What would happen if she turned? The heat from Tristan's hand hovered just above her cheek.

He let her hair drop.

"Alice."

"Yes?"

He didn't answer but she knew his eyes were on her. She turned toward him. Then she felt his lips on hers. Soft, exploring. He kissed her more gently than he'd ever kissed anyone, stroking her face with his fingertips.

Alice smelled the soap on his skin and felt the familiar, worn material of his T-shirt. When she opened her eyes, all she could see were the stars.

CHAPTER NINE

The kettle in Tudor House's bright, homey kitchen shuddered and clicked off as the water boiled. Tally poured it over her chicken and mushroom noodles and pushed them about with her fork, breathing in the cloud of savory steam. *Mmmm.* Instant lunch. Being allowed to cook meals for yourself instead of eating dining-hall slop was one of the best perks of junior year—even though "cook" was something of an overstatement, considering that the kitchen's only appliances were a toaster, a kettle, and four painfully slow electric burners. That was all part of a conspiracy by Mrs. Traphorn, St. Cecilia's headmistress, to coax the girls to eat in the cafeteria despite their so-called "independence." "The community that dines together, shines together," she was fond of telling prospective parents. Obviously she'd never had to eat the mush that the dinner ladies doled out.

As Tally prepared to take a mouthful of noodles, a piece

of paper detached itself from the opposite wall, where it had been tacked, and fell to the floor. She picked it up. It was a photograph of Dylan Taylor—an absolutely hideous one. Dylan looked like a sea monster, with clumps of seaweed hanging off her ears, sand matted in her hair, one eye closed, and an entire nipple exposed.

Tally almost snorted her food up into her nose. There was no doubt about who was behind this little project. She placed the picture on the kitchen counter. There were probably dozens more copies of it plastered round the house. Sure enough, looking next door, she saw one hanging crookedly underneath an *Atonement* poster.

Just then, someone started clapping for attention. The charity meeting in the common room was about to start. Inside, the other girls in their class had already claimed seats and were fidgeting and screeching so loudly it reminded Tally of the pigeons in Trafalgar Square. Every chair was taken. Juniors were perched on the window ledges and on top of the radiator and scrunched cross-legged on the floor. Tally trod over Clemmie Lockheed and Farah Assadi. Clemmie, one of the biggest nerds in the class, was holding a pad and pen awkwardly over her knee, and looked poised to start scribbling notes.

With a gasp, Tally realized that the Dylan photo she'd seen from the kitchen really was only the beginning: The entire common room was smothered in color photocopies. She scanned the place. Dylan hadn't yet arrived.

"You are such a bitch." She shook her head at Alice, weaving her way toward the maroon sofa where Alice was saving her a seat.

Alice chuckled. Then, suddenly, seeing Gabrielle Bunter about to plop next to her, she slapped her hand down.

"Excuse me," she hissed. "Taken."

"Oh, sorry." Gabby lumbered backward. She hunched against the wall, a frown line creasing her chubby forehead.

Alice rolled her eyes. There was no doubt about it, Gabby Bunter was the weirdest girl in the school. When they'd all first arrived at St. Cecilia's, in sixth grade, she used to waddle about the grounds wearing giant Bose headphones over her stringy hair, preventing anyone from ever speaking to her. (Not that anyone wanted to.) One time, as an experiment, Alice and Mimah had snatched the headphones off her head and hidden them. Gabby had gone totally hysterical—so hysterical, in fact, that their housemistress, Miss Wilde, had threatened lockdown on everyone till the headphones were returned.

"That was close," Alice whispered loudly as Tally dropped onto the couch next to her. "Scabby Gabby almost sat here."

"She never gets any less freakish," Tally muttered. "I can't believe Mimah got stuck sharing a room with her. Anyway, what's your news?" Tally and Alice had been at separate lessons all morning and hadn't had time to chat. "What happened last night? Where did you run off to?"

"Everybody shut up!" a voice barked suddenly above the racket. It belonged to Sonia Khan. She was standing in front of a collage of four Dylan pictures, glaring round the room. The little diamond studs she wore in her ears flashed in the light from the windows behind her. Tally giggled. Sonia's mean expression didn't go with her dinky new button nose. She looked ridiculous, like a kitten trying to imitate a tiger. Tally still didn't understand why Sonia had gone to the lengths of a nose job to fix something that hadn't been all that bad to begin with, but Sonia insisted that all the women in her family got them; it was practically *de rigueur* once you turned sixteen. Besides that, she seemed convinced it'd help her finally find a boyfriend. And that would be a relief for everyone.

"Right," Sonia was saying, "as I've been appointed Charity Representative, I need to let Sharko know by this afternoon what we're doing for our October House Event. Obviously we'll all have to agree on whatever it is. But my idea gets first consideration since I'm in charge."

Tally rolled her eyes. She knew Sonia was going to suggest something to do with a film or a TV show. Sonia was obsessed with becoming a director, even though the only thing she ever shot on her £10,000 digital camera was footage of them all getting ready for parties or brushing their teeth before bed. "Real-world cinema," she called it. Real-shit cinema, Tally thought.

"Here it is." Sonia took a deep breath. She'd been planning

this for the past two days and was desperate for it to go well. "Our very own version of *Pop Idol*, presented by . . . the junior class. Most people will play the contestants," she rushed on, trying to get out all the details before someone butted in. "Everyone'll sing a few lines of music and then be critiqued by the judges. At the end, the audience . . ."

"Hang on, hang on, this sounds complicated," complained Farah Assadi in her low, grainy voice. A lot of boys said it was sexy. "Who exactly get to be the judges?"

Sonia stopped short. Of course it was Farah who'd cut her off. Skinny bitch, with her pretentious razor-chopped haircut and big, overly made-up eyes.

"We'll decide later," Sonia said, pursing her lips. Not that there was anything to decide. She already knew who the judges were and it wasn't going to come as a surprise to anyone. There was no way in hell *she* was getting up and singing in front of the whole school. She stole a look at Alice. *Pop Idol* was just the kind of cool plan she'd love.

Except that Alice wasn't listening. She didn't even seem to have heard the idea. She was whispering intently to Tally, the side of her cheek slightly flushed. For a second, Sonia stopped hearing all the questions being shot at her from the meeting as she strained her ears and squinted toward her two best friends. What were they saying? And why wasn't she in on the secret?

Alice paused, then leaned in closer to Tally. Someone was staring at her; she could feel it. "Listen, don't tell anyone about me and T just yet," she said softly. "I don't want everyone gossiping."

Tally waved her hand dismissively. "Okay, okay," she rushed. "But how did it happen? Were you planning it for a while? I sort of suspected you had a crush—"

"Of course I didn't!" Alice cut her off. "It was a total surprise. I mean, it's *Tristan.* There we were, just having a spliff, and he jumped on me. Confessed he's been in love with me for years and years. He was practically crying. I was like, 'Oh shit.' I didn't know what to do. I swear I'd never even thought of him like that."

Alice listened to herself; the story sounded good this way. Clearly Tristan had been thinking all these things even if he hadn't said them, and that meant she was telling the truth.

Tally was shaking her head. "Oh my god, he's so stoic," she breathed. "I never would have guessed! When did it start, did he say?"

Alice considered gravely. "He didn't really. But I think it might have been way back during that Easter of eighth grade when our families went on safari together. Remember? I got the feeling he was lusting after me the whole time."

"Wow, poor T. That was almost three years ago. He must have really been pining for you."

"I suppose so." Alice raised her right eyebrow suggestively. "That would explain how passionate he was. He must have been so pent up!"

"Oh my god!" Tally squealed. They both started giggling.

"Shhh," Alice choked out between laughs.

"Excuse me!" snapped Sonia's piercing voice. She was rapping on the TV with the flat of her hand. "Order!" The noise in the common room died down. They'd still decided nothing. "Look, if no one likes the *Pop Idol* idea, then come up with some suggestions yourselves."

People started shouting things out.

"Bake sale!"

"Borrring."

"Oh please! Everybody does that."

"We could make jewelry and sell it."

"How about putting on a play?"

"What play? And when would we rehearse?"

"I have an idea," Alice said loudly, raising her chin in the air. The room fell silent. She waited a beat. "We should do a fashion show. We've already got loads of clothes. All we'd need is a catwalk and I reckon we could sort that out."

There were murmurs of approval.

"But a fashion show would just be us strutting round wearing our own stuff," Zanna Balfour whined. "Who'd pay to see that?"

"I agree, we need an *angle*," Farah Assadi chimed in.

"Here's your angle." Heads turned. The husky voice had come from the back of the room. Mimah Calthorpe de Vyle-Hanswicke was leaning against the door frame with her arms crossed. "Pashminas," she said.

"Pashminas?" Sonia sneered.

"Yes. Congratulations, you speak English," Mimah shot back. "We all wear them, don't we? Between us, we must have hundreds in different colors. So we make a rule: The only things allowed down the runway are us, wearing our pashminas. Only our pashminas, wrapped around our bodies in as many ways as we can imagine. We work out dance routines. People will be talking about it for years."

"Wicked idea!" Clemmie Lockheed chirped, clapping her hands.

"Pashminas to the rescue for charity. I love it," Zanna cried.

"Hang on, that's what we should call it!" Tally exclaimed. "'Pashminas to the Rescue.'"

"If we can get permission," Sonia mumbled. But by now people were nodding and talking all over the room. "Fine," she conceded grudgingly. "Let's put it to the vote. Everyone who likes the idea, raise your hand."

Mimah looked to where Tally and Alice were sitting. They were smiling with their arms straight up in the air.

Perfect! Mimah laughed to herself. Those bitches. Did they really think she was going to sit back and let herself be dumped?

"Tell me I didn't miss the meeting," Dylan panted, clattering up to Mimah five minutes later as the juniors poured into the corridor. The room's warm, stuffy smell rolled out after them.

"I *could* tell you that," Mimah said, "but it'd be a lie. Where were you?" She stood in front of Dylan, blocking her way.

"In the art building talking to Miss Baskin about joining her class. Art's my favorite subject. I've always loved sculpture."

"Oh my god, really?" Mimah nodded exaggeratedly. "That is so fascinating. Tell me more."

Dylan folded her arms. She didn't get Mimah; the girl was as hot and cold as a pair of faucets. But she was the only person so far who'd even pretended to be friendly, so it wasn't as if Dylan had much choice.

"'Scuse me," she said, attempting to make her way into the common room.

"Why?"

"Umm, because I'd like to sign up for some charity stuff before it's too late?"

She pushed forward.

"Wait," Mimah blurted out. "Don't go in there."

"Huh? Why not?"

"It's just . . . we should get lunch first. It's fish and chips day. You can sign up later."

"But we're here now."

Just then, three girls walked out of the common room. When they saw Dylan, they froze, gasping. Clemmie Lockheed tittered.

"Mimah," Dylan narrowed her eyes. "What is going on?"

Mimah sighed. "You might as well see for yourself. Go on, have a look."

Dylan stepped through the doorway. For a few seconds, she stood there, taking in the dozens and dozens of photos lining the walls. It was like her worst nightmare: bad hair. Bad face. Bad pose. Her fucking *nipple*.

No, actually it was worse than a nightmare—there'd be no waking up.

"Who the hell did this?" Dylan choked, ripping down the nearest photo and crushing it in her hand.

Mimah shook her head. "You mean you can't guess?"

CHAPTER TEN

*T*ally hadn't worked in the school library for terms and terms and now she was suddenly remembering why. It felt like a tomb. The windows in the cavernous main reading room were so high you had to stand on tiptoe to see out of them. The only sounds were whispers and the rustle of pages. And there were too many books. Far too many books, all looming down and shoving in your face everything you'd never bothered to read and probably wouldn't understand even if you tried.

But today was going to be different. Tally passed into a series of smaller rooms and wandered toward the poetry section. Back when the school had still been a grand stately home owned by Lord and Lady Cornwallis, this part of the house had been a cluster of elegant drawing rooms used for entertaining. St. Cecilia's first headmistress had tried to keep their style intact, obviously deluded into thinking that girls concentrated better when they felt at home. What planet was she living on? Tally snickered quietly as she spotted Bella Scott snoring gently on a windowseat, her head lolling to one side and her math textbook crushed facedown on the floor.

She padded on over oriental rugs, past an unlit fireplace with a painting of a horse above it, past velvet armchairs and carved antique desks adorned with porcelain lamps. All this *was* rather nice for a school library. Tally had been impressed by it when she'd first arrived from Moscow three years ago; it was so perfectly . . . English. But she'd got used to it.

A bank of brand-new Apple computers blinked from the far wall. Tally hadn't checked her e-mail in at least half an hour. The poetry could wait. She tapped her St. Cecilia's ID into the system.

Where is my scarf? read the title of a new message. From her mother. Tally sighed. She clicked it.

> I can't find my yellow Pucci scarf. If you took it, send it back now.
> I hope you are not coming back for half-term. Boris and I are going to Cyprus for that week and we don't want you in the house when we're not there. Tell your father you need to stay with him.
> Mum
> PS Send the scarf

Tally shut her eyes for a second. She hadn't been planning on going back to Moscow till the Christmas holidays, but still . . . Did her mum always have to be such a bitch? She'd started acting like this around the time Tally turned thirteen. Tally could remember it as clearly as if she had it on film.

One day she'd gone to the set of *Da! Fashionista*, the glamorous talk show her mum hosted in Moscow. Not that her mother needed to work, obviously. Tally's grandfather took care of them all with his immense oil fortune. Lyudmila just adored the fame and attention. She loved strutting around on set in her knee-high boots and miniskirts, flirting with fashion designers and male models and having her face plastered on posters all over the city.

That afternoon three years ago, Tally had been on her way to a friend's birthday party. She was wearing a black satin minidress with snakeskin stilettos and no tights. Her white-blond hair flowed loose over her shoulders.

"Yeah baby!" the film crew catcalled her. She'd known them all for years. "Work it, girl! Look who's all grown up!"

"Better watch out, Lyudmila," the producer had joked, slapping his fleshy hand across her mum's shoulder. "Soon we might ask your daughter to take your place!"

Tally watched her mother's jaw tighten. Six months later, Lyudmila had sent Tally off to England to live with her dad for good.

A low, male voice punctured Tally's reverie. "Hiya—it's Natalya, isn't it?"

Tally whipped her head round. Mr. Logan! A little gasping sound escaped from her nose.

Shit. Had he heard? Her e-mail was still open. Hurriedly, she closed it.

"Hard at work?" Mr. Logan asked. He'd shoved his hands into the pockets of his corduroys. His shirtsleeves were rolled up to his elbows, exposing his strong forearms.

"Posh in here, isn't it?" he carried on, jerking his head at their surroundings. "Chandeliers and everything. You wouldn't find any of those where I taught before." He looked at Tally expectantly, waiting for her to ask where that was.

Tally rubbed her right ankle with the bottom of her left loafer and fixed her clear, gray eyes on Mr. Logan. There was no way she was doing a repeat of her mortifying blushing fiasco from earlier in the week. "Oh really?" she asked coolly. "Where did you work bef—"

"State school in Tower Hamlets," Mr. Logan interrupted. He tossed his head back dramatically and ran his hand over the unruly curls at the front. He smelled faintly of aftershave, or maybe it was cologne. "Try bringing those kids here. They wouldn't know what had hit 'em."

"Yes, we're very lucky," Tally said. She groaned inwardly. What a fucking boring thing to say.

"They were a difficult lot," Mr. Logan carried on, not seeming to have heard her. "Rowdy. Boisterous. But there was some raw intelligence in that classroom like I've never seen before. It felt good to know I was giving those kids a chance." He glanced down at Tally again. "So what brings you to the library? The vast pursuit of knowledge?"

"I came to find that poem you read us in class the other day," she answered. "By Yeats, I think. Where he's talking to his girlfriend or whoever it is, about his dreams."

"Ah yes. It's called 'He Wishes for the Cloths of Heaven,'" Mr. Logan said. He breathed deeply and struck a pose, then, gazing into the middle distance, began reciting. His voice sounded soft and throaty, as if he'd drunk too much milk. It made Tally feel strange.

"Indeed, that's a beautiful poem," Mr. Logan said once he'd finished. "But too many people like it. It always wins plebeian competitions, like The Nation's Favorite Love Poems and things like that. It's become a bit of a cliché. Why not try reading some on your own? Then you can tell me what you think. Here, come on."

Tipping his head sideways, he beckoned, then disappeared round the bookshelf before Tally could answer. She followed.

"Let's see, what might you like? Have you read any Keats?" he asked, running his index finger over some spines.

Tally pretended to think, then shook her head.

Duh. Of course not. This was the first time she'd ever taken any voluntary interest in English. Schoolwork and all that crap weren't things you bothered with unless you had to. Even Alice knew that, and she was the one who was so obsessed with getting high marks and glowing report cards.

But now . . . well, for some reason Tally was desperate to have Mr. Logan approve of her. She wanted to win his praise.

He'd taken down a thick hardback—*John Keats, Letters and Poems*, it said—and was flipping through it, his head bent in concentration. She looked at his neck. Her eyes traced the line of his wavy brown hair to where it met his collar and flicked up into little curls. It looked like he hadn't had a haircut in ages. Maybe he didn't care about insignificant things like that.

"Here is a haunting poem about a man bewitched by a beautiful woman," Mr. Logan said, meeting Tally's gaze. "Because, as you know, beautiful women are dangerous."

Holding the book straight out in front of him with both hands, he cleared his throat and read in a silken voice:

"Oh what can ail thee, knight-at-arms,
Alone and palely loitering?
The sedge has withered from the lake,
And no birds sing"

Mr. Logan glanced at Tally again, then jumped his eyes farther down the page.

"I met a lady in the meads,
Full beautiful—a fairy's child,
Her hair was long, her foot was light,
And her eyes were wild.

71

I made a garland for her head,
And bracelets too, and fragrant zone;
She looked at me as she did love,
And made sweet moan. "

On the words "sweet moan," Mr. Logan shut his eyes, then closed the book abruptly.

"So," he said. "What do you think?"

Tally gulped. She realized she'd been staring at him. She'd never had a man read poetry just for her before. She'd let herself imagine that he was speaking to her, that she was the beautiful lady on the page and he was her lovelorn knight.

"Er . . . ," she murmured. *Say something. Say anything.* "It's very . . . scary, isn't it?" she ventured. No, that sounded lame. "It's quite, what's the word . . . enigmatic?" Tally felt a shock of pride—even though she wasn't particularly sure what *enigmatic* meant.

A muscle twitched in Mr. Logan's forehead and his look brightened. "That is a very astute comment," he told her. "Well done. Perhaps you have a talent for poetry."

Tally glowed. A talent. Well, why not? Just because she'd never set her mind to working didn't mean she wasn't clever. Maybe she was even a secret genius. She pictured herself winning the school Poetry Prize. Her name would be inscribed on the heavy wooden tablets in the Main Hall. They'd read it out at Parents' Day. She'd walk up the aisle between everyone's seats to collect her certificate, and people would crane to see her, murmuring, "Wow, who's that girl? She doesn't look like a nerd. She must be naturally gifted." *Naturally gifted.* Her father would be so surprised that he'd actually pay attention to her for once.

"Listen, Natalya," came Mr. Logan's voice.

"It's Tally. Please."

He smiled at her. "Tally. What are you thinking about uni? Do you know where you might apply next year?"

"Umm, well," Tally said. It was a bit embarrassing, but she'd hardly thought about university at all. Whenever teachers started going on about it she just sort of tuned out, always falling back on the vague idea that she'd return to Moscow after school was finished. But now, considering it, she wasn't quite sure she wanted to.

"Because," Mr. Logan said, "I'm always looking for eager young minds to nurture." He had his milky voice on again. "If you ever have any questions, or read something you want to discuss, come and see me. My door's open to you."

Tally opened her mouth to thank him. But she was interrupted by the five-thirty bell ringing for supper.

CHAPTER ELEVEN

Over in Hasted House's dining hall, the racket was deafening. Tristan knew that even if he yelled and swore at the top of his lungs, no one would ever hear him. He rested his cheek on his hand. This, right here, was the problem with school: Sure, it was brilliant fun when you were in the right mood, but it was an absolute bloody nightmare when you just wanted some space.

Next to him, boys in all years were elbowing each other to get at the big steaming platters that had just been set down, shoveling themselves piles of shepherd's pie and peas before everything disappeared. There were no chairs at the long tables—just flat wooden benches that ran alongside. Everyone was squeezed in together, making it impossible for people to get in and out of their seats, and easy to shove off the idiots who sat at the ends. Rowdy food fights kept breaking out at the front of the hall where the younger students sat. They'd chuck bread rolls and butter pats at one another and send saucers clattering down the table. Then suddenly the stern voice of a housemaster would pierce all the other noise in the room. The talking would deflate for a few minutes, but it was never long before another bubble of roaring and laughing and clanging swelled up to bursting-point again.

Tristan's crew sat near the end of a long table, a few seats away from their housemaster. Mr. Brand was with two other members of the math staff, and their corduroys and checked shirts stuck out like lurid blossoms in the field of navy and white uniforms. The three of them were probably discussing Pythagoras or some other hellishly boring subject that numbers geeks were obsessed with.

Seb Ogilvy was reaching across three people to ladle a mountain of carrots onto his plate. "Hey, Meters, that was a really cool party invite you sent out on Facebook," he was saying to George Demetrios, his voice dripping with sarcasm. He waved the serving spoon around with a dramatic flourish. "'Demon Demetrios's Birthday Extravaganza.' Yeah, great name, mate. I'm sure everyone can't *wait* to come."

Jasper von Holstadt howled with laughter and banged his fist on the table, making the dishes shake. Tristan flinched a little.

"Demon Demetrios!" Jasper gasped. "That is unbelievably lame. What were you thinking?"

"I don't know what you mean." George looked hurt. "I thought it was a good nickname. I wanted something catchy."

"You can't give *yourself* a nickname, you jackass," groaned Seb. "You're meant to wait for other people to do it for you."

"Classic!" Jasper laughed, shaking his head.

"Shut up, you fuckwits, or I'll disinvite you. Anyway, are you coming? It's next weekend. At my parents' house in London."

"'Course we're coming," Tristan said, without looking up from his plate.

"Just make sure you bring all the hot girls along." Jasper punched Tristan's arm. "That means Dylan, T. Bring her. She'd better live up to everything you told us over the summer."

"Yeah, what's happening with Dylan anyway?" Seb looked at Tristan curiously. "I thought you'd be back together with her, since she's here."

"She must be gagging for it by now." Jas grinned.

"Arrr. Gagging for it!" chimed in George Demetrios, laughing obnoxiously and spraying flecks of potato onto Tristan's blazer.

"Hey, man, that's disgusting." Tristan frowned and shoved him away. He wiped his sleeve on the edge of the table and kept eating his food in silence.

Jasper and Seb looked at each other.

"So?" Jas prodded. "What are you gonna do? I'd go for it. You said she was a brilliant shag."

Tristan let his fork drop. "Look, I told you about that before

I knew you'd *meet* her," he said. "Leave it alone. I feel a bit shitty talking about her like that now."

George guffawed. "Haha! You're such a pussy."

Jas and Seb burst out laughing too. "Yeah! What the fuck is up with you, T?" Seb said. "Are you in looove with her or something?"

"Woo! T's in love. T's in love."

"No!" Tristan protested. "I dunno, it just feels wrong, you know? Leave it."

He poured himself a cup of the watery orange juice the school served at every single meal, and ignored the fact that Seb was staring at him. The Dylan situation had been gnawing at T ever since he'd checked her Facebook page that afternoon. Dylan had listed only one friend at St. Cecilia's: Mimah Calthorpe de Vyle-Hanswicke. Fantastic. She'd been adopted by a social pariah. Not that Tristan should care, but he felt he'd got sort of close to Dylan over the summer while all that stuff was happening with her mum and dad, and although it definitely wasn't ideal that she'd moved here, he felt like a bit of a bastard just dropping her. Leaving her to the St. Cecilia's wolves.

On the other hand, what right did Dylan have to plant herself down the road and make him feel guilty? This was exactly what he hated most in the world: having obligations to people. Having people rely on him.

Tristan glared at the oak-paneled wall opposite his seat, feeling agitated by the whole situation. Then suddenly an image popped into his head: Alice, in Italy this summer. She was holding a champagne flute, running down the wave-smoothed beach at dawn after they'd stayed up all night, her arms flung wide, her face turned toward the rising sun.

No question about it. He was young and free. The important thing was doing whatever he wanted.

CHAPTER TWELVE

*J*emimah! Jemimah," Miss Sharkreve called, waving frantically at Mimah Calthorpe de Vyle-Hanswicke's retreating back. She set off across the Great Lawn, her hair whipped by the wind and her skirt flapping out behind her like a loose sail. Mimah, who had been running in the direction of the school theater, slowed down and swung round, sighing.

"Where are you off to?" Sharko panted. She pretended to cough a few times to hide how unfit she was. "They're expecting you at lacrosse practice."

Mimah scraped the dry ground with her toe and didn't say anything.

"Well, go on, you'd better hurry and change, or you'll miss the beginning," Sharko prompted.

"I'm not playing lax this term," Mimah said.

A furrow appeared in her housemistress's freckled forehead.

"You can't be serious. You've been on the team since freshman year. You're our *star*."

It was true. In fact, Mimah had competed in every school sport at one point or another: tennis, football, lacrosse, hockey, netball. But lax had always been her best. Everyone knew she'd be made captain next year when they were seniors.

"Not anymore." Mimah shook her head defiantly. "I'm finished with it."

Miss Sharkreve stared at her, concern misting her light blue eyes. "Mimah, are you all right?" she asked. "And Charlotte? I know some things have been difficult at home with—"

"I'm fine," Mimah almost shouted. "We're fine." She'd pulled it together a little, but her voice sounded strangled, the way it would if she sprained her ankle in practice but didn't want to be pulled off the team.

The truth was, *fine* was a massive overstatement—at least in her sister Charlotte's case. Charlie was only fourteen and had been hit hard by their father's public disgrace. Just last Easter, she'd been a total joiner at St. Cecilia's—always doing school plays and singing in the choir and playing sports—but now Mimah hardly ever saw her around the school grounds. Charlie used to talk a lot too, but not anymore. At first, she'd kept asking their mother stupid questions, like when Daddy was coming back, and whether he and Mummy were still in love. Finally, their mum had slammed her ever-present whisky onto the table and shouted at Charlie to shut the fuck up.

And Charlie had. Lately, she'd fallen in with a freakish,

stringy-haired crowd in her year who listened to garage and drum 'n' bass. She'd started wearing skinny jeans and high-top sneakers. Her eyes looked sunken. Mimah was pretty sure she was popping pills, and wondered if she was doing other things too.

Miss Sharkreve glanced at her watch and nodded slightly. If Jemimah said she and her sister were fine, then it certainly wasn't her concern to pry. In any case, it was tidier when the girls kept their personal problems to themselves.

"All right then." She gave Mimah a long look. "I'm disappointed, but I can't force you to play lax. I hope you'll reconsider. You really have a duty not to let your school down."

Miss Sharkreve liked the way those words sounded. *Duty. Reconsider.* It was her job to get the girls thinking about right and wrong for themselves. "Well, I must go," she said briskly, turning in the direction of the art studios. It was almost time for the Saturday-afternoon life-drawing club that she supervised for the seniors. She had to meet the male models; it wouldn't do for the girls to see them unsupervised.

Mimah stood still for a second. Then she rolled her eyes and took off toward the theater again. It was none of Sharko's fucking business whether she played sports or not. It was nobody's business. Why was it that the people she wished would pay attention to her insisted on ignoring her, and the people she wished would leave her alone were always on her back?

CHAPTER THIRTEEN

*D*ylan had almost given up waiting when she finally saw Mimah jog through the line of gnarled oak trees round the side of the theater. If Mimah had stood her up, that would have been one less friend she had at this snobby school. And one less pretty much meant zero.

"Do you have the stuff?" she called in a loud whisper. She jumped up from the bench she'd been slouching on and ran over.

"Shut up!" Mimah scowled.

"There's no one around. At least, I don't think there is. All the Saturday-afternoon clubs started like ten minutes ago." Dylan looked anxiously back at the empty stone patio outside the theater. Damn. It seemed like she was always making stupid mistakes here, being too loud or too friendly or too obvious. These English girls didn't seem to get her, and she sure as hell didn't get them.

"Just be quiet for a minute, okay?" Mimah snapped. "We have to look innocent, like we're going for a stroll. If we get caught, we're fucked." After dealing with Miss Sharkreve, she wasn't in the mood for stupid people. "By the way, what on *earth* are you wearing?" She gaped at Dylan's getup of fluorescent pink leggings, black leg warmers, black leotard, and pink headband.

"What do you mean? It was for dance studio. This is what you wear. How else are you supposed to move around?"

Mimah sniffed. Dance Club was for losers. "Well, I just hope you're good. Because you look like a joke, walking round dressed like Exercise Barbie."

Dylan bit her lip. Sometimes it seemed like Mimah only wanted to be friends with her so she'd have someone to bully. Trying to block out the swishing sound that Mimah's ballet flats were making over the grass, she looked down over the school spread beneath them. An elegant avenue led from the Great Lawn to the chapel; gardeners in overalls beetled about the grounds, and a little farther away, on the games fields between the white goalposts, girls wearing long socks ran back and forth in patterns like migrating birds. At the side of one field stood a ring of younger students, cheering on the lax team at practice. One girl ran and turned a cartwheel. The others skipped up and down and applauded. They were about her sister Lauren's age, and they all looked the same: skinny with glossy ponytails, bootcut jeans, and lacy little tops.

Dylan missed her sister. Lauren had sent her a hungover-sounding e-mail this morning: Her new friends from school had taken her out last night to the pub in Notting Hill and got her drunk on pints of Fosters that someone's older brother kept buying them. Something that fun would never happen here. Those girls by the games field looked like they'd rather eat shit than let a new member into their clique.

Abruptly, Mimah turned off into the woods bordering the hill. She ducked through some barbed wire, and beckoned furtively to Dylan. "This way."

Dylan surveyed the fence. Cruel metal asterisks glinted along it, and she could see tufts of hair sticking out. Or was it fur? Wild animal fur. Dylan shuddered. The English countryside was a little bit like hell. What if she got snagged and turned rabid and Mimah abandoned her and she collapsed, foaming at the mouth? This wasn't where she wanted to die.

"Umm, actually I'm okay." She backed away. "This seems a little complicated. Maybe we should go home and make popcorn or something. Isn't *The Simpsons* on?"

Mimah rolled her eyes. "Come on, you wuss; you're not in New York anymore." She trod on the bottom strand of the fence and yanked the top one upward. "Look, you can get through there. You're not a fatty. Or are you?" She laughed sourly. "Your ass does look a bit big."

Bitch. Dylan squeezed her eyes shut and scrambled through the opening. Soil and dried leaves were clinging to her when she straightened up on the other side, but before she could brush them away she noticed a black blob scuttling up her leg.

"Arrrgh!" she screamed. "There's a spider on me, there's a spider on me! Get it off, get it off, get it ooooff!"

Mimah stared. She couldn't believe her eyes. Didn't these bloody Americans ever go outside?

By now Dylan was galloping around, shaking her leg like an epileptic dog. She looked like an escaped lunatic.

"What if it gets into my pants?" Dylan yelled. "What if it gets into my *underwear*?" She slapped her palm down hard on her thigh. A smudge appeared on the pink material of her leggings.

"Ewww! Gross!" she squealed, wringing her hands. "It's dead!"

"Of course it's dead, you idiot," came Mimah's voice. "You murdered it. Now will you stop fucking screaming?"

Dylan looked at her in surprise, suddenly turning red. What was she doing, losing it like that? Over a bug? With a pang, she thought of her friends back home. This little outing *so* wasn't their style. Sneaking out to the woods to get stoned? The closest they ever came was sneaking out to a café to get lunch.

"That's better. Are you finished?" Mimah asked.

Dylan nodded. "I, umm . . . ," she said lamely. "Our apartment in New York is really clean. Our maid makes sure there are no cockroaches or anything."

"Yes, well, maybe you should have brought your maid with you here. She could walk ahead of you with a dustpan and brush and sweep up any creepy crawlies before they got within two meters of you. And you might want to watch out for that horse shit," she added.

Dylan looked down. A big pile of manure lay on the ground right next to her shoe; she'd almost stepped in it. She gasped and jumped to one side.

Mimah chuckled. "I take it you don't ride horses."

"Of course I don't."

"You absolutely must learn to. It's like tennis: If you ever come to stay at our country house, everyone rides and you've got to join in. Alice and I were both in Pony Club when we were younger. I was better than her. I always beat her in eventing."

"Oh. Really? What's eventing?" Dylan asked.

"You must be joking," Mimah muttered. Without answering, she plunged into the trees, down what she seemed to think was a path. Dylan hurried behind, darting her eyes around for any dangling webs or suspicious leaf-shaking. After a while though, she let her guard down. The forest was like a strangely still room that smelled sweet and a little musty. They passed through streams of cool air and then warm air, where prongs of light pierced the leaves, spotlighting tree trunks and cushions of moss. They walked for a long time, until Dylan started to worry that Mimah was leading her round in circles.

"Are you sure you know where we're going?" she asked.

"Yes, obviously," Mimah said. "I come here all the time. This is my favorite smoking spot." She looked pointedly over her shoulder at Dylan. "I only tell the people I *trust* about it. See? We're here."

They'd come to a tiny clearing where a stream flashed in the light. A few feet away were some flat rocks and, piled behind them, the remains of a low stone wall. It made the perfect sitting area. If anyone came, you could duck and be momentarily hidden. That was a relief. Dylan didn't dare think what her mom would do if they got caught.

Mimah settled down cross-legged and dug in her pocket for the two joints she'd pre-rolled. She lit one. Dylan watched her take a deep toke, hold her breath, then let out a rich cloud of smoke. She looked so cool. That made Dylan nervous since she, on the other hand, was about to make an asshole of herself. She'd only got stoned once before. At least, she thought she'd been stoned; she might have just been trashed. It was two years ago, at her first boyfriend's party, and she'd ended up drunker than she'd ever been in her life. At about four in the morning, everyone sat in a circle passing around a pipe of weed. Brandon and his friends had started daring her and the other girls to kiss in front of them. Dylan had ended up making out with her best friend, Jessie, for two full minutes while the boys pounded the floor and cheered them on. Then she'd spent the rest of the night throwing up in the toilet.

Mimah passed Dylan the spliff. Dylan balanced it between her index and middle fingers like a cigarette but it wobbled and fell. Probably because she didn't smoke cigarettes either.

Mimah giggled. "Hold it with your thumb."

Dylan nodded and took a shallow puff. Then she held her breath with her eyes wide open, like she was underwater.

"I'm sort of bad at smoking," she said. She hadn't breathed out, and her voice sounded constipated.

"Oh really? I'd never have noticed," Mimah shot back. "First of all, you've got to take more than that. And chill out."

Dylan tried again. She coughed.

Mimah cracked up next to her.

"What? Am I doing it wrong?"

"Why didn't you tell me about your little ballerina hobby?" Mimah cackled, pointing to Dylan's leggings again. Dylan glared and tossed the joint on the ground between them. She was at the end of her fuse.

"Why do you have to be so mean?" she retorted. "If you don't want me here, I can leave, you know."

"Oh please. Keep your shirt on," Mimah snorted. But when she spoke again, her voice sounded friendlier. "Seriously, are you any good?"

Dylan started to nod, then awkwardly crooked her head to one side just in time. You were never supposed to say you were good at anything in this weird country, even if you'd won Wimbledon or something. How could she forget, after finding that out the hard way? The other day she'd walked into the common room and found Zanna Balfour and Sonia lounging on the sofa.

"Dylan, are you gonna go for any school teams?" Zanna had said, craning her neck round on the cushion. "I thought all Americans loved sports."

"That's a great idea; I'm definitely good at sports," Dylan had said. "I could probably get onto the hockey team or something. I've always been awesome at—" She'd stopped suddenly, noticing that Sonia and Zanna were grinning snidely at each other, sharing some kind of private laugh. It hadn't taken her long to find out that the joke was her.

Now, in answer to Mimah's question, she looked down demurely. "Oh, no. I'm a terrible dancer, I have no rhythm whatsoever. I don't even know why they let me in the class."

"Don't be so modest, silly; I'm sure you're fine." Mimah leaned back and appeared to be thinking, her black fringe tumbling over her eyes. Without warning, she sat up straight. "Hold on, I have a brilliant idea! Let's do our own special dance together in the 'Pashminas to the Rescue' show. We'll be partners. It'll be so fun!"

"Umm . . ." Dylan shook her head, trying to sound diplomatic. "I don't think so."

"What do you mean? Why not?"

"I wasn't planning on getting involved. It just doesn't sound like . . . my thing."

"What, dancing?"

"No. Getting laughed at in front of the whole school. Everyone would make fun of us."

"Of course they wouldn't. Go on," Mimah urged. "If we choose a good song and work out an amazing routine, they'll all look like spazzes compared to us. Say yes, say yes!"

Dylan glowed with the flattery, despite the fact that she found it unnerving when Mimah switched moods like this out of the blue. The thing was, Mimah was good to know. Over the past week, she'd been the only person Dylan could sit with at meals, the only one who'd save her a spot in class or whose door she could go knock on when everyone else in Tudor House was curled up gossiping in each others' rooms.

She'd also been the only one who hadn't found it funny to stick up pictures of Dylan's bare nipple all over the school.

"I hear they're inviting all the Hasted House boys," Mimah wheedled.

That did it. Dylan had been trying to think of a way to attract Tristan's attention. It wasn't exactly easy, trapped here in the middle of a bunch of fields, and dancing in the PTTR show could be the perfect chance to remind him what he was missing out on.

"Okay," she sighed, not wanting to seem too eager. Mimah might suspect something. "I guess I'm down with that. Let's listen to some music tonight and come up with a song."

"Wicked! I'll lend you some of my pashminas. I have a dusty-rose-colored one that'll be gorgeous on you. Oooh, I can't wait! Here, let's smoke some more."

She handed Dylan the spliff again. Dylan took a third drag, then a fourth. Then a fifth. Then something started happening.

"Heehee," she giggled, feeling giddy. "Heeheehee!" She couldn't stop herself. Not that she wanted to. Were there birds twittering or was it her imagination?

"Birdies," Dylan called. "Where are you, birdies? Heehee."

"Who the hell are you talking to?" Mimah's voice floated across to her.

"Huh?"

"Never mind. Want to come to a party next weekend?"

"Huh?"

"What's wrong with you? It's at George Demetrios's house. He's one of T's good friends."

"Beeest frieeends," Dylan sang. She gave a high-pitched giggle. "Who?"

"Tristan and George!" Mimah sounded like she was shouting from far away.

"Sounds nice, I'll go," Dylan said. "Wait. Are you sure I'm invited?"

"You're invited now. And stop hogging the spliff. You've definitely had enough." Mimah plucked the dead joint out of Dylan's hand and relit it.

Dylan propped her head on a rock and lay with her mouth hanging open, listening to the stream hum its happy song. Suddenly she felt something dribbling down onto her top. She lifted her fingers to her face. Was it drool? She smeared it away, then tried to shut her jaw by pummeling her chin with her hand.

"God, you're a mess," Mimah groaned. "I hope you don't act like this at the party."

"What party?"

"The one next weekend." Mimah sighed. This was getting ridiculous. "We'll go up to London straight after Saturday-morning lessons."

"Oh," Dylan murmured, "can I come? Sounds fun."

Mimah stretched out on the grass with her hands behind her head, ignoring her gibbering companion. She had other things to occupy her—like how it would be to see Seb Ogilvy at the party. He hadn't spoken to her since those rumors had started circulating, and she just *had* to sort things out.

"Fun isn't the word," she mumbled to no one in particular. "Parties are what this fucking school is all about."

CHAPTER FOURTEEN

ome on, Tals." Alice pouted into the locker-room mirror, admiring how her netball skirt complemented her long, tanned legs. "We'll be late for class. Don't make us end up doing warm-ups with all the losers."

"Can't find my bloody socks," Tally mumbled from the slatted wooden bench she was hunched on. Why did this always happen to her? She rummaged through her bag, sending shoelaces and bandages and rumpled T-shirts flying to the floor. Fuck. She'd promised herself she was going to get it together this term. Well, actually, she promised herself that every term—and she never did.

"I can't stand watching this!" Alice declared. "Let me put you out of your misery." Reaching for a shelf in her neatly ordered locker, she plucked out a perfectly rolled-up pair of socks and chucked them to Tally. "Here, borrow these. But don't ruin them. And this time, wash them before you give them back to me. And don't you dare lose them."

"Thanks, sweetie." Tally pulled them on, pretending not to hear the bossy strain in Alice's voice. *Voilà!*"

"Oh. My. God." Alice snorted with laughter. Tally's netball ensemble was a wreck. Her T-shirt was too small for her and was clinging in all the wrong places. Her skirt looked as if somebody's cat had been mauling it, with loose threads hanging off the bottom and a cigarette hole in the middle of the thigh.

"I'm a total mess, aren't I?" Tally burst out. "I should have bought new stuff last term, but I forgot."

"Don't be ridiculous; you look great." Alice slipped her arm through Tally's. *At least, for someone who gets neglected by their selfish mum and cokehead dad,* she added in her head. Not that she'd ever say that, of course. Honestly, Alice didn't know how Tally could bear having such dreadful parents. Her own mum and dad weren't exactly perfect, but at least they were dignified. At least they acted like *adults.*

Tally giggled, bumping her shoulder into Alice's bony one. "You still haven't told me what you were whispering to T about on the phone last night. I heard you sneak out to have your secret midnight chat. 'Nighty night, Lover Boy. Miss you. Kiss, kiss, kiss . . .'"

"Shut up!" Alice squealed. Her heart was fluttering wildly at the mention of Tristan's name.

"No way. Spill it!"

"I can't. It's private."

"Oh, go on!"

"Okay. It was amazing." Alice blushed, swinging open the glass door of the locker-room building. "He told me I was beautiful. And that all he could think about was being naked with me."

"Oh my god. Romantic!"

Alice nodded. "He kept saying how much he wished he could sneak out of school into my bed. And then he read me some new love-song lyrics he was writing. I think they were about me, Tals. I've never felt this way before."

Alice took a deep breath, feeling a pang of nervousness as she heard her own words. It was all true—things were going brilliantly with T—but she'd suddenly started to worry that they were moving too fast.

And then there was Dylan. For some reason, she couldn't get the bitch out of her mind. Every time Alice saw her, a cloud of jealousy shrouded her brain and she lost the ability to think straight. In fact, ever since this morning, the same hideous scene had been looping over and over in her head: Dylan and Tristan on the beach, shagging on a fluffy white towel under the round moon. Tristan, *her* Tristan, was slipping his hands all over Dylan's body, murmuring into her ear.

Not that Alice knew for sure whether the two of them had had sex. But she didn't need to know. It was logical; Dylan looked like the kind of slut who'd give it up to anyone.

A whistle blew across the field.

"Oh shit. Hurry up!" Alice broke into a run. It'd be awful if they were late. She hated being told off, especially in front of other people.

Tally jogged after her, dragging her Green Flash sneakers over the lawn and letting her eyes linger on the landscape. The day was the chilliest yet this term, and the sky was gray and flat.

On the concrete court, their manly gym teacher, Miss Colin, was wearing her usual lilac shellsuit, ushering everyone into teams for warm-ups and shouting instructions in her flinty Yorkshire accent. She was stocky but surprisingly agile, and the girls respected her even though she had a mullet and a pug nose that made her look like a bulldog wearing a wig. Fear of her sharp tongue kept people in check.

Glancing down at Alice's netball skirt, Miss Colin made a loud tutting sound. Every year these girls got tartier and tartier. This was a playing field, not a bloody nightclub. "Alice Rochester, team three," she pointed.

Alice followed the direction of her finger. Victoria Lindley and Sarah Renault, two utter losers, were doing clumsy-looking stretches, and right behind them was Dylan, bending over to tie her shoe with her ass sticking straight up in the air.

Alice planted herself as far from them all as possible. Fantastic. A team full of losers, plus her arch nemesis. To make matters worse, Dylan wasn't wearing the shorts that went with the regulation netball uniform; she was wearing frilly underwear instead, and Alice couldn't stop staring at them. They were white with red hearts sprinkled over them and little bits of lace puffing out. What a joke. Someone should stamp Dylan's stupid ass into the ground.

Alice spied round. Perhaps she could covertly dart onto a different team while Miss Colin had her back turned. Florence Norstrup-Fitzwilliam and Emilia Charles were chatting nearby, comparing the gold charm bracelets they both had on. Alice was friendly with both of those two—especially blond, vacant-looking Flossy, whose grandparents owned a villa near the Rochesters' on the French Riviera. She tensed up, ready to bolt over. But before she could make a move, Miss Colin tweeted her whistle again.

"Each warm-up group choose a leader," the gym teacher ordered. "When I call out your group, I want the leader to say her name. That way I'll know who to pick on when it all goes tits up."

Victoria and Sarah giggled. It was terribly funny when Miss Colin used common terms. That must be how they spoke in Yorkshire. Alice frowned as they turned their cowlike, questioning faces to her, deferring to her to be the leader. As she nodded regally without looking at them, the end of her ponytail flicked against her razor-sharp cheekbones.

"Team one?" Miss Colin kicked things off.

"Arabella!"

"Team two?"

"Flossy!"

"Team three?"

That was Alice. She paused for a split second before answering, a brilliant idea suddenly slithering into her head.

"Dylan!" she said.

Miss Colin blinked. "Who on earth is that?"

"You know, Dylan," Alice replied. "The new girl."

"No!" Dylan whispered in alarm. "What the hell are you talking about?" She'd turned bright red and the entire class was staring.

"Oh, yes." Alice shrugged selflessly, struggling to keep a straight face. "Dylan volunteered herself. She's been telling us all how talented she is at sports and how she thinks she should be team captain. I'm sure she's got loads to teach all us . . . *amateurs.*"

Snickers broke from Flossie and Emilia's direction.

Miss Colin squinted at Dylan, sizing her up. "Of course, Dylan the American. I've heard about you. You sound very confident indeed. What position do you play?"

"N-no," Dylan stuttered. "I don't know." She shot her eyes around. People were laughing. How did the *entire* cool crowd know about her remark to Sonia and Zanna the other day? "I've never played netball before. I don't even know the rules. Except there's no, like, dribbling, right?"

"Of course there's no dribbling!" Miss Colin's eyes glinted. "Are you making fun of a venerable English sport?"

"No! I never . . . I'm not . . ."

"Stop stammering. Time wasters aren't welcome in my

lesson. Netball may be a game, but it is not a joke!" Miss Colin had worked herself into one of her rages and was practically foaming at the mouth. "Sarah, you take over for team three. I don't want to hear another word!"

Tally chuckled as she trailed behind her teammates. Poor Dylan. Alice clearly wasn't going to get over her vendetta easily. And George's party was coming up this weekend . . . Tally dreaded to think what was going to happen when the two rivals and Tristan were all in the same room.

A wedge of sunlight parted the clouds behind the court and all of a sudden Tally caught sight of a silhouette on the sidelines. Mr. Logan was standing there, lit up like some kind of angel. Tally caught her breath. Luckily, she was wearing the T-shirt she'd managed to shrink in the wash and she could feel it clinging sexily around her boobs. Thrusting her shoulders back, she bounced out to catch the ball.

CHAPTER FIFTEEN

*H*ello?"

"It's me, darling." Alice bit her lip, smiling as she heard Tristan's lazy, mumbly voice. He sounded even better over the phone than in real life. "Can't you see my name pop up when I call?"

"Yeah, yeah, I can." Tristan glanced at Jasper von Holstadt and Tom Huntleigh, who were watching Spurs get thrashed by Man United, and reluctantly hauled himself up from the common-room sofa. Alice was giggling into his ear.

"Why do you pretend you don't know who it is then? I think you should give me a special ringtone to remind you."

"Huh? Remind me of what?" Tristan said, stretching.

"Are you listening to me?" Alice snapped. "If you don't want to talk, just say so."

"Hold on, of course I'm listening to you!" Tristan protested. "I've been thinking about you all day."

When he heard this, Seb Ogilvy shifted round on the sofa

and rolled his eyes. Alice, Alice, Alice—these days, she was always interrupting. After dinner the other evening, Tristan had confided in him about their night together, and in Seb's opinion, the whole thing was bloody weird. Tristan caught his look.

What? he mouthed. He flicked Seb two fingers and walked out of the room. "Anyway, what are you doing?"

"Wouldn't you like to know." Alice's voice oozed like honey through the phone.

Tristan grinned. "Wish you were here."

"So do I. We've only got two more days till George's though."

Two more days. That reminded him. Tristan rubbed the back of his head. "About this weekend. I wanted to ask. Erm, maybe . . ."

"Go on, babe."

"Well, you know how my parents are having my bedroom repainted . . ."

"Mmhmm."

"How about I plan to stay at yours after George's party? I can't wait to have you alone and it might be our only chance for . . . *you know* . . . for weeks."

Alice felt her palms turn clammy. "Oh. Yeah." She swallowed. Why hadn't she seen this coming? She blinked, realizing she'd been staring at one of her posters on the opposite wall. It was of a painting called *Olympia* that she'd bought on a History of Art trip to Paris, showing a tarty naked woman lying on a bed. Alice sat up suddenly. "I'd have to let you know though. I need to check."

"Check what?"

"With Mummy, silly. You know, in case we have guests."

"But I wouldn't have to sleep in any of the spare rooms. Dom's girlfriends never do."

"Okay, *fine*. Why are you turning this into a competition with my brother?"

"Competition?" Tristan frowned. "What are you on about?"

"I'm not on about anything. You're the one who's acting like a twelve-year-old." Alice bit her lip. She knew she sounded like a mental case. "Anyway, better go. I have to take a shower."

Tristan looked at his watch. It was four thirty in the afternoon. "You do that," he told her. Unbelievable how moody she was being. It was probably that time of the month. "But seriously, Ali, let me stay with you in London. It'll be amazing. I promise."

Amazing? Alice thought. *As amazing as it was with Dylan?*

"Don't you want to?" Tristan urged

"Hmm? Sorry? You're cutting out. See you on the weekend," Alice said, gripping her phone. "Gotta go. Bye."

The connection went dead. Tristan looked at his screen pensively. The thought of being with Alice was what had kept him going over this last dull-as-hell week at school. But now he suddenly felt guilty, and he couldn't work out what on earth he'd done wrong.

CHAPTER SIXTEEN

I hear *someone* in this room has a party to go to later." Victor Dalgleish leered at Dylan across the lunch table. It was Saturday afternoon. They were sitting in the Taylors' brand-new kitchen, and Victor's vulgar, bleached teeth were sparkling garishly enough to give the custom-made marble countertops a run for their money.

I think someone *should go back to the kennel where he belongs,* Dylan thought, and carried on eating her smoked salmon in silence.

Victor snorted with laughter. "I know what you've got on *your* mind," he grinned, clearly not noticing he was the only one in the conversation. "You can't wait to get your grubby mitts on some English boys, can you? Oy, oy!" He jerked back in his chair and guffawed, slapping his hand on Dylan's mom's thigh. "At least we know you can't get up to anything naughtier than this little kitten and I do every night!"

"What the fuck? That is disgusting." Dylan dropped her knife onto her plate with a clatter.

"Don't be a prude. Sex is marvelous—it's a force of nature," Victor proclaimed. "Go to any farm you like. The cows and sheep are always jumping on each other, trying to have it off. And rabbits . . . don't get me started. They're horny little buggers, at it all the time."

"Mom!"

"Vic, darling, thank you. I think you've made your point," Piper Taylor said, rubbing her lover's fingers hard on top of the table. "And don't swear, Dylan."

"I can't believe this is happening," Dylan muttered, scraping her chair back. "I'm going out."

"Dilly. Dill Pickle, sit down," Piper pleaded.

"How many times do I have to tell you not to call me that? Leave me alone." Dylan stomped up the stairs to the ground floor and over the black-and-white marble tiles of their entrance hall. The whole damn place still smelled of fresh paint and sawdust, and it was making her nostrils burn.

Dylan's mom had bought this huge pile in swanky Holland Park a few months ago, but she'd only moved in over the past two weeks while Dylan was at St. Cecilia's. Dylan didn't know why she'd bothered. Lauren reported that their mom spent most of her time at Victor's shag-pad anyway.

It had been surreal this afternoon, when Dylan had walked in and dropped her weekend bag at the foot of the carpeted staircase. Looking round, she knew she'd never be able to think of this house as home. The oversized vases of lilies on every table, the bathrooms with their little round colored soaps, the two grand living rooms with their rich cream furniture—it all seemed like paraphernalia from someone else's life. She hadn't unpacked anything, except her toothbrush. That bedroom way up at the top, where her mom hadn't even bothered to hang curtains, would never feel like hers.

Grabbing her wallet and the dusty-rose pashmina Mimah had lent her, Dylan swung open the door and stepped into the afternoon.

The rack of condoms loomed at Tristan in the basement level of Boots on Notting Hill Gate. He'd never bought condoms before, and was finding the whole experience incredibly embarrassing. His mind boggled at the absurd amount of choice they had: ribbed, large, extra-large, flavored. Even vibrating ones. It was enough to make you wonder if the world was full of perverts. How about a type that just said *Normal* on the box? You know, for normal people. Like him. Then he wouldn't have to stand here for so long looking like an overprivileged sex-addict with a scruffy prepster quiff.

Oh god. The lady behind the cash register was definitely staring at him.

Tristan's iPhone shook in his pocket and he slid his finger

across the screen to unlock it, grateful for the distraction. He hoped the message was from Alice.

It wasn't.

Jas's house pre-party. 8 sharp. No girls said Seb's text. No totty? Tristan narrowed his intelligent eyes, trying to work out what was going on with Seb these days. Girls were the reason they'd come to London. He had no intention of sitting around getting lean at Jas's house, playing *Guitar Hero* on the Wii and watching Jas mix lounge beats—badly—on his decks. Jas was convinced he was the music industry's next major mogul, even though Seb and Tristan were the ones who could actually play instruments and who were bothering to start a band.

Anyway, T wanted to go out for mojitos before George's party, maybe to that new Brazilian bar near Piccadilly Circus. And, more important, he wanted to get to the bottom of whether Alice planned to let him stay at hers tonight. The day was starting to gnaw at Tristan. Not because he was the kind of anal guy who needed to plan out every second of his life, or even who needed everything to go his way, but because this evening, he had some pressing business on his mind.

Such as: if there was any point in him buying these stupid condoms at all. He grabbed the simplest-looking pack and turned it over in his hand. Might as well go for it. He knew he'd kick himself if he got the chance and was caught empty-handed.

Out on Notting Hill Gate, Tristan stuffed his Boots bag noisily into the pocket of his baggy jeans and turned down the pavement toward Holland Park. Cars and buses exhaled past. It was only five o'clock. He had hours to kill.

Dylan blinked in the gloomy light of the Duke of Edinburgh pub. It was hard to see, coming in off the sunny street, but she slowly made out the wood paneling, the faded green upholstery, and the afternoon customers watching a football game on a small flat-screen at one end of the bar.

Excellent. This was an awesome place to have her first ever drink alone. She'd told herself she was going to go easy on the booze after a few embarrassing experiences in New York, but here, it just felt impossible. To hell with being a good girl.

"Jack and Coke, please," she told the bartender, slapping down a five-pound note. He looked down at her dubiously. Dylan held her breath, wondering if she'd remembered to pocket her fake ID.

"What's that then?" the bartender grunted. He sneaked a glance back at the TV. The lamps hanging above him were reflecting unattractively off his bald head. Dylan hesitated. Maybe this wasn't such a good idea after all.

"Um, Jack and Coke. You know, like, whisky and Coke? Jack Daniel's?"

"Oh, right. JD and Coke. Why didn't you say so?" the bartender replied absently, plopping two tiny ice cubes into a glass. Dylan pursed her lips. Everyone here was always correcting what she said. Surely she wasn't *that* hard to understand. Maybe they did it to all foreigners on purpose, just to make them feel unwelcome. They were real experts at that.

She swallowed and mustered her courage. "Do you think I could have a little more ice, please?"

The bartender gave a bitter sort of scoff and added a third cube to the glass. Out of the corner of her eye, Dylan spotted an empty table surrounded on two sides by a padded booth. Lucky no one had taken it. Funny too though, she thought, considering that all the less cushy seats around it were full. She threw down her bag and stuck her straw in her mouth, chewing on it a little with her front teeth, just like she always did. It felt comforting. But suddenly, looking up, she gasped. Literally everyone in the room was staring at her. No joke. Twenty or thirty people, mostly men, were gawking in her direction as if she'd stumbled onto the stage in some kind of seedy burlesque club. Dylan turned from one side to the other. She couldn't see anything weird. What was their problem? Starting to panic, she raised her eyes. There, straight above her head, was a second, giant plasma screen on which men in long socks were scurrying back and forth on a grass field. Fuck. Of course, she was the moron who'd sat right under where they were showing the football match.

Just then, the room erupted in shouts and waving fists aimed at the TV. One man jumped to his feet, roared, "Blaaargh!" and hurled his cardboard Stella Artois coaster toward her. Dylan squealed and dived out of her seat. Nearby, a salt-and-pepper-haired man started cackling madly.

"Watch it there, girlie! That's it, get your ass out of the way!"

Dylan retreated to a table in the far corner. Still blushing fiercely, she traced a skull and crossbones pattern on its surface with her finger, careful not to chip any of the pale pink nail polish she'd put on for the party to go with Mimah's pashmina. She'd taken to wearing the thing everywhere to remind herself that she had at least one friend. It was so lonely being a stranger in a strange land. So lonely and so very, very cold. She shivered delicately and bit her lip, waiting for the tear to fall, *plink*, into her glass.

"Hi there," came a familiar, playful voice.

Dylan shook back her blond hair and found her wet blue eyes gazing into a boy's chestnut ones. Tristan. He was holding a pint and wearing a striped scarf wound several times round his neck. His hair, standing out sexily in all directions, looked longer than she remembered it, and even better than it did in all her fantasies of the summer.

"Hi," she whispered.

Shit. She was supposed to be angry for the way he'd treated

her. But somehow she couldn't be, now that he was standing right there.

"Nice surprise seeing you. Mind if I sit down?" Tristan gave Dylan his sweetest repentant look and slid into the adjoining seat.

CHAPTER SEVENTEEN

Alice emerged from her bathroom smelling of her favorite gardenia body cream and wrapped in her flowery kimono-robe. Her legs felt silky smooth as she glided into her bedroom and shut the door; she'd just shaved them meticulously in the shower in preparation for—well, she didn't know *what* for, exactly, since she was still having major jitters about letting Tristan stay over this evening. Last night, lying in bed half-dreaming about him after putting away a bottle of cheap Pinot Noir in her room at school with Tally, she'd come *this close* to sending him a booty-text. Literally. She'd even typed a drunken draft on her phone: Baby u know I want u. Here. Now. AND FOREVER. Thank god she'd passed out in a red-wine haze before she'd sent it.

Tonight, Alice had no idea what to wear. Maybe she should go for her new, low-cut babydoll dress—the one that showed off her cleavage (well, would have shown it off, if she'd had any). She perched on her queen-size bed next to Tally and stared at the clothes in her open wardrobe. Like every other room in the Rochesters' massive house, Alice's was decorated with tasteful antique furniture—most of it family heirlooms—and slightly worn but extremely valuable oriental rugs. Sculptures and pots and masks from places like India and Zimbabwe were scattered throughout the house's seven floors. They'd been handed down by Alice's grandfather and great-grandfather and great-great-grandfather, who had all been traders in the British Colonies—before, as her father put it, everything in those parts of the world went to seed.

The two tall windows that looked onto the garden behind Alice's bed shed their golden evening light onto *Tatler*, the high-society rag that Tally was devouring. Every month, she and Alice ran out to buy the latest issue and combed through it for people they knew—which, of course, always constituted at least half the magazine, what with people's friends, enemies, parents, cousins, siblings, half siblings, pets, and so on. It was how everyone at school kept up with who was in, who was out, and who was throwing the best parties.

But even *Tatler* couldn't distract Alice today. Picking up her toenail clippers from the bureau, she pensively snapped them open and shut a few times before starting to trim.

"Um, y'know the first time you had sex?" she asked finally, trying to sound offhand. A piece of her big toenail landed on Tally's jeans, but Tally didn't notice.

"Mmmhmm."

"How did it happen?"

"You know how it happened," Tally yawned, turning a page. "You were there. It was that French guy Jérôme in Barbados."

"Duh. I don't mean who was it with," Alice replied. Obviously she hadn't forgotten Jérôme. He was heir to a perfume fortune, tall and bony and sensitive-looking in that *très sexy* French way, with a shock of curly brown hair and light green eyes.

They'd met him on the beach last Easter while Tally was on holiday with the Rochesters. The girls had taken a midnight walk down the sand from their villa, stumbling on Jérôme and his friend Vincent as they swigged rum on sunbeds under the moon, outside the island's swankiest hotel. They were so stylish it was to die for. Especially Jérôme, in his white linen trousers and sky-blue linen shirt, and that leather cord he always wore hung round his neck. Anyone could tell that he and Tally were smitten with each other right away. That had left Vincent for Alice—not exactly ideal. Vincent was the worst kind of French person, with garlic breath and puffy lips that he used instead of his tongue when he kissed. After the first five minutes Alice hadn't liked him in the slightest, but she'd made out with him anyway. It would have been a bit rude not to.

Tally and Jérôme hadn't slept together till the girls' last night in Barbados. Sometime after the music from the hotel had died down, he'd taken Tally's hand and led her off along the beach. They'd been gone so long that eventually Vincent had walked Alice home by herself, jumping at the opportunity to rub up against her for a while near their villa's security gate until she'd shoved him off.

Alice made a face at the memory.

"I meant, how did it happen?" she said. "How did you decide you wanted to?"

"I didn't really." Tally let *Tatler* fall onto her chest. "It just happened. He was giving me that adorable crooked smile. We were naked and it was so nice and he had a condom and I thought, Why not? Much better than doing it with some dirty English boy who I'd have to see everywhere."

"But didn't you want your first time to be with, like, a boyfriend? Someone you loved?"

Tally laughed. "No way! The only boyfriends I've ever had have been awful. Seriously, can you imagine having sex with any of the immature guys we know?" She caught sight of Alice's face. "Oh fuck, Ali! I didn't mean it like that. I'm an idiot. I'm sure T won't be terrible."

Tally looked so mortified that Alice burst out laughing. "He'd better not be," she said a little too loudly. Staring down at the colorful woven rug that her brother had brought back from his gap-year trip to Nepal, she gave a deep sigh. "But I'm sort of nervous, Tal."

Tally sat up, straightening her mum's yellow Pucci scarf, which she'd knotted round her hair. Alice hardly ever admitted weakness. "Oh my god. Why's that?"

"I don't know. What if it's not good?" But that didn't sound quite right.

"I'm sure it'll be incredible!" Tally said, giving Alice a squeeze round the shoulders. "And even if it's not, who cares? Once you do it, you won't be a virgin anymore. And being a virgin is so last year! Come on, I reckon you're the only one of us left who hasn't had sex. Well, besides Sonia. How awful can it be?"

She looked at Alice. Nothing. Her pep talk was a definite failure.

"Plus, it's T," Tally said kindly. "It's gonna be amazing. And you look so hot today. He'll be, like, ecstatic that he got rid of Dylan."

"Oh great, thanks for bringing Dylan up."

"What? He's probably forgotten all about her. She's so lame compared to you."

Alice closed her eyes and nodded. "You're right, she's utterly lame. There's no way Tristan likes her anymore."

No way, she repeated to herself. And tonight was going to prove it.

CHAPTER EIGHTEEN

*H*ow about another drink?" Tristan asked, watching intently as Dylan slurped up the last of her rum and Coke. Her cheeks were looking a bit flushed and her hair had more bounce in it than usual. It suited her.

"You bet your ass," chirped Dylan. This was her third drink and it wasn't even seven thirty. She shoved her glass playfully toward Tristan, but misjudged the distance and sent it flying onto the carpet instead.

"Oops!" she giggled, covering her mouth with her hand.

Tristan zigzagged his way to the bar. He was feeling a bit tipsy too, after only eating a bag of salt and vinegar chips for lunch and then downing three pints in the space of about twenty minutes. Maybe that was why he was remembering how much he enjoyed spending time with Dylan. She seemed so . . . open compared to most girls. So guileless. It was refreshing.

Dylan stared at Tristan's back as he leaned casually toward the bartender in his slouchy Carhartt jeans and white polo shirt with the collar popped up. It was amazing to see him again. Somehow he made everything fun, even stupid English football. During the match he'd explained all the teams to her, and afterward he'd been so sensitive and considerate, asking about her dad and her sister and of course Madison, her golden retriever. He hadn't met her mom—Piper had been in London with Victor for the entire summer—or he would no doubt have asked about her, too.

Dylan stroked the soft fabric of the booth where Tristan had been sitting. It was indented and slightly creased and still a little warm. On the seat, he'd left a small blue and white plastic bag with letters on it. *B-O-O* . . . Curious, she pulled it toward her.

"'Scuse me," Tristan said abruptly, snatching the bag away and throwing it onto the bench behind him. He looked momentarily panicked, but quickly shrugged it off as he set their drinks down.

"Here you go. One JD and Coke for the lady." He winked, making Dylan's tummy do somersaults. "Cheers."

"Cheers." She hiccuped.

"To us." Tristan was sitting much nearer to her than before and Dylan watched his lips as he took a slow first sip of his lager. A golden stream of bubbles fizzed on the glass.

"Listen, Dyl," the lips suddenly said. Dylan dragged her gaze upward.

"Er, if I upset you . . . ," Tristan said stiffly. He cleared his throat. "You know, it wasn't intentional."

Dylan stared at him. He had such beautiful eyebrows; why had she never noticed?

"Whatever," she slurred. "I mean, I guess you were like, not cool, but . . . we'll work it out." She inched her fingers toward his thigh.

"Wicked." Tristan drank off about half his pint. Now that the football match was finished, the pub was filling up with a Saturday-night crowd of riotous single people. He could stay here all night. Screw Jas's house. Screw the party.

Dylan sucked up the last of her drink and shuffled closer. Tristan felt her head nestle onto his bicep.

"I keep thinking," she said coyly, "it was such a shame things didn't work out on your last night in East Hampton. Maybe we should try again."

Tristan stiffened. He didn't want to be reminded of that night. It had been the most shameful one of his life. After making him wait most of the summer to have sex with her, Dylan had decided that their final evening together would be the one. He'd thought it was pretty stupid to shag just when he was about to leave, but he wasn't about to pass up the chance.

Then he'd messed it up. Totally messed it up. Maybe it was the condoms, stupid things. Maybe he was just nervous; it was his first time if you didn't count that one-night stand in the orchard at Jasper's country-house party, and he'd been so drunk then that he couldn't even remember it.

Dylan breathed on him and her breath smelled sweet and sugary. There was a splash of Coke on her top lip and all he could think about was reaching out his tongue and licking it off. Tristan swallowed. Then he was kissing her. He pulled her toward him, remembering the fun they'd had over all those long, sultry summer days. It was impossible to get enough.

"Oh shit!" Suddenly he came to his senses. He jumped up from his seat like it was an electric fence. "What am I doing? I've got to get out of here."

"No. Come back!" Dylan cried, watching him bolt through the pub.

She slumped backward. Something rustled behind her. He'd forgotten his plastic bag.

CHAPTER NINETEEN

*D*arlings? Aliiice? Where are you?" Sonia
Khan whined into her BlackBerry. "Ring
me as soon as you get this. I'm waiting."

Muffled beats emanated into the street from George
Demetrios's Mayfair mansion, where she'd been loitering
like a friendless loser for five whole minutes. No doubt the
music was loud inside, but the Demetrios family's thick, sound-
proofed walls strangled it before it could piss off any of their
eminent neighbors.

A Porsche roared past, blowing its exhaust on Sonia, and
she tutted in indignation. She'd come straight from school
this evening because, unlike Alice and Tally, she'd had actual,
important work to do planning every last detail of *Pashminas
to the Rescue*. The show was exactly two weeks away now and
Sonia was determined for it to be the event of the school
year. Not trusting the other girls on the charity committee,
she had personally booked the auditorium, drawn up a guest

list of parents and Hasted House boys, ordered the flowers and crepe paper for decoration, and handed instructions for refreshments to the caterers.

And Alice couldn't even be on time for a party. Sonia knew whose fault that was: Tally's. Selfish cow, always making everybody late. Why should she wait around for them?

She rang the bell. After a minute, George Demetrios flung open the door.

"Sonia! My angel," he cried, his eyes going straight to her cleavage before he kissed her clumsily on both cheeks.

"Careful! My nose," Sonia said, curling her fingers round it protectively.

"Your schnozz looks hot, darling. It's a real beauty."

George had done five shots of his parents' shockingly pricey Rodnik vodka and was looking sloshed. His pink check shirt, hanging out of his jeans, had a few too many buttons undone and Sonia found herself transfixed by his notorious forestlike chest.

At that moment the Wyndham-Rhodes sisters, both wearing hot pants, scurried over shaking bottles of Dom Pérignon. They were students at Malbury Hall, a prestigious school about an hour's drive from St. Cecilia's.

"Oh Sonia darling, how *lovely* to see you!" drawled Olivia. "Mwah. Mwah."

"You're looking *fab*," echoed Melissa, steadying herself against the wall.

"So are you," Sonia said. "I just adore those feathers in your hair, Messy. You're such a clever thing."

"Blah blah blah." George draped one arm round each of the sisters and beckoned to Sonia. "Come on, you three. None of you are nearly hammered enough. I know where there's a stash of tequila."

"But we have champagne, you devil."

"Rubbish! You need something stronger than that."

Sonia watched them lurch backward like an ungainly six-legged goat. She wasn't about to follow. Messy and Livs were not only beautiful but also incredibly stupid, and she couldn't compete with that lethal combination.

She surveyed the place for allies. The ground floor was buzzing with people: Bathsheba Fortnum was pulling her skirt down to show her new tattoo to Gerald Coombes, Flossy Norstrup-Fitzwilliam and Jamie Darlington were chasing each other round a giant antique urn, Oliver Rylands was prancing about in eyeliner and the Spandex Batman outfit that he'd taken to wearing to parties. And there was Mimah Calthorpe de Vyle-Hanswicke, flirting with horsey-looking Freddie Frye. Sonia started to walk over to them, then remembered that was out of the question. They weren't friends with Mimah anymore.

She stood twisting her handbag awkwardly for a few seconds. Across the room, Seb, Jas, and a cute boy she didn't recognize were watching YouTube videos on someone's phone. She clopped toward them over an ornate floor mosaic depicting

Poseidon, the Greek god of the ocean, heaving a schooner out of a stormy sea. It was meant to be a tribute to the Demetrios shipping fortune.

"Well hello, boys," Sonia said, with a catlike smile. "Which one of you is going to make me a drink?"

"I'll take care of that," Seb answered. He always liked to get involved where booze was concerned. "What'll you have? Wine? Champagne? G and T?"

"A white wine, thank you, sweetie." Sonia kissed him on the cheek, giggling as a bit of her lip gloss rubbed off. As she leaned in to wipe it away, she realized how sexy Seb looked tonight. He was wearing a flattering gray V-neck sweater and his face was plastered with that sweetly baffled expression that appeared whenever he was drunk. Seb was watching her and blushing. But before Sonia had time to wonder why, someone grabbed her elbow.

"Are you with Alice?" Tristan asked. He looked pale.

Sonia glared at him. "Oh, how charming. Nice to see you, too."

"Whatever. Seriously, is Alice here?"

"Of course I am," a voice behind them said.

CHAPTER TWENTY

*T*ristan was so nervous as he turned round to face Alice that he thought he might chuck up the sausages he'd eaten for dinner. He could taste them rising in his throat.

"Hi," she whispered shyly, leaning in to kiss his cheek.

Tristan burped quietly.

"I meant to call you back about tonight. Sorry I didn't." Alice pinched a fold of Tristan's sweater between her fingers. *Sorry* might be her least favorite word in the universe. But for him, she was prepared to make an exception.

"Yeah, good to see you, too," Tristan mumbled. He wasn't listening to a word Alice was saying. He was too busy trying to act normal.

Alice's eyes started to narrow.

"T darling! How are you?" Just on time, Tally danced up to them, throwing her arms round Tristan from behind.

"Tals, old girl." He hugged her in relief. "I've hardly chatted to you in eons. How the hell are you?"

"Fantastic! I feel like going mad tonight," Tally gushed, oblivious, as always, that she'd interrupted something. "Come on everyone, let's go insane! Here's to that!" She took a swig of her drink, a livid pink concoction that she'd scooped from the punchbowl on the way in.

"Careful!" Alice shrieked. "You have no idea what could be in there."

"Of course I do. Fruit juice and booze. What more could a girl want?"

"Urine," Alice said.

Tally looked confused. "But I don't want—"

"No, you minger. Everyone knows you should never drink from punchbowls. Boys like to piss in them for fun."

A few feet away, the tall stranger who'd been chatting with Jasper had stopped mid-sentence and was gazing at them. Or, to be more precise, he was gazing at Tally, who looked like a Hollywood starlet tonight. She'd styled her hair into waves and was wearing a tight gold satin dress that belted at the waist, with gold shimmer and eyeshadow to match. Alice nudged her, and Tally stole a glance at the boy over the rim of her plastic cup. He had dark, wavy hair and eyes like blue sea-glass. He reminded her ever so slightly of Mr. Logan. Except that Mr. Logan was older. And hotter. And way more . . . *experienced.* She wished he were here—then she could bring a whole new meaning to the words "teacher's pet."

"Tals, this is my Cousin Rando," Jasper said, dragging the boy over. "He's just joined us at Hasted House."

Rando shifted a bit, then held out his hand. "Pleasure," he smiled. He had pointy teeth that gave him a dashingly cheeky air.

"Rando?" Tally scoffed. Oops. She'd meant to say, "Nice to meet you," but something had gone wrong.

"Well, it's Tom Randall-Stubbs actually," Jasper's cousin replied smoothly. "Rando's my nickname."

Tally rolled her eyes sarcastically. "Oh, nickname. Is that what it's called?"

There was an awkward silence. Tally turned in panic to where Alice had been standing, but she and Tristan had mysteriously disappeared.

Then Rando burst out laughing.

"*Touché,*" he congratulated her. "That was rather funny."

"Why, thank you." Tally's eyes shone. "*Nastrovya!*" she toasted in Russian, downing her drink.

"Don't touch me," Mimah ordered, slapping Freddie Frye's hand away as he tried to sneak it round her waist. She'd put a stop to their incredibly boring conversation and had maneuvered Freddie onto the dance floor at the back of the Demetrioses' huge, open-plan lobby.

Behind them, party guests were spilling through the glass doors onto the patio, and above them, revelers on the mezzanine were chucking down bits of chips and chocolate into the crowd. From here, Mimah commanded a better view of the territory.

"Why not? What's your problem?" Freddie bleated. He wiggled his ass in delight as Amy Winehouse came on and a general cheer went up.

But Mimah didn't answer. She'd caught sight of Sonia Khan and Seb Ogilvy smoking near an open window. They were actually *sharing a cigarette*. Mimah watched as Sonia took it out of his lips and put it between hers. She'd been in love with Seb for fucking ages. How dare her psychotic ex–best friend try to steal him? Mimah felt the rage boiling up.

"Vodka jelly!" Gerald Coombes's voice rang out above the music. He dashed from the kitchen carrying a tray and cut a swath through the masses.

"Hurrah!" People rushed him, trampling each other as they tried to grab the cups. Delphinia Atwood tripped on her six-inch shoes and slid over the floor into a carved table, cracking one of its legs right off.

Luckily, George wasn't there to witness any of this. He'd disappeared ages ago with the Wyndham-Rhodes sisters, into another wing of the house.

"So . . . do you still want to come back with me later?" Alice fluttered her eyelids up at Tristan. She'd drawn him behind a pillar, away from the others, and was standing with one leg crossed over the other, trying to suppress the urge to pee.

Battling her nerves and being seductive at the same time took astonishing skill.

"Er, yeah," Tristan said. "Of course."

"That's great, darling. Do you like my dress?"

Tristan checked it out. Alice was wearing one of those awful loose things that seemed to be in at the moment, tight at the top but shapeless and puffy everywhere else. Just like a fucking maternity tent.

"Adore it," he said.

Alice kissed his neck and shivered. Tristan smelled of his usual soap, and, beneath it, of something warm and mysterious and delicious. Under her babydoll dress, she'd put on her sexiest black lace underwear; they had a gold lollipop charm hanging off them, and she felt a thrill whenever she thought of Tristan playing with it later. Things were going to be fine. He was gorgeous and he was her oldest friend and he was in love with her.

Slipping her hand under Tristan's sweater, Alice hooked her pinkie tentatively over the top of his trousers. She heard him gulp. He was probably overcome with excitement.

Dylan stepped out of her black cab at the Mayfair address that Mimah had given her. She was so late. After getting home from the pub, she'd fallen into a snooze, woken up at ten, rushed like crazy to get ready, and drunk half a bottle of wine to get her courage up. Now she was tipsy. More than tipsy. Again.

Posh gas lanterns illuminated the front of the house as Dylan stood uncertainly outside, wondering whether she was meant to knock or what. Judging by the flashing disco lights in the windows and the stifled music thumping through the walls, knocking wasn't likely to attract anyone's attention. Then the door flew open and two people fell into the street, passionately sucking each other's faces off. Problem solved.

"Excuse me," Dylan said. They blanked her.

"Move it!" She raised her voice. The alcohol was getting to her. Maybe she shouldn't drink any more tonight, but fuck it.

"Piss off," said the girl in the couple.

"Slut." Dylan maneuvered round them.

Inside, the place was teeming with people. Dylan stayed close to the door, seeing no one she knew. Then she caught sight of Mimah dancing near a bucktoothed blond boy. The boy was trying to grind with her, but Mimah was ignoring him and gazing menacingly across the room. Dylan followed her eyes. Sonia. She was sitting on a windowseat with her legs draped over a sandy-haired guy wearing a gray V-neck sweater, and it looked like they were about to lock lips.

Dylan had no clue what new drama was brewing between her classmates. And she didn't give a shit; she'd just seen Tristan. He was standing by himself up on the mezzanine with a pensive expression on his face. Maybe he was thinking about her. She smiled drunkenly and climbed the stairs.

* * *

"They've run out of champagne so I got you vodka," Alice said, pushing aside some rowdy boys practicing river-dancing, and handing Tristan a drink. She'd finally rushed off to the toilet to relieve her bursting bladder and had poured them both stiff ones on the way back.

"Vodka's always good," Tristan said, guzzling half the cup.

"Easy there, tiger," Alice chuckled. She drew him toward her and kissed him, savoring his taste. He rubbed the small of her back with his free hand, pulling her closer.

"You're irresistible," Alice said. "Oh my god. What's wrong?"

Tristan had stiffened, and was gawking past her with a horrified expression on his face. An object came hurtling toward them and skidded along the floor. Alice looked down. It was a box of condoms. She started to laugh, until she saw that Dylan was standing right there, her eyes on fire, wearing some ratty pink pashmina.

"You left those in the pub," Dylan spat at Tristan bitterly. "I wouldn't want you to be without them. Seeing as you'll be needing them for tonight." She gave Alice a dirty look.

"What is going on?" Alice hissed.

No one said anything. Dylan's jaw was trembling.

"Answer me!" Alice growled. "Have you been seeing *her* behind my back?"

"No," Tristan protested. "Those aren't mine."

"Liar. Of course they're yours," Dylan burst out.

Alice looked at her coldly. "How do we know *you're* not the fucking liar?"

"How do you know? Because of this." Dylan dug into her purse and pulled out a piece of paper. "There. *Tristan Murray-Middleton*. Says it right on the receipt. And you know why? Because he bought them with a stupid credit card! What kind of moron buys condoms with a credit card? And I'll bet he doesn't even pay the bills. I'll bet *Daddy* pays them. Is Daddy financing your two-timing sex habit, Tristan baby?"

Alice gaped. She hadn't suspected that Dylan had such spark in her. Then she turned to Tristan. He was staring at the ceiling, looking like he wasn't even paying attention anymore.

"Well?"

"Ali, it's not what it looks like, I promise."

"Yeah, right." Alice was almost crying.

Before Tristan could defend himself further, a ruckus erupted below.

"What are you doing?" Sonia shrieked from the ground floor.

Mimah had grabbed Sonia by her long, dark hair and was dragging her off of Seb's lap.

"You bitch," Mimah snarled. "You slut!"

"Slut?" Sonia screamed. "I'm not the one who *paid* this poor boy to have sex with me. There's a word for that, you know. It's called prostitution."

"No it isn't, you moron," Mimah mocked. "It's called *solicitation*. There's a big difference."

"Oh, of course. You *would* know something like that." Sonia's eyes gleamed with malice. "The Calthorpe de Vyle-Hanswickes are experts on the sex trade. All you have to do is copy your dad."

With that, she turned her back and faced the crowd of wide-eyed party guests. Holding her head high, she began wobbling on her heels in the direction of the bathroom.

Mimah said nothing. Instead, she calmly stepped forward and shoved Sonia, hard, from behind. Sonia reeled drunkenly, crashing her face into a nearby column. Then she collapsed, clutching her bleeding nose.

CHAPTER TWENTY-ONE

*R*espect, respect, respect," droned Mrs. Traphorn, the headmistress of St. Cecilia's, rolling her *r*'s with relish. It was Monday morning, and The Trap was making her weekly address to the school's 250 students during Chapel. As usual, she'd chosen a bland moralistic theme and was squeezing all remaining life out of it.

"Respect comes in many forms," she intoned, leaving what she obviously thought was a pregnant pause between each sentence. Interminable was more like it.

"Let us list the many different forms in which respect may come. Number one, self-respect. That is very important. Number two, respect for your peers. That is also very important. Number three, respect for your superiors—such as teachers. Also. Very. Important."

Tally yawned and squirmed on her hard wooden pew, wishing The Trap would shut it. This was the worst speech she'd ever heard. Plus, not only was she dying for a fizzy drink and a cigarette, she desperately needed to fix the wedgie she'd given herself as she rushed to get dressed. Pulling up your tights while shaking your ass to Justin Timberlake while sneaking a few puffs of a cigarette out the window was not the most efficient way to end up looking neat and tidy. But Tally's morning routine kept her sane. She'd never changed it—not even after three years at St. Cecilia's—and she wasn't planning to anytime soon. Best leave sensible things like that to Alice.

Which reminded her: Where on earth *was* Alice this morning? She'd completely disappeared.

Bella Scott tapped Tally's knee and leaned in. "Have you seen Sonia's nose?" she whispered.

Tally nodded.

"How does she look?"

"Like Hannibal Lecter."

Bella giggled.

"What?" Clemmie Lockheed nudged her from the other side. "What are you two saying?"

"Sonia looks like Hannibal Lecter. Tally says."

"Like who?"

"Hannibal Lecter. You know, the cannibal from *Silence of the Lambs*?"

"Cannibal? But Sonia's a vegetarian."

"Oh forget it," Bella sighed. Little Clem was so sheltered, she'd probably never even heard of *Silence of the Lambs*. Most people felt protective over Clem, because, at age fifteen and a half, she was by far the youngest girl in their year. She was a bit like a mascot. She still wore her hair in braids and spent her free time grooming her pony and reading horsey magazines. Everyone knew she'd never even kissed a boy.

"In conclusion," The Trap's voice banged on monotonously from above, "respect makes the world go round. I urge you all to think about that this week. And now for the announcements."

Clearing her throat, Mrs. Traphorn at long last picked up a sheaf of papers from the lectern. She smoothed the front of her white blouse, over which she wore a sleeveless green cardigan. *Teacher fashion never changes*, Tally thought. "Miss Baskin's pottery classes will resume tonight in the small art annex," The Trap read. "Please sign the sheet on her door if you plan to attend. . . . This next one is from Miss Wilde. Auditions for *The Importance of Being Earnest* will be held at lunch tomorrow in the auditorium. Interested GCSE students should see her by the end of today."

Tally gave an exasperated sigh and cupped her chin in her hands. Hadn't The Trap ever heard of e-mail? This system of reading out the notices was so unbelievably antiquated. Hoping for distraction, she looked round at the Chapel's ornate decorations. The place had been built back in 1882 for Lord and Lady Cornwallis, St. Cecilia's founders, and most of its detailing was intact. Well, as intact as it could be with thousands of pairs of shoes shuffling down the marble aisle every year, thousands of fingers jabbing into the stone carvings, and thousands of asses fidgeting along the benches.

"Oy," Bella whispered.

"What?"

"Is it true that George Demetrios shagged both of the Wyndham-Rhodes sisters on Saturday? At the same time?"

"That's what I heard," Tally said. "He's such a man whore. Have you ever seen him dancing?"

"*He's* a whore?" Bella choked. "They're sisters! How could they be so foul?"

"Maybe they're lesbos," Clemmie joined in.

Bella rolled her eyes. "Do you even know what that means?"

"Did Mimah come back to school last night?" Tally interrupted.

"Yeah. No one's talking to her. I pushed my chest of drawers up against my door in case she tried to strangle me in my sleep. I think she's a crack fiend."

"Girls! Quiet," Miss Sharkreve hissed from the end of the row.

"The weekend before half-term," The Trap continued, "there will be a literary excursion to Dublin. The trip has only eight spaces so book early to avoid disappointment. Juniors wishing to go must tell Mr. Wagon straightaway." She squinted doubtfully at the piece of paper. "Oh, pardon me, that's Mr. *Logan*. Not Mr. Wagon. Strange handwriting some people have."

Bella tittered; Mrs. Traphorn was always cocking up the announcements, mispronouncing everyone's names. She nudged Tally.

"See? She's illiterate," she snorted.

"Shhh," Tally ordered. At the sound of Mr. Logan's name, her teeth had practically started chattering in anticipation. Dublin with her crush for two whole days? How utterly perfect. They'd take long walks through the rain-heavy city, drink Guinness late into the night, stay in cozy adjoining rooms at a B&B with a crackling fireplace. Maybe he'd even read her more poetry. Tally didn't have a clue what poets came from Dublin, but she was sure Mr. Logan knew all the best ones. Who cared if half-term was weeks away? Digging a pen from her pocket, she scribbled a reminder on her hand: ♡DUBLIN♡

"And lastly," declared Mrs. Traphorn, "we have a message from Sonia Khan about the junior class's upcoming charity event. Sonia? Where is she?"

Tally, Bella, and Clemmie craned their necks as Sonia emerged from the choir stalls. She looked less than her best, to say the least. Dr. Essex, the Khans' famous plastic surgeon, had put a cast round her nose, and above it her two bruised eyes loomed like black holes. Tally made a Hannibal Lecter sucking noise with her tongue.

Blinking down at the assembly, Sonia drew a deep breath. "Boverdy," she announced. At least, that's what it sounded like. "Boverdy is nod a joke."

"What the hell is she saying?" Tally mouthed. Bella gave an exaggerated shrug. Sonia's voice was all blocked and nasal.

"Boverdy is a very serious broblem," she said. "When we bicture boverty, we bicture blaces like Africa and India, where beoble have disgusting diseases that make us not wand to douch them. And that's derrible. Because boor beoble deserve do be douched. Boor beoble need a lod of love. Yes, even if they are disfigured."

On the word *disfigured*, Sonia paused dramatically. Tally clapped her hand over her mouth and cracked up.

"Sonia's talking about herself again," she whispered.

Up on the dais, Mrs. Traphorn was furrowing her forehead. She stepped forward as if she might intervene.

"But none of thad is the boint," Sonia carried on, stopping the headmistress in her tracks. "The boint is, there is boverdy in England, too. Like, some beoble can't even afford do buy bedrol for their cars. And that is why we, the juniors, have chosen to subbort the London-based charity CrisisAid. Blease help us. Blease buy dickeds to our fashion show, *Bashminas to the Rescue*, in two Saturdays' time. I'll be selling them all this week. Beace," she made a peace sign with her fingers, "and thank you."

A long, unimpressed silence filled the chapel. Several people coughed. Then came a halfhearted smattering of applause.

"That was crap," Bella remarked.

"Yeah, I thought the point was to make PTTR sound *glamorous*," whispered Clem. "She's just grossed everyone out."

"And she didn't even say what it is. I mean, maybe she's upset about her nose, but that's no reason to ruin everything for us."

"Whatever," interrupted Tally, standing to file out of Chapel behind the rest of their row. "Everyone'll come anyway. It's school. What else is there to do?"

She jabbed her fingers into Bella's back. "Hey, hurry up." She had ten minutes to catch Alice before their first lesson began.

CHAPTER TWENTY-TWO

A cloud of dust blasted out as Alice rammed her heel into the old attic door, forcing it open. She cringed and listened for a second, making sure she was alone. No one ever came up here, into the eaves of the art block, but if anyone got suspicious it would be the end of the Grubhouse, her and Tally's favorite and most secret smoking lair.

She stepped over the familiar broken floorboard and into the loft. The place looked the same as ever: crammed with disused easels and workbenches, still-life drapery and canvases, lit by two garret windows and a skylight that hadn't been cleaned in years. It smelled the same as ever too: slightly sharp but musty, like dried paint encrusted with dust.

Alice sank down onto her and Tally's lookout post. That was what they called the rough-hewn bench that they'd dragged over last summer from under a pile of crusty palettes, and to which they nipped off whenever possible to spy down on the

Great Lawn. Alice hugged herself at the thought of lurking up here all alone, just a pair of all-seeing eyes, when no one else at St. Cecilia's had any idea.

The door banged open. Tally burst in.

"Hey, babe! I knew you'd be in the Grubhouse. Saw you running off after Chapel."

"Shhh! Keep your voice down," Alice said. "How on earth did you know?"

"I didn't think you'd be in the mood for news hour today."

"Yeah. Bunch of lame bitches talking about lame shit." With her fist, Alice smudged a circle clean in the filthy window-pane. Normally she had a wicked time at news hour, the fifteen-minute gap between Chapel and lessons when the whole school milled about on the Great Lawn, scrambling to catch up on the weekend's gossip. She held court in the most prestigious spot, the steps leading to Quad. But today, considering her private life *was* the gossip, she'd made a dash for it. Sprinting in three-inch heels was possibly the most indispensable skill of boarding-school life, and she was legend at it.

Tally sat down next to Alice, fishing out the hip flask she kept stowed in her satchel. "Here, have some of this."

"Thanks. What's in it?"

"Lemonade."

"Excusez-moi?"

"Duh. Obviously it's whisky, darling."

141

"Thank fuck," Alice laughed, taking a swig. "You're a life-saver."

"Have you heard anything from T?"

Alice lit up a cigarette and opened the window a crack. A few flakes of paint drifted to the floor. "No. He hasn't texted me since after the party."

"I don't get it. Maybe he's giving you some space."

"He can do whatever he wants. I don't give a shit."

Tally watched Alice take a puff of her cig and blink calmly. Typical of her to pretend everything was fine. But her face told another story. Which was a nice way of saying she looked rough. Her skin, instead of its usual glow, had an ashen tint. Her eyes were bloodshot. There was a frown-line on her forehead. As far as Tally knew, Alice hadn't cried since Saturday, when she'd stormed out of George's party and spent five hours bawling hysterically onto Tally's shoulder. But she was obviously still cut up about T. She really should have worn more makeup if she didn't want people to know.

"They're all so predictable," Alice sighed. She was watching the girls clot together on the Great Lawn.

"Yeah, look at Sonia, totally milking her nose situation," Tally snorted. "Know what I found out on the way here? She has to wear that hideous cast for an entire week. What a joke. Do you think her nose'll go back to the shape it was before the plastic surgery?"

"I bloody well hope not. We'd never hear the end of it. I'd

have to punch her myself to shut her up." Alice took another slosh of whisky and wiped her mouth with the back of her hand. "Maybe I should punch her anyway. That might fix the stupid thing for good."

Tally giggled. "A nose job courtesy of Dr. Alice Rochester. You could send her the bill."

"Exactly. I never give out my services for free."

"Hey, look at the losers convention." Tally was peering out the window in the other direction. In the shadow of an oak, way off to one side, stood Dylan and Mimah. Dylan was still wearing that stupid pink pashmina. It was like she had no other clothes or something. "No prize for guessing who the outcasts are."

"Mimah should be a sumo wrestler," Alice sneered. "Her shoulders are so massive."

"Nah. She'd look too ugly in a loincloth."

"Oh my god. What the *fuck* is Dylan doing?"

Dylan had whipped off her scarf and was using it in a dance move. She was slinky, fluid, as if each part of her body had its own set of controls. When Alice tried to dance like that, she looked like a robot whose wiring had gone wrong. "Exhibitionist," she growled. "What, does she work in a strip club?"

As if on cue, Dylan grabbed the tree trunk and started gyrating in circles round it, then dipped all the way down and touched the ground with her ass.

"Whoa!" Tally's voice was admiring.

Alice snatched the cigarette out of her hand and took a drag. "How many people do you think she's slept with?" she snapped.

"Oh, loads. At least six."

"Six? Random. Where'd you get that from?"

"Well, Bathsheba Fortnum has slept with five. And I bet Dylan's shagged even more than her. Slut."

"What the fuck are *they* doing?" Alice's voice squeaked even higher as Emilia Charles and Farah Assadi skipped over to the oak tree.

"Probably telling Dylan to put it away."

"They'd better be." But Alice pressed her nose closer to the window, wishing she could hear the conversation on the grass. Nobody was safe around Dylan.

The first bell chimed. It was ten minutes to nine.

"Hurry up! English," Alice cried. She prided herself on never being late.

Tally uncoiled herself. "Cool. What did you write about for your *Othello* prep?"

Alice froze. "Oh fuck. Fuck!"

"What?"

"I haven't done it! I haven't even finished the play."

"You haven't read the play?" Tally couldn't believe her ears. She was the one who messed up assignments, not Alice. "But Mr. Logan reminded us on Friday."

"I know, I know. Shit. I've been so preoccupied. What should I do?" Alice was practically hyperventilating.

"Okay, don't freak. I'll tell you what happens." Tally screwed the top back on her flask, concentrating. "It's very tragic actually. Othello's obsessed with the fact that his wife is cheating on him, even though she's not. He's just insecure."

"Why's he insecure?"

"Er, because I guess he's always been the best at what he does. Popular and admired and everything. But now he's in love and he has no idea how it works. So he messes it all up."

"And?"

"That's it."

"That's it?"

"Yep."

"I thought it was meant to be, like, a masterpiece."

"It is a masterpiece." Tally nodded enthusiastically. "You really have to read it to get it."

Alice glared at her. "Oh, I have to read it, do I? Now why didn't I think of that?" Her phone buzzed in her pocket.

"Oh my god. It's from Tristan." Alice's heart leaped, but she twisted her face into a sneer. "What does *he* want? Bastard. Does he think he can cheat on me and then just contact me? He can go fuck himself."

"What does it say?"

"Nothing much." She held the phone out for Tally to see:

Hey Ali, u alright? Let's talk soon. Maybe drink this week? T.

"I knew it!" Tally squealed. "If you waited long enough, I knew he'd come crawling back. What are you going to do?"

"I don't know." Alice shut the window with a smug smile. "But let's make *him* wait now."

CHAPTER TWENTY-THREE

I call it the Man Muncher." Dylan was practically shouting on the Great Lawn, struggling to be heard above the bell. She was explaining to Farah Assadi and Emilia Charles the impossibly raunchy dance routine she'd just demonstrated, which was, at the moment, number one in her arsenal of sexy moves. She couldn't get over the fact that Farah and Emilia were talking to her like normal people. They were the first popular girls who hadn't spat in her face since she'd arrived at St. Cecilia's. Dylan hoped Alice was watching. But Alice didn't seem to be in her normal spot, on top of the wide, flat stairs leading to Quad.

"No man has ever survived it intact," she added, feeling the back of her skirt to make sure it hadn't ridden up too far with all the gyrating.

"Oh man." Emilia's eyes were wide. She started twitching her pelvis tentatively, as if tempted to try out the Man Muncher for herself. She looked like she couldn't dance for shit, though. Not on those toothpick legs.

"Where did you learn it?" Farah asked.

"Oh, nowhere. I made it up myself." Dylan shrugged breezily. "It was for a contest at my school in New York. I was president of the tenth-grade dance team."

"Excuse me," Mimah interrupted shrilly. She was smirking the way she always did when she reckoned she had something clever to contribute. "What exactly did you say you called this move?"

"The Man Muncher. So?"

"So?" Mimah let rip a vicious laugh. "Sounds suspiciously like something else, doesn't it?"

There was a silence. No one seemed to be following her.

"Hello? *Rug* muncher perhaps?" She grinned obnoxiously at Farah and Emilia, waiting for them to laugh. No go. They were too rapt with Dylan's stupid story to care.

But Dylan cared. She shot her friend a hurt look.

"Umm, anyway," she went on, "I might use the Man . . . er, that routine in *Pashminas to the Rescue*. It's not hard to learn. Just lock your abs and rock your hips. Like this." She lifted her arms in a graceful arc and bumped her butt in circles. Her breasts—they must have been at least double-Ds—bounced in time with her movements. She looked just like an exotic belly dancer, except without the belly.

"Hot," Farah said. "That move should definitely be rated R."

"You go, girl!" Emilia cried.

Mimah glared at them. "Ooh, I'll bet I know who enjoyed

that," she snapped. "Tristan Murray-Middleton. Especially when you did it underneath him."

"What?" Dylan stared at her.

Mimah put on a deep, breathless voice. "'Dance for me, Dylan. Dance while I'm inside you. Work it, baby.' Is that what he said?"

The others giggled.

"Of course not!" A familiar cold rage flashed behind Dylan's eyes. "Actually, sometimes at the end of the routine I like to add a flourish. Like this."

She did a high-kick in the air, landing her toe right near Mimah's chin. Mimah stumbled backward. "Oops. Sorry, sweetie." Dylan feigned concern. "I didn't hurt you, did I?"

Immediately, she felt surprised at herself and a little ashamed. Dylan used to lose her temper all the time when she was younger. She'd thought she'd got it under control, but if the last few days were anything to go by, that wasn't the case. Plus, Mimah's face had a particularly nasty air right now. Maybe that was because of the birthmark under her left eye: It seemed to channel all of her vitriol at moments like this. Just as Dylan thought things might get ugly, a male voice broke the tension, resonating off the red-brick buildings at the back of Quad.

"Enough chatting!" shouted Mr. Vicks, the Head of Physics, charging among the loiterers. He was clapping his hands at them, as if they were a pack of hounds. "Get to lessons. Lessons! That means you lot, Jemimah."

Without giving Mimah a second to respond, he strode

past and thrust his balding head in Dylan's face. His gray eyebrows were wedged together so that all the little wisps of hair stood straight out.

"And you, my girl—save the kicking for when you really need it."

Dylan gasped. "Yes, sir."

Farah rolled her smoky, almond-shaped eyes as Mr. Vicks set off after another group. He was always spouting vaguely ominous comments that made it sound as if the Apocalypse was about to hit. He probably believed it was. He was crazy enough. The school should really fire him, but he was one of those institutionalized teachers who'd been there for so long he'd probably wither up and die in the real world.

"I've got to get to German," Mimah grunted, stalking toward the Main School. "See you later."

Farah turned to Dylan. "Moody cow, isn't she? What've you got?"

"Free period."

"Awesome. Emilia and I were going to cram for our Chemistry quiz on the Great Lawn. Feel like joining us?"

Dylan nodded eagerly. She'd been longing for an invitation into a Great Lawn study set ever since her first day, when she'd seen cliques of girls dotted round like they were posing for the cover of a perfect school prospectus.

When they reached the sunniest patch of grass, right out in the middle of the lawn, Emilia pulled a charcoal gray pashmina out of her bag and folded it neatly. She lived in constant fear that her ass would get smudged with grass stains.

"I wonder what Sonia's going to do if her nose isn't normal again by the time she has to compère," she said.

"Who cares?" Farah asked. "Serves her right for being such a stuck-up bitch."

They both chuckled. Dylan couldn't believe her ears. Farah bad-mouthing Sonia? Maybe Alice's crew weren't as untouchable as she'd thought.

"I feel sorry for Sonia though," she ventured, "because no matter how hard she tries, she'll never be as big a bitch as her idol: Her Majesty Alice Rochester." She chortled loudly.

Then she realized the other two weren't laughing.

"Oh, Alice is really cool once you get to know her," Emilia said defensively.

"She knows everyone there is to know. And she throws the best parties. Her sixteenth was at Shantytown. You know, the club that Sir Randolph Lindley's grandson owns?"

"Practically no one can get into Shantytown," Emilia panted. "He only let her have it there because her aunt is married to his cousin, and also, it'd obviously make the place look good to have Rochesters in it."

"And you know, if you have a party and Alice isn't there, that basically means it's a failure."

Dylan had gone red. What was it with Alice? Did she have the entire fucking country under her thumb?

CHAPTER TWENTY-FOUR

I've got a surprise for you lot." Mr. Logan's voice wafted down from the low stone wall he was crouching on. This morning, he'd had the bright idea of bringing his students out from their stuffy classroom and into St. Cecilia's sunken garden, which was famous for being one of the most beautiful in England (at least, if you believed the virtual tour on the school website). Rare plants burst from every square centimeter of its soil, their leaves and petals flashing like colored glass in the late-September sun. Even Mr. Logan's wall had blossoms sprouting out of it. He'd taken a flying leap up there as soon as the students had reached the garden, sending pebbles and bits of chalk showering into the front row of the class and, more specifically, into Alice's face. Alice glared at his tatty loafers. She was certain she'd seen him purposely scuffing them on the paving stones outside the staff room. No doubt he'd bought them last week and messed them up so he'd look more like a bona fide intellectual. Pathetic.

"Get ready, everyone," Mr. Logan ranted on. "Today, we're going to read some of *Othello* aloud. I'll cast the roles and we'll act out the scenes. See? English really can be fun!"

Alice scoffed to herself. No, English really couldn't be fun. Especially not today, when her entire life felt like it was going to shit. If high marks hadn't been so important to her father—and to her, naturally—she'd have skipped this class and gone sunbathing. Her tan from the South of France could do with a little topping up. During the Summer Terms, she, Tally, Sonia, and Mimah had always lain out on the grass in this area of the grounds, hiking up their skirts and unbuttoning their blouses, under which they wore tiny push-up bras to titillate the gardeners. There was one gardener in particular over whom Mimah and Tally fought—but that was only because they were so fucking man-starved at school. In the real world the guy wouldn't have stood a chance with either of them. He was about nineteen and looked identical to the string beans that he cultivated in the vegetable patch: long, skinny, and slouched. He was a good person to know, though; he never minded picking up a few bottles of gin or vodka for their posse on his way into school in the mornings, and occasionally, he was up for letting them into his shed to share a spliff. Their seminaked sunbathing was sort of his payment.

If you wanted to put it vulgarly, that is.

"Alice!" Mr. Logan's voice seemed to break over her head. "You've been grinning at me like an automaton for ten minutes now. May I help you?"

Alice snapped open her pen and scribbled down *automaton* to look up later. You got extra points in exams for using long words. "Oh. No, sir," she said. "I was just interested in what you were saying."

"I'm so glad. In that case, why don't you be the first to answer my question?"

"Your question." Alice cleared her throat. "Which question was that?"

"The one I just asked: Which theme in *Othello* did you write about for your prep?"

"Ah yes." Alice took a deep breath. "Actually, I meant to talk to you about that."

"Indeed?"

"Yes. Well, you see, there are just so many themes in *Othello*, and I find them all so terribly fascinating, I couldn't choose which one to write about."

Mr. Logan tapped his foot impatiently.

"So I wanted your advice before committing."

"Bullshit!" Mr. Logan yelled. Alice jumped.

"Do I seem like an amateur to you?" he choked. "Do I seem so stupid that I'd buy into that transparent excuse?"

"Y-yes. I mean no!"

"You'd better mean no." Mr. Logan's face had gone a nasty

red underneath the designer stubble he'd cultivated over the weekend. Alice hadn't bargained on this.

"Where's your essay?" Mr. Logan shouted. "Show me what you've done."

Alice bit her lip. "Please, sir, I'll have it for you soon. Honestly. I just need a bit more time."

"Time," Mr. Logan snarled. "If I don't see that piece of work on my desk by Break today, I'm putting you in detention."

Alice paled. Vindictive bastard. There was no way she could do the essay by Break. Nor could she, under any circumstances, go to detention. It would spoil her spotless record. What would her father do? What would *Oxford* do? Hopefully, Oxford didn't look at your junior year report cards, but you never knew. You didn't get where Oxford was by not being thorough.

"No, please, Mr. Logan," she gasped. "I can explain. Please, please give me a chance!"

"See me after class," Mr. Logan snapped, spotting the tears welling in Alice's eyes. He turned hurriedly away and started assigning parts. He couldn't stand the sight of women weeping.

Tally put her head on Alice's shoulder. "You all right, honey?"

"I hate him," Alice sniffed imperiously. She'd pulled herself together now. Tally's hair smelled of fruit.

"Oh, I'm sure he doesn't mean any harm. I think it's really sexy when he gets pissed off." Tally gave a lingering sigh. "Have you decided what you're going to write to T?"

Alice shook her head.

"Natalya," Mr. Logan butted in. He was smiling his dimpled smile. "I'd like you to play Desdemona in this pivotal scene."

"Fabulous!" Tally immediately jumped up, almost knocking Alice over in her hurry. "Where do I start?"

"Right here. But first, could you remind us of the context, please?"

Tally squinted at her copy of the play. "Oh yeah. This is where Desdemona's maid, Emilia, is preparing Desdemona to go to bed with Othello. The next act is their big showdown. Where he murders her. Most foully."

Mr. Logan nodded approvingly while Tally took her place on the stage, a raised slab around the fountain and did a little curtsy.

Alice picked some daisies out of the soil and ripped their heads off. Tally was so pathetic in front of Mr. Logan. And the acting around the fountain was so bad she could hardly bear to watch.

"I have laid those sheets you bade me on the bed," read Gabby Bunter as Emilia. Lord knew why Mr. Logan had cast *her*; she was too fat to be anybody's personal maid. Gabby was muttering her lines with zero expression. Her book started to shake uncontrollably. What a nerd.

Meanwhile Tally had adopted some kind of breathy, low-pitched voice that she obviously thought sounded tragic.

"O, these men, these men!" she huffed, putting on a mopey face.

Tragic was right.

Finally, when the scene was over, Mr. Logan dashed onto the stage, applauding loudly.

"Natalya, that was wonderful." He brushed straight past Gabby, who drooped her head to one side and slunk away.

"I've rarely heard Desdemona read with such . . . pathos." Mr. Logan was practically drooling.

I'm going to be sick, Alice thought.

"Oh, thank you." Tally blushed demurely. Jumping down from the stage, she flung herself back on the grass next to Alice.

"Hey," she whispered, "I've been thinking. About Tristan. Why don't you give him the benefit of the doubt?"

"Why the fuck should I?"

"Because he's a good guy. He was probably telling the truth about not shagging Dylan."

Alice winced.

"And you know what I've just realized?" Tally went on. "You can never prove it if someone's been faithful to you. You can only prove it if they've been *un*faithful."

"What on earth are you talking about?"

"You know, like if you'd actually seen T in bed with someone else—that's proof. Then you'd know for sure that he was cheating. But there's no way of knowing for sure that he's *not* cheating. Being suspicious of someone is an endless quest. Sometimes, you have to trust people or you'll go mad."

Alice nodded slowly. Maybe there was some wisdom in that.

Just then, the bell rang in Quad and reverberated around the grounds.

"You." Mr. Logan beckoned to Alice. "I haven't forgotten."

CHAPTER TWENTY-FIVE

*A*lice waited till the rest of the class had exited the garden, then gathered her things into the boho-chic tote that she and Tally had snapped up on their Saturday-afternoon shopping spree in Harvey Nics. She was doing her best not to freak out. Not visibly at least. Members of the Rochester family never showed weakness. That was why they were so respected in society.

She thought back to the time when her older brother, Dominic, had been suspended from Hasted House and stripped of his position as Head Boy for smoking weed. (In fact, Dom had been the biggest pot dealer at school, but he was too wily to get nabbed for something as serious as that.) Their mother had gone to collect him in the Mercedes, keeping her mouth sealed about the incident all the way back to London, and to this day, no one in the family had ever mentioned what had happened—not even during the week that Dom was home serving out his punishment. He was doing brilliantly now: reading Land Economy in his first term at Edinburgh, keeping at least three girlfriends on the go, and acting as head of Edinburgh's Hasted House Old Boys Club.

Because that was another thing about Rochesters: They always ended up fine.

Alice looked Mr. Logan in the eye.

"I apologize," she told him stiffly. "I can do the essay by tomorrow morning. If you like."

Mr. Logan said nothing, but reached into his forest green canvas bag and drew out a sheet of paper. He held it to his chest so that Alice couldn't see what was on it, just like a six-year-old who doesn't want anyone to copy his prep. Lame. Still, Alice could see why people thought he was attractive. Sort of. Up close, he looked much younger than he did at the head of the classroom. The angles of his face hadn't hardened yet. He had curly brown hair, shiny hazel eyes, full lips, and a little cleft in his chin that could possibly be called cute. But he was so fucking pleased with himself that it canceled everything else out.

"I don't appreciate you making me look a fool in front of everyone," Mr. Logan commenced in his deep voice. "Didn't you listen to Mrs. Traphorn's address this morning? You should respect me." He paused, presumably to let that piece of wisdom sink in. "I expect to have your essay on my desk by the end of the week. Meanwhile, I want you to volunteer for something."

Volunteer! That didn't sound like detention. Alice had known it all along: He wouldn't dare.

"Umm, doesn't *volunteer* imply that something's *voluntary*?" she asked. "Whereas I'd say you're forcing me into this. Whatever it is."

The light in Mr. Logan's eyes wavered. He regarded Alice coldly, giving her upturned mouth, shiny hair, and long legs the onceover. He'd got the lowdown on her in the staff room: father had inherited the family's immense trading firm, mother came from old nobility. Bunch of toffs, never had to work for anything in their lives.

His gaze was making Alice uncomfortable. She smoothed her skirt, and her silver bracelets jingled on her wrist.

"Nobody's forcing you," Mr. Logan said evenly. "You could always choose detention instead."

"Fine. Do I get to know what I'm volunteering for?"

"Naturally." Mr. Logan took the sheet of paper away from his chest, leaving Alice to stare at his hideous candy-striped button-down shirt. It looked like something an estate agent from Essex might wear out on the pull. Maybe he'd only been holding the paper there to hide it.

"On Wednesdays," Mr. Logan explained, "I usually take a group of ninth-grade girls to visit the old people's center in town, as part of their Duke of Edinburgh Award scheme."

Alice shrugged. Wednesday was Elective day, when lessons finished after lunch so the girls could practice sports, go on educational outings, or do community service.

"This Wednesday, I'd like *you* to take them instead."

"What? Why?" Alice cringed. She hated old people. They smelled like mothballs and they liked dark places. She even hated visiting her grandmother's estate in Hampshire.

"Why? Because I can't send them by themselves. And since you're a junior, you're allowed to lead an outing. School rules."

"No, I mean, why can't *you* take them?"

"That is a private matter. Let's just say I have an engagement I can't miss."

Alice crossed her arms. This was unbelievable. Not to mention unprofessional. She should really report Mr. Logan. Except she couldn't, or they'd know that she hadn't done her essay. It would be like a car thief complaining to the police about another car hitting him from behind. She shut her eyes for a minute.

"Okay. I'll do it."

"Deal." Mr. Logan handed her the paper. "Here are instructions and a list of students. The school bus will bring you there and back. I'll let the office know that you so generously offered to help out." He winked. "Don't be late."

They were done. Alice scooped up her handbag and swept out of the garden, stalking past the Chapel to the Great Lawn. When she reached it, she glimpsed, in the distance, Farah and Emilia sitting with someone.

Dylan Taylor. That man-eating bitch. Alice got out her

phone. This, at least, was in her control: There was no way she was letting Dylan win.

How about tonight? she replied to Tristan's text. A drink in town.

Then, hesitating a minute, she added: AR xox.

CHAPTER TWENTY-SIX

*I*t was dusk, and Alice was on the last leg of her escape from St. Cecilia's to the nearby town of Hasted, thinking how much she could do with a fucking strong rum and Coke. Sneaking out to town was a trick that Alice had mastered in her second term and now, after five years of practice, she was famous for having never been caught. Her favorite route was to dart into the woods at the side of the Great Lawn, making sure that crazy old Mr. Vicks the physics teacher and his three Norfolk terriers were nowhere to be seen. Then she followed the woods till she emerged onto the road, safely round a bend from the entrance to St. Cecilia's and all its high-tech security cameras that snooped in every direction. Even then, Alice never walked the last mile to town in plain view. You never knew which prying teacher might drive past. It was far better to stay hidden in the underbrush lining the road, or to take the precaution of walking in the fields that ran alongside it.

Right now, Alice was in the old part of town; she always avoided the new center, where Waitrose and Jessops and WH Smith inhabited soulless glass shopfronts. Hasted was looking particularly picturesque, its faded brick buildings and cobbled streets melting together in the dim light. Smoking a nervous cigarette, she glanced at her reflection in a window. Tally had helped her choose the perfect sexy-but-casual ensemble: gray skinny jeans, a soft, electric blue sweater that was so thin you could see the outline of her bra nudging through it, and blue stilettos that made her teeter on the cobblestones. Their heels were covered in mud from sinking into the ground every few meters—one of the pitfalls of country life. Alice didn't really mind though; she liked the outdoors. People were always surprised by that, probably because she seemed like such a society girl. Well, just because she liked to party didn't mean she couldn't be into other things, too.

Turning down an alleyway, Alice pushed open the door of Shock Box, the grimy spot where she'd arranged to meet T. The place was narrow inside, with a bar running along one wall and a row of small booths set against the other. It was decorated with kitschy neon palm trees and flamingos, and a fifties jukebox that still worked.

Downstairs was the world's shittiest disco. On Saturday nights, you paid three quid for the privilege of dancing to dreadful music while getting wasted on cheap vodka and even cheaper beer in plastic cups. It was always absolutely rammed with St. Cecilia's girls in their tiniest outfits, trying to seduce

Hasted House boys. The place was so badly ventilated that people's sweat condensed on the ceiling and rained down onto the dance floor. In fact, you'd be hard-pressed to think of a bodily fluid that wasn't exchanged down there.

Still, everyone came anyway. It wasn't like there were other places to go in Hasted.

"Ali! Over here." Tristan waved from the booth he'd occupied, right at the back of the bar.

Alice squinted. "Why'd you sit all the way in Siberia?"

"Thought it was more private, I suppose."

"Whatever you say." Alice threw down her Prada pouch bag, containing wallet, phone, cigs, and lip gloss, and slid into the opposite side of the booth. She wasn't going to sit next to him. Not yet. First he could stew a little. And grovel.

"I've ordered you a rum and Coke. I thought you might want one," Tristan said. "Is that cool?"

Alice shrugged. God, he was amazing. He always knew what she wanted. He knew her better than anyone else in the world. That was why she'd fallen in love with him. It was why she was still in love with him now, even if he *had* acted like a bastard. Maybe soon they could go on a dirty weekend together: hop on a plane to Croatia and hole up in a hotel by the sea. They'd emerge only to go for gentle strolls along the port at sunset, or to feed each other oysters and drink crisp white wine.

"So . . ." T was studying her. "How are you?"

He was wearing a scruffy blue hoodie and had a few days'

worth of stubble. It looked so soft she wanted to reach out and caress his cheek. He'd probably been too busy torturing himself over her to even think about shaving. These last few days had been so tragic, it made her want to cry.

"I'm fine," Alice said, trying to sound it.

"Honestly? It's me, remember. You don't have to pretend."

"Don't I?"

"Come on, Al. Of course not."

"I don't know. How can I ever trust you again after what happened on Saturday night? What am I meant to think?"

"I'm sorry about that," Tristan said. "I really am. But let me explain, it's just a misunderstanding."

Alice put her head in her hands. "You don't know how hard it is, seeing that slut every day at school."

"Hang on, Dill's not a slut. I promise."

"What the fuck?" Alice couldn't believe she was hearing this. "How can you say that? I knew you still liked her! I knew you cheated!"

"That's lies!" Tristan raised his voice, a rare occurrence for him. "I haven't even been near Dylan Taylor. There's absolutely nothing between us."

"Fine. If that's true, then how did she have your . . . that bag?"

Tristan sighed. "Okay," he said staunchly, "I'm going to tell you the truth. Promise you won't get angry?"

Alice clutched her drink.

"I did buy those condoms," Tristan said. "But they were for us. In case you and I ever wanted them."

Alice lowered her eyes.

Tristan took a deep breath.

"Then I went to the pub 'cause the football was on, and Dylan happened to be there. I don't know what she was doing—having a drink by herself, it looked like." He started fiddling with the string on his hoodie. "She came over and wouldn't leave me alone. I had to let her sit down. But it was only for a minute. I literally downed my pint and ran off. And stupidly I walked out without the bag of . . . of, well, you know. All I wanted was to get away from her."

"Promise?"

"Cross my heart. I swear it, Squidge."

Alice smiled. Squidge was the special name T had given her when they were four years old and used to build mud castles in each other's gardens. Now he only used it very rarely, when it was just the two of them at their closest. He'd never do anything to hurt her. She touched the back of his hand.

A muscle twitched in Tristan's cheek. "Listen, Al . . . We're best friends, right?"

"Of course. I love you, T. As a friend," she added hurriedly. "That's why being together is so amazing. It makes things really special."

Tristan swallowed and took his hand away.

Alice's eyes shot to his face. "What? Don't you agree?"

"I . . . I don't know. Look, I'm sorry. That's what I wanted to talk to you about tonight. I don't think this is a good idea: I think we should just be friends."

"What?" Alice thudded her glass down on the table. She felt as if all the blood had been sucked from her body, like water down a plughole.

"I think we should break up." T was looking at her as if he were a thousand miles away. "I don't think we're ready."

"What do you mean? How can we not be ready?"

"I mean it's too difficult. You must agree, come on."

"*You* come on! You're such a coward!" Alice burst out. "I should have known you'd do this. As soon as something isn't incredibly easy for you, you run away!"

"I'm not running away," Tristan said. "I've thought about this loads."

"Yeah, right. It took you two whole days to decide. You don't care about me." Alice felt herself breaking down.

"Ali, I do care about you. That's why I don't want this. I don't want to ruin our friendship."

"Fuck that. It's ruined already!"

"I hope that's not true."

But Alice didn't seem to be listening. She was twisting her glass round and round, leaving a trail of watermarks.

Tristan fidgeted. "Hey, are you all right?"

No answer.

"Maybe we should go find you a taxi?"

"No." Alice's voice sounded flat.

"Okay, well . . ." Tristan sat staring at the jukebox for

a minute. "I guess I'm gonna go then." He stood up and awkwardly put his hands to his pockets.

She couldn't let him leave. She couldn't bear to see him turn away. "When I said I loved you, I meant it," she whispered.

Tristan nodded slightly. Then he was gone.

Trying desperately to control herself, Alice dialed Tally on her phone. "Tal . . ." She could hardly get the words out between sobs. "Tal, he—"

"Babe, what's wrong?"

"He finished it."

"He what?"

"He . . . he . . . he dumped me."

"Oh my god! How dare he do that? Did he say why?"

"No!" Alice almost screamed.

Tally had never heard her like this. "Sweetie, come back to school. You'll feel better when you're here. I'll make you toast and tea. I have Nutella."

"I don't want Nutella. I'll starve myself. I'll never feel better again. I loved him, Tally. I—I loved him."

"Oh, Al . . . I'm so sorry. Hey," Tally suddenly said, "I know what'll cheer you up! Let's go to Paris! I'll book us Eurostar tickets now. We'll go this weekend. Everything will seem better in Paris."

Alice got her breathing under control. Paris was nice. She pictured them strolling past Notre Dame, drinking *chocolat chaud* in the Marais, shopping for winter coats at Colette.

She'd take her new superslim digital Canon. Then she could post pictures on Facebook to show Tristan what a good time she was having without him.

"O-Okay," she said. "Wait—Tal?"

"Yeah, sweetie?"

"Make sure you book us first-class seats."

CHAPTER TWENTY-SEVEN

*T*he night was thick and still as Tristan stole back from town through the side gates of Hasted House. He'd only had a short distance to walk. Some of the school's buildings were even situated within the town, so Hasted House students, wearing their gray suits and club ties, were a familiar sight as they walked in twos and threes down the cobbled streets. Once Tristan was inside the school grounds though, he felt removed from all that. He stood staring at the lake and the dead-quiet boat sheds, then past them to the dark lawns and the even darker fields further off. He shuddered. Who knew what was lurking out there beyond the trees' inky contours? At times like this, it felt like there was no barrier between him and infinity.

With his fingertips, Tristan scooped into the pocket of his hoodie for a spliff. He'd meant to smoke it earlier to mellow him out for his meeting with Alice, but he'd been so stressed that he'd forgotten. He lit it now and inhaled, blinking at a halo of light on the rugby field. At the beginning of home matches, that was where he and his team paraded in front of the whole school, with everyone cheering them on. Alice always came to support him for the big games. Last year (his first as team captain) she'd painted a huge banner in his honor, which Tristan still kept rolled up under his bed.

God, Alice had looked so upset in Shock Box just now. Maybe he shouldn't have left her. He'd never felt like such a shit in his life.

"Hey T," a voice boomed. It was George Demetrios, with Seb Ogilvy. "Why the fuck are you lurking all the way out here? You look like you're about to nick someone's wallet."

"All right, T," Seb nodded, giving his standard greeting. His haystack hair and rail-thin frame made him look like a scarecrow next to George's athletic bulk.

Tristan threw down his joint. "Just getting some air," he said. "You guys?"

"Same," George said. "Christ, you're looking glum."

"Did you do it?" Seb tossed his lighter up and down in one hand.

Tristan nodded. "Yeah."

"Yeah what?" George demanded.

"I broke up with Alice."

"Fuck me. That was quick. Why?"

"It was too heavy, man. I couldn't deal." T paused. "She just made me feel guilty all the time."

"Well, maybe that's because you had something to feel guilty about!" George punched Tristan's shoulder and laughed. "Did you? Did you? Eh? Dirty boy."

"Unbelievable. And you wonder why I never tell you anything."

"Break it up!" Grinning, Seb flung a skinny arm round each of his friends' shoulders. "Come on," he told Tristan. "We're going to The Oakes to drown your sorrows."

"At least someone's being sympathetic," T grumbled. He'd been planning to go back to his room to play his guitar, maybe work on some of the tortured love ballads he'd written recently for his and Seb's and Rando's band—their first gig was just a few weeks away. But when he thought about it, the songs seemed jaded now that his whole *life* was a tortured love ballad. Far better to go to The Oakes, the elite club founded almost three hundred years ago off in its own corner of the grounds at the same time as Hasted House itself. Officially, The Oakes was an intellectual society where the juniors and seniors who'd been invited read poetry, declaimed about philosophy, and smoked cigars just like their fathers and grandfathers had done before them.

Unofficially, it was a den of vice. All the teachers knew that the boys who belonged smuggled in liquor and worse, but they turned a blind eye. If The Oakes ever got busted, its past members—some of the most powerful men in England—would kick up a fuss like nobody's business.

Seb gave the secret knock and led them in.

"Oy! Over here," Jasper called from one of the room's leather couches. The whole place looked like a shabby gentlemen's club, with a piano in one corner, a pool table at the back, and several brass lamps casting pools of light onto the worn rugs.

Jasper was sitting with his cousin Rando, from whom he was inseparable these days. "What took you so long?"

"We found T on the way over."

Jasper inspected Tristan. "You're looking a bit worse for wear."

"He just split up with Alice."

"That's a shame, mate. Here, have some of this." Jasper poured some Jameson into Tristan's glass. "Sort of saw it coming though. She's a firecracker. Think you two will ever work it out?"

"Don't know," Tristan muttered, swirling the tawny liquid. "I really hope we can still be friends."

"You hope you can still be fuck friends, you mean!" George roared. "Enough of this bullshit. Here's the question we've all been waiting for. Who was the better shag, Dylan or Alice?"

"Shut up!" Seb broke in. "That's out of order. Why would you objectify people like that?"

"They're not people. They're girls!"

"I have a question," Rando said suddenly. The other four looked at him. "Has anyone ever been out with that Russian bird, Tally? I thought she was the most beautiful thing I've ever seen. Like an angel."

Jasper laughed. "So do we all. Remember when she first arrived and she wore those thigh-high leather boots around everywhere?"

"Such a prick-tease," George said.

"We all love Tally," Seb added, "but she refuses to go out with anyone in our group. Good luck if you like her."

Rando's face fell. "I was hoping to ask her out."

"Don't give up." Jasper patted his knee comfortingly. "Remember, we've got that dinner at St. Cecilia's on Thursday night."

"What dinner?" Tristan grumbled. "I wasn't invited to any dinner."

"Actually, I've been meaning to ask about that," Rando said. "I saw the invitation but I don't get it—what's the deal?"

Jasper rolled his eyes. "Oh, just you wait. This is one of the great 'privileges' of the junior class. Every month or so, our tutors arrange these chaperoned do's for us with girls' schools. You know, so we'll be prepared to socialize in the real world when we're not locked up in an eighteenth-century, all-boys boarding school anymore. The whole thing's meant to be very civilized—we're served one minuscule glass of wine each and have to make charming small talk round the table. Come to think of it, that's probably why they didn't invite you, T—you're incapable of charm."

"Hilarious."

Jasper turned back to Rando. "Anyway, you'll see Tally there."

"Wicked," Rando said. His usually mischievous eyes had gone dreamy.

"Uh-oh." Jasper shook his head. "We've got a case of love-sickness on our hands."

CHAPTER TWENTY-EIGHT

*J*emimah Calthorpe de Vyle-Hanswicke strode into the hallway of the art block, ramming straight into a freshman girl who was balancing a pot of paint in her hands.

"Shove off!" Mimah barked.

The girl dropped her cargo, splattering thick tendrils of orange over the linoleum tiles. "Ow! Help!" She screwed up her nose and took in shuddering gulps of air, the way people do when they're about to lose their shit.

Mimah pulled her into a supply room and gave her a shake. The girl's French braid flapped wildly against her back.

"What's your name?"

"C-Camilla."

"Listen up, Camilla. Don't you dare cry. This is boarding school. It's not a nursery. It's not home. Your mummy isn't coming to save you. Got it?"

The girl nodded tearfully.

"Good. Now dry your eyes and piss off. And not a word of this to anyone."

There was no room for wimps at St. Cecilia's, not even eleven-year-old ones. The sooner you toughen up, the better.

Mimah swept back into the corridor and up the light-filled stairway, whose walls were plastered with the charcoal portraits the juniors had drawn of one another. Miss Baskin required her Advanced Art set to do the "portrait project" every year. She always said that if you could draw someone's character, you could draw anything. Most of the attempts hanging here had about as much character as leeches. That either said something unfortunate about the juniors' artistic talent, or something even more unfortunate about their personalities.

Reaching the third floor—where she noted with satisfaction that she wasn't out of breath from all the stairs, despite chucking lacrosse this term—Mimah heard strains of music. She traced the sound down the corridor until she came to the doorway of one of the smaller studios, half of whose roof was glassed over like a conservatory. It was empty except for one person: Dylan Taylor.

"Hey," Mimah said, hovering.

Dylan didn't turn. Probably because she couldn't hear over the iPod speakers that Miss Baskin had allowed her students to hook up. Or maybe she was still ignoring Mimah after their fight at news hour yesterday.

Mimah watched her for a minute. The glass roof above

Dylan's head channeled the day's gray light and illuminated the dust motes swirling round her as she worked. Mimah's eyes widened when she noticed what Dylan was working *on*. All around her she'd pinned up dozens upon dozens of pictures of men. Or, to be more precise, of men's six packs. She was hoarding tear-outs and postcards in every shape and size, ranging from Renaissance sketches to modern paintings to sex-crazed Dolce & Gabbana ads from *Vogue*. She was pasting some of them together into a huge collage, and every so often stood back, glue stick in hand, inspecting her design.

Despite the subject matter, for the first time since Mimah had known her, Dylan looked at peace. Mimah realized she was playing *Wish You Were Here*, the Pink Floyd album that Mimah had burned for her last week. Mimah was obsessed with rebellious music from the seventies and she was trying to convince Dylan of how awesome it was too.

Suddenly, standing there unnoticed, she felt a deep pang.

"Hey," she said again, loudly.

Dylan looked up and stared at her. Then she turned the music down.

"Hey."

"What on earth are you doing?" For some reason, Mimah always ended up being rude, even when she was trying to be nice.

"What does it look like I'm doing? I'm examining depictions of the male torso throughout history," Dylan replied icily. "Then I'm going to create my own personal interpretation."

Mimah burst out laughing. "What a load of shit. You're using school supplies to take your porn collection to the next level." She stopped herself. "Er, no, really Dill, I'm only joking. Can I talk to you for a minute?"

"Depends what you want to say."

"Just that I'm sorry for cussing you yesterday. I didn't mean to act like a bitch. I'm PMS-ing. You know how it is."

Dylan sighed. She'd spent most of her free time here in the art studio during the past twenty-four hours, with only cutouts of people to keep her company. Headless people, more often than not. Spending time by herself was fine, if it was a choice. If not, it was the loneliest thing in the world.

"There was something else too," Mimah went on. "I'd love you to teach me your dance routine—I really did think it was hot. We could use it in PTTR."

Dylan smiled slyly. "Maybe. If you think you can do it."

"Of course I can do it. You just swing your hips like you're having sex, right?" Mimah gave her hoarse giggle. Then her face lit up. "Actually, why should we stop there? I vote we add even juicier moves and use it as our secret weapon."

Dylan raised her eyebrows.

"Sonia wants to take all the credit for the show herself," Mimah elaborated, "even though it was *my* idea. And she's a bitch to you. We'll totally upstage her with the Man Muncher. She won't know what's hit her."

"What kind of 'moves' do you mean?" Dylan asked.

"Oh, I have a few ideas." Mimah winked. "Just you wait."

She glanced back toward Dylan's collage. "Can I see what you've made so far?"

"Sure."

Finally stepping into the room, Mimah walked over to the easel. She shuffled through a pile of images and picked out an ancient black-and-white Calvins ad, showing Mark Wahlberg in tiny Y-fronts clutching his crotch.

"Whoa, where did you find this?"

"Just on Google. It's so retro, isn't it?"

"He is *hot*." Mimah held it up. "Mind if I keep it?"

CHAPTER TWENTY-NINE

*W*e're from St. Cecilia's School," Alice enunciated as clearly as she could, shooting an exasperated look at the ninth-grade students clustered round her. It was Wednesday afternoon, and they were standing in the recreation room of the old people's home in Hasted, trying to communicate with one of its elderly residents. "We're just here to chat with you for a while. Is that all right?"

"Pardon me, dear?" The lady Alice was talking to cupped her liver-spotted hand behind her ear. "Who are you?"

"Students from St. Cecilia's."

"Pardon?"

"St. Ce-ci-lia's!" Alice shouted for the fourth time.

"Ooh, no, don't know anybody by the name of Cecil," the woman said, an air of confusion clouding her already cloudy eyes. "Are you sure it isn't someone else?"

Alice shut her eyes for a moment, ready to scream in frustration. This woman must be at least two hundred years old. There was no way they were going to get her to under-stand. She sighed. It wasn't that she didn't like old people. It was that being around them brought back memories of the miserable Christmases her family used to spend at her grandmother's mansion in Hampshire, before Alice and her brothers had refused to go anymore. The place was so huge and so gloomy—Grandma Lucinda refused to open any curtains or turn on any overhead lights—that Alice was terrified even to walk down the hallways alone. Grandma Lucinda was as hard of hearing as this woman here. She never spoke, in fact; just rustled silently from room to room, glaring at anyone she came across.

Alice turned toward the girls whom Mr. Logan had made her chaperone, wondering how she could escape this hellhole. Thank fuck there were only two more days till she and Tally dashed off to Paris. They were taking the 7:32 p.m. Eurostar on Friday. Their hotel was booked and their excuses were sorted: Alice had already forged the notes from their parents getting her and Tally off Saturday-morning lessons. She'd used the great-aunt-keeling-over-and-dying story. Teachers could never check up on things like that—it'd be too insensitive.

Alice's eyes fell on Charlotte Calthorpe de Vyle-Hanswicke, Mimah's fourteen-year-old sister. The fact that Charlie was here was another piece of bad luck. Back when Alice and Mimah had been friends, Alice used to spend weeks at a time at the Calthorpe de Vyle-Hanswickes' mansions in Wiltshire and Spain, so she knew Charlie well. Just last Easter, the girl had been innocent and boisterous—still a kid—but she seemed to have taken her dad's notorious philandering to heart. Today, typically, she was wearing black eyeliner so thick it looked like she'd smeared it on with a spatula, and a gray school skirt that barely covered her thighs. Her coal-colored hair hadn't been cut in months.

"Excuse me, dear," the old woman said, smiling hopefully at Alice. "Would you like to see my collection of teeth?" Behind her thick spectacles, her eyes seemed to be blinking out from fish tanks.

"Er, no thanks." Alice backed away. But the woman was already reaching into her pocket, pulling out a plastic tortoise-shell box.

"Here you go. Lovely, aren't they?" she smiled, shaking the box. The lines of white dentures inside it rattled like dice.

Alice's eyes darted toward the glass doors.

"Know what?" She nudged Charlie. "I reckon I'll go for a walk."

"You can't," Charlie argued. "Your job is to stay and supervise us."

Alice regarded her coldly. Younger students weren't meant to talk back to their superiors. Trust a Calthorpe de Vyle-Hanswicke to disregard the status quo.

"Wrong," she said. "I can and I will. Tell the others I'll be back at five."

With that, she pushed past Mimah's sister and the rest of her charges, and booked it for the center of town.

CHAPTER THIRTY

*I*t wasn't until twenty minutes later as she wandered past New Look—Hasted's sad attempt at a trendy store—that it occurred to Alice how risky it was being here at this time of day. Sometime around now, several afternoons a week, Tristan came into town for lessons with Dr. Grott (or Grotty, as generations of boys had nicknamed him), the legendary Latin and Greek teacher at Hasted House. Dr. Grott was a lunatic—he wore an eye patch and sometimes broke into Wagner arias while he was lecturing—but for some reason T worshipped him. Alice suspected it was because Grotty was everything T wanted to be when he got older: intellectual, original, and so clearly above what other people thought.

Grotty had been teaching translation and pronunciation for decades in his book-strewn house next to the church. He'd had a small stage built, where he made the boys stand to declaim ancient poetry while he waved his cane in time with their recitations like a mad conductor. When they pronounced something wrong, the tip of the cane (which he'd had cast in steel) rapped down on the floorboards, signaling that you had to start all over again. Tristan had told Alice that if you ever did a recitation straight off with no mistakes, the entire room would explode in cheers, with boys jumping on the tabletops and Grotty dancing a jig round the piano. Alice had laughed in his face. He'd looked so excited talking about it that anyone would think he'd been describing a Daft Punk concert and not a Latin lesson.

Tristan. Fuck, she missed him. Alice snatched a corner of her yellow pashmina—the one that matched perfectly with her school uniform—and dabbed furiously at her eyes, willing the tears not to well over. Falling apart like this was completely unacceptable. If she didn't pull it together, everyone would dump her, just like they'd dumped Mimah last term. People had tried to be supportive of Mimah for a few weeks when the scandal about her dad and that prostitute broke. Alice and Tally and Sonia had even treated her to a girly spa day at Bliss, which she'd ruined by bitching at them and snapping at the masseuses and crying so much the manicurist couldn't even do her nails. In the end they'd all agreed: The girl had become a hopeless bore. She hadn't even made an effort to get over it. Did she expect everyone to put up with her drama-queen depression forever?

Just then, Alice rounded the side of the church. She froze, her heart clanging against her ribs. It was him, Tristan, no more than six meters away. He was standing with his back to her but she'd know him anywhere, from any direction: his longish, unruly hair, his striped scarf wound messily round his neck, his school trousers, accentuating the hard, lean muscles in his legs, and his stance, with his hands in his pockets and one foot crossed in front of the other.

She shrank into one of the building's alcoves, watching greedily. Tristan was talking to Seb. He laughed, throwing his whole body backward the way he always did when something was particularly hilarious. Alice gripped the church's stone wall so hard that her fingers turned white. How dare he be finding anything funny when she was feeling like this!

After a minute, the two friends drifted off. Without thinking, Alice slipped out of her hiding place and clicked briskly after them over the cobblestones, trying to keep them in sight. She lost them round a corner, speeded up, then emerged a minute later at the busy crossroads near the turn-off to Hasted House.

Too late. No sign of the boys. She hesitated. Maybe it was lame to track them any farther.

Suddenly, someone rammed into her side, knocking her bag off her shoulder.

"Ow!" she growled, bending over to retrieve it.

"Gosh, sorry."

Alice stiffened. She knew that voice: Seb.

"Shit, hey Al," he said, recognizing her as she straightened up. "How come you're here?"

She darted her eyes round. No sign of T.

"Oh, you know"—Alice kissed Seb on both cheeks, trying to stay calm—"claustrophobia, I suppose. Sometimes school gets too much. I needed a break."

"Wicked. Me too. I was just with . . . I mean, er, I was by myself and decided I really wanted a drink." Grinning in his characteristic sheepish way, Seb jerked his head at the Badger & Hounds placard hanging from the pub behind them. "What do you say?"

"Well, I suppose . . ." Alice hesitated. It was unexpectedly cool of Seb not to take sides. "All right, quick though, go in! I don't want to get caught."

They chose an almost-hidden table at the back of the pub, tucked into a nook behind the curving staircase that led to the hotel bedrooms upstairs. Alice had always wondered what kind of losers stayed here. You'd have to be pretty desperate, considering this was the oldest and shabbiest establishment in town. Her bench had been sat on so many times that the wood actually felt soft in some places, and the wallpaper, once a floral pattern, now looked like the faded remnants of some ancient food fight. Alice pictured the beds upstairs having no springs left, their frames groaning under the weight of horny guests trying to shag.

"I got an invitation for some fashion show next Saturday at St. Cecilia's," Seb said, clinking his glass with hers. "Pashminas Save the World, or something? Sounds bizarre. Does it have anything to do with you?"

"We're all in it, the whole year." Alice watched as Seb downed his whisky in two gulps and then held the glass up, looking disappointed it was gone.

"Better have another." He wiped his mouth and slid his chair back. "Anything for you?"

"No thanks," Alice said. People talked about how Seb was a total lush, but she'd always treated it as a joke. Now it occurred to her: What kind of normal person goes to the pub near boarding school at four in the afternoon on a Wednesday? By himself?

Seb had been a raver for as long as Alice could remember. Even now that they were sixteen, he seemed to care more about getting drunk and stoned than about girls. Perhaps he got it from his father, Sir Preston Ogilvy, who owned one of the biggest wine cellars in England, amassed over his lifetime from all corners of the globe. Even Alice was impressed by the way it unfurled under the whole of Seb's house in Kensington, each rack filled to the ceiling and cooled to the optimum temperature for whatever vintage ripened on its shelves. Last year, when Sir Preston was off on one of his many trips, Seb had thrown a now-famous dinner party. He'd cracked open forty-seven bottles of wine among sixteen people and served nothing but Kentucky Fried Chicken on silver trays. More wasted than anyone, Seb had ended the night dancing naked on top of the dining-room table, waving cigarettes round like sparklers in both hands. His pals had posted the pictures on Facebook as evidence, but Seb had made Jasper and T take them down.

"So," Alice giggled as Seb started in on his second drink, "tell me about Sonia."

He turned red. "What about her?"

"You tell me. Doesn't she look lovely with her new nose?"

"Yeah, I suppose. She's pretty. She always was."

"And?" Alice smiled archly.

"And nothing! I can't go near her now, can I? Not after that drama at George's."

"Come on, Sebby! You're always thinking up some excuse not to go for it with girls. What are you so afraid of? She likes you. The way she was sitting on your lap at the party? So obvious."

Seb tugged on the frayed end of his school sweater, thinking how long and bony his fingers looked. He wished he could light up a cig to go with the warm whisky seeping its way through his body.

So what if he was reluctant to get involved with women? They were nothing but trouble. Look at the rumors over the summer about him sleeping with Mimah. Look at the mess that was Tristan and Alice. That had been inconvenient for his social life while it was going on, and it was even more of a disaster now. Dating clearly fucked everyone's friendships up, and he was pretty happy with the way things were.

Besides . . . there was something else. Something that he wasn't quite sure he was ready to deal with yet.

"Speaking of liking people, how about you and T?" Seb

changed the subject, taking a swig from his glass. "Do you think you two will ever be friends again?"

"I don't know. Why?" Alice felt her face go hot. "Does he think we will be?"

Seb hiccuped. This would have been awkward, except that he didn't give a shit, thanks to the whisky.

"'Course he does," he slurred. "You just gotta give him some time. T is the best guy in the world. The best! Why can't you understand—you people, you women . . ." Seb was waving his hands about now, choking to get the words out. "Let me tell you, us men, we need our freedom! We need our freedom to be men!"

That was fucking ridiculous. Alice opened her mouth to protest. But instead, her jaw dropped.

Right in front of them, coming down the bottom few steps from the bedrooms, was Mr. Logan.

"Man is a hunter!" Seb cried.

"Shut up!" Alice gripped his arm. "That's my English teacher."

She ducked to conceal her face behind the table's rim, straining to see who Mr. Logan was with. There he was at the exit, holding open the door—and there, brushing past him with her head lowered, was a woman.

Who the hell could it be? Alice peered harder. A scarf covered the woman's hair. All she spied, before they vanished, was the ripple of its yellow silk in the breeze.

CHAPTER THIRTY-ONE

*D*ylan flung open the door of Tudor House, soaked to her underwear from the rain that had been pouring down ever since lunchtime. She peeled off her Burberry trench coat and hung it from one of the many hooks in the front hall, nailed there for exactly this purpose. If there was one thing the English knew how to do, it was prepare for wet weather.

Wringing out her hair, which had slickened and darkened with the water, Dylan sloshed into the kitchen to make a cup of hot chocolate. As she spooned out the powder and heated the milk—skim, of course—she heard heckling and chatter spilling from the common room next door. A clump of juniors were in there, a tangle of legs and arms and long hair on the maroon sofas. They were watching *Neighbours*, that smug Australian soap that everyone seemed to love in this country. Dylan had no clue why. As far as she could tell, it was a hash job of cardboard sets, stilted scripts, and unbearably suburban characters.

"Just you wait," Mimah had told her. "It's like crack. Once you try it, you're hooked."

Dylan still hadn't given in. But today, she noticed that Farah Assadi was among the group on the couch. Maybe she'd try to join in.

"Excuse me."

Dylan whipped round. Sonia was standing behind her, looking pointedly at the tea kettle. Her cheeks, still puffy from the bruising round her nose, gave her the air of a muskrat.

"I said excuse me," Sonia repeated, her nose cast quivering. She'd just found out that Alice and Tally were jetting off to Paris without her tomorrow night and was having trouble controlling her jealousy. Talk about kicking a girl when she was down. "I'd like to make some tea?"

"Oh, sure." Dylan stood aside, deciding to ignore Sonia's hostility. She was in a good mood, having spent most of the afternoon in the art block with her collection of half-clothed men. Her study of torsos was looking set to be a big hit. Miss Baskin was already rapt by it—she came by to check out Dylan's collage at least once an hour.

"Hey, Sonia?"

Sonia carried on filling the kettle without turning round. She fitted it pertly back onto its stand.

"I was thinking," Dylan bubbled on. "You know I'm doing Advanced Art? Well, I'd love to help out with—"

"Urrrgh, nasty," Sonia interrupted, flapping her hand disgustedly across the front of her school sweater. "Look what you've done. Why do you have to stand so close to me?"

"Oh, sorry." Dylan struggled to see what the fuss was over. In her excitement to make her offer, she'd flung her arm into the air, spraying a few tiny drops of rainwater from her sodden sleeve onto Sonia's clothes. All of a sudden Dylan felt like a drowned puppy next to her roommate who, as always, was impeccably turned out. Sonia's hair was devastatingly straight and shiny. Her manicured hands flashed with gold rings. Her shirt cuffs protruded to just the right degree from under her sweater.

"But . . . but anyway," Dylan continued, careful to keep her arms still this time, "if you want any help with the sets for *Pashminas to the Rescue,* I'd love to come up with some designs. I was thinking we could make some big white screens. I'd cut them into silhouettes of dancing girls and then we could project different colored lights onto them to echo the colors of the pashminas. It'd look really hip."

Sonia was staring at her.

"Hip?" she sneered. "By 'hip' do you mean a total rip-off of the iPod ads?"

Dylan felt like she'd been slapped. She focused on the trail of crumbs snaking along the counter near Sonia's arm.

"I think you'll find that's plagiarism," Sonia said. "Worse, it's intellectual property theft. And we don't need 'help' like that. Thanks." She slit open a packet of Earl Grey and placed the tea bag deliberately in her mug.

"Fine," Dylan muttered, grabbing her hot chocolate and storming toward the staircase.

Across the hallway in the dining room, a school caterer was laying out the plates and silverware and candlesticks for tonight's dinner with the Hasted House boys, who were due to arrive in just under two hours. Dylan was getting jittery at the thought. According to Mimah, these social dinners with boys' schools were organized on a rota, with different juniors asked to each one. The girls in Dylan's corridor had been invited this time, which meant that Sonia and Tally and Alice Rochester would be there in full force. Way to ruin the evening. At least Tristan wasn't among the guests. She'd triple-checked the list to be sure.

Reaching the first floor of Tudor, Dylan turned the corner to her bedroom and passed directly in front of Alice and Tally's door. Usually they kept it shut—except to a select few—but this afternoon Dylan could see right in. Alice was leaning over her bed in front of a half-packed Anya Hindmarch weekend bag. She seemed to be staring at nothing, lost in thought. Behind her, the window was streaked with rain and the trees outside were bowed over in misery. As Dylan slowed down to get a proper look, Alice raised her eyes, met Dylan's, then walked forward and clicked the door shut.

*   *   *

"Hey, Dilly!" Lauren Taylor chirped from Dylan's computer screen as her face popped up on Skype. From downstairs, Dylan could hear the whiny theme tune of yet another soap, *Home and Away.*

"Hi." She grinned at her sister. Keeping her hands underneath the desk so Lauren couldn't see, Dylan dipped into her drawer and fished out the bottle of Bacardi Superior that she'd nicked from her mother's stash in London. She cracked open the seal on the rum and topped off her half-finished hot chocolate to the brim. Dylan hadn't been expecting to find such useful stuff in her mom's pantry; it was only since Piper had met Victor that she'd started keeping booze around the house. Now she was obsessed with it. When Dylan had rolled into the kitchen last Sunday morning with a horrendous hangover, she'd found them both guzzling Bloody Marys with their breakfast.

"How are you?" Lauren gushed. "Oh my god, is that your room I can see? Boarding school looks so cool. How's it going?"

"Great!" Dylan lied. "Yeah, school's awesome. People are being so much nicer to me now."

She stirred her cocktail with the end of her pen. She wouldn't normally be drinking at six in the evening, but she could hear laughter down the hall from Alice and Tally's room. The others were probably choosing outfits and starting to get wasted in preparation for dinner. It was bad enough being lonely without being sober, too.

"I might even design the set for this fashion show that we're putting on," Dylan said. "My roommate saw my artwork and asked me to help her. But I'm not sure if I have time."

"That's fantastic!" Lauren exclaimed. "You're so talented, I knew people would realize. Wait, that show's next Saturday night, right? I think we got an invitation. Yeah, here it is." She held up an elegant black card with swirly gold writing on it:

Please join us at St. Cecilia's for an evening of Fun, Frolics, Philanthropy, and . . .Fashion!

"Did you design this?"

"Sort of." Dylan stared. It was the first she'd seen of the invitations.

"Lauren!" a voice called in the background.

"One second, I'm talking to Dylan!" Lauren yelled. "Mom's going out." She turned back to the screen. "She and Vic have some cocktail party with media types. I swear, her social life is better than ours."

"*Vic?*" Dylan coughed. "Excuse me, but since when do you call him Vic?"

Lauren flushed. "Since . . . since he asked me to. He's kind of a sweetheart, Dilly. He gave me tickets to the taping of his show last week. It was so cool!"

"I'm glad some of us can be bought," Dylan glared. She

couldn't believe her sister was defecting to the other side. They'd both agreed from the beginning: They hated Victor Dalgleish and wouldn't rest till he was history—he and his fucking sideburns.

"Don't be like that," Lauren insisted. "Anyway, Mom's still crazy about him. He isn't going anywhere and neither are we. So forget about escaping back to New York."

Dylan was about to hang up on Lauren when her mom burst into the frame.

"Dill Pickle, is that really you?" Piper Taylor twittered. She thrust her face right into the camera so that her eyes bugged out on Dylan's screen. "Remarkable! It's like futuristic video-conferencing. I feel like I'm in *Star Trek*!"

Dylan rolled her eyes. "Hi, Mom."

"Mom, guess what?" Lauren told her. "Dylan's designing the sets for that fashion show at her school next Saturday."

"No, no, not really—" Dylan started to protest.

"Honey, how thrilling! In that case we'll definitely come. Vic will be delighted—he loved the look of St. Cecilia's when we dropped you off."

I'll bet he did, Dylan thought. Now that her mom had backed away a little, Dylan got a glimpse of her outfit: platform shoes and leggings with a frilly bubble dress over them. Totally age-inappropriate. She looked like she'd been on a spree at H&M.

"Umm, maybe you shouldn't come," Dylan suggested. "I don't know if anyone else's parents are."

"Nonsense. We'll be there. We're dying to meet all your friends! Anyway, Pickle, I must go. Kiss kiss. Wish you were here!"

"Me too," Dylan said, but her mom and sister had already disappeared from the screen. She sighed and drained the rest of her now-cold hot chocolate.

CHAPTER THIRTY-TWO

I'd like to propose a toast," Jasper von Holstadt roared above the din in Tudor House's dining room, staggering to his feet. No one paid the slightest attention, so Jasper seized Dylan Taylor's dirty butter knife from the next seat over, and pinged it insistently against his glass. "Toast! Toast!"

The party of twenty-four boys and girls suspended their conversations and turned to him expectantly.

"That's more like it," Jasper declared. He stood there with a fuzzy look on his aristocratic face, made handsome by its long, elegant nose, and cast his droopy, disdainful eyes about the room. Before getting aboard the bus to come to St. Cecilia's, Jasper and Rando had knocked back several shots of Tequila Gold up in Jasper's bedroom, and the effects hadn't exactly worn off. But by the looks of it, they weren't the only ones who'd indulged in that sort of preparation. Everyone was completely wasted, and it certainly wasn't from the stingy glass of revolting school wine that they'd been allowed with dinner.

"Well, make your speech, then," jeered Rando. "Go on."

"You go on!" Jasper bellowed. "Ahem. As I was saying. Girls . . . No, no, what am I talking about? *Ladies*, thank you for inviting us into your humb—humble abode." He hiccuped, then began to sing in a deep baritone, "For auld lang syne, my dear, for auld la-ang syne!"

"Stop! It isn't New Year's," ordered Rando. "That's worse than opening an umbrella indoors."

Jasper tipped the dregs of his wine down his throat. "Who bloody cares!"

"Hear, hear!" cried their classmate Olly Rylands, chipping in from the other side of the room. He jumped up from his seat and started to unbutton his fly.

"Bloody hell, Ryles, put it away!" Jasper banged on the table. "Any excuse to take your clothes off." It was true. Ryles was famous for his mania about getting naked whenever possible. If you went round to his house for a dinner party, it was guaranteed that at some point during the evening he'd bring out the cards and insist on a game of strip poker.

As people started shouting over each other again, Rando turned to Tally and gave her an embarrassed eye-roll. "Please forgive my friends' antics."

"Don't worry." Tally smiled. "I'm used to it. Remember, they're my friends as well. I'd probably have a heart attack if they *didn't* act like animals."

Rando nodded, staring raptly into Tally's silver-gray irises. They sparkled like deep seas kissed by the sunrise. He couldn't believe he was this close to someone so perfect. In Rando's memory of Tally from George Demetrios's party, she was the most ravishing girl he'd ever laid eyes on. Now he realized he hadn't done her justice. She was the most ravishing girl *anybody* had ever laid eyes on. Her marble-smooth skin dimpled ever so slightly at the corners of her mouth when she smiled. Her tiny, perfect hands fluttered about when she talked. He wanted to capture them in his own and hold them forever.

Rando congratulated himself yet again on being cunning enough to nab a seat next to her tonight. As soon as the Hasted House bus had arrived here, he'd pretended to need the bathroom, then dashed straight to the dining room to swap his seating card round. Now to his delight, when most other people had got bored of their neighbors and were leaning across each other to talk to their real friends, he and Tally were still chatting away.

"Tell me more about yourself," Rando said, pushing his plate and its pile of soggy ratatouille to one side. He'd hardly been able to eat anything for the entire meal, his heart was beating so fast.

Tally blushed. She wasn't used to boys asking for personal information. Usually, they were either too nervous to speak to her, or too arrogant to realize they *should* be nervous. The arrogant ones didn't generally ask questions. They just plied her with alcohol till she kissed them. But Rando was different.

He kept smiling at her attentively, and she was growing to like his pointy little teeth.

"So, my parents have been divorced since I was four," she resumed her story. "My dad got remarried last spring. His new wife's an ogre but I have to be nice to her or they might not let me stay with them when I'm in London."

"Wonderful. Fascinating," Rando said. "Do you have any brothers or sisters?"

Tally shook her head.

"For fuck's sake," someone groaned behind them. It was Alice Rochester, wearing a tiny purple dress and an irritated scowl across her face. She plonked herself in an empty chair and drew it round till she was between Tally and Rando. "This is completely interminable."

Rando frowned. Talk about cock-blocking. He only had one more hour to get Tally's number. At ten thirty on the dot, his housemaster, Mr. Brand, was due to emerge from his civilized dinner in Miss Sharkreve's flat next door, and drag his inebriated students back to Hasted House.

"Sounds like you need a refill." Tally winked at her friend. "There's more wine upstairs in our trunk."

"But Tally," Rando broke in, putting on a selfless voice, "Alice looks so tired. Why don't you and I go and get some for her?"

"No," Alice sighed. "It won't help." She directed a death stare across the room. "Just look at that slut. What does she think she's doing?"

At the other table, Dylan was wearing a low-cut top that looked like someone had vomited black sequins all over it. Her hair was hanging loose over her shoulders. She was pawing Jasper's hand and holding it up to a candle, apparently trying to read his palm.

"I always knew she was trashy," Alice sneered.

Dylan laughed brashly and leaned forward. Her melon-sized breasts practically tumbled onto Jasper's dessert plate.

"Hmm. She's quite hot," Rando commented, staring. "Yeah. Really hot. I can definitely see Jas going for a girl like that."

"As if you have any idea," Alice snapped, obviously forgetting that Rando and Jasper were related. As she spoke, Jasper left Dylan and rambled over to their group.

"See?" She crowed triumphantly.

"Mate." Jasper draped his arm round Alice and breathed a cloud of wine fumes into her face. "That Dylan character is awesome. She's so cool. Why don't you ever invite her out with us?"

Alice and Tally exchanged looks.

"Excuse me." Alice lifted his arm away. "I think I will get that wine after all."

Were all boys so fucking insensitive, she asked herself as she headed out the door and stomped up the stairs, or just the ones they knew? Just then, she bumped straight into someone on the way down: Mimah Calthorpe de Vyle-Hanswicke.

"Hey," Alice said.

"Hey," Mimah replied. She felt a little thrill; that was the first word Alice had spoken to her in months.

Letting her ex-friend pass, she crept down the stairs and peeked into the dining room. Dylan was sitting by herself, the chairs around her deserted, skimming her finger through the flame of the candle in front of her.

Mimah gave a little smile. Dylan wasn't the only one playing with fire.

CHAPTER THIRTY-THREE

When Alice woke up on Saturday morning, the Paris sunshine was pressing through the long curtains into her and Tally's suite at the perennially cool Pavillon de la Reine Hotel in the Place des Vosges. It was seeping across their soft, billowy duvet and over the gigantic feather pillows into which they'd sunk their tired heads the night before.

"Time for *le petit déjeuner!*" Alice chirped, flinging off the covers and jumping out of their four-poster bed.

"Urrrgh," Tally groaned. "No breakfast. Just a little longer..."

Alice prodded her. "You can't. Otherwise we'll waste the whole day."

"Sleep isn't waste," Tally yawned, regretfully kicking herself free of the duvet. She sat up, her white-blond hair flying out like a firework, and blinked round their room. Dark antique beams lined the ceilings, fragrant flower arrangements popped out of glass vases on the tabletops, and custom-made black-and-white paper adorned the walls. She and Alice could have got separate rooms, of course—this was a no-expenses spared type of weekend—but they'd decided to share. After all, the whole point of being here was girly bonding, and what better way to have fun than to stay up till five in the morning, giggling, gossiping, and ordering room service champagne before falling asleep across one gigantic bed?

"Hurry!" called Tally, bouncing up and down as Alice vanished into their massive tiled bathroom to brush her teeth. "I need the bathroom."

Half an hour later, dressed and armed with their credit cards, the girls strolled hand in hand out of the Pavillon's courtyard and into the Place des Vosges, the city's stunning square of sparkling lawns and fountains. They fitted in seamlessly with the chic crowd of breakfasters and shoppers. Tally was wearing skin-tight jeans with knee-high boots, a cropped leather jacket and a scarf, while Alice had on a dark green wool minidress and ankle boots with gloriously high heels. Her whole outfit was totally mod. She considered herself, like the French, to be an expert in dressing simply yet elegantly.

Underneath the Place des Vosges' covered arcade, next to one of its cafés, a string quartet was playing Pachelbel's Canon.

"Ooh, let's sit near the band." Alice ran daintily over. Recently, she'd been trying to cultivate a taste for classical music so she could add it to her cultural repertoire. "Dinner-party ammo," she called it, and you could never have too much.

"Smile, darling." She produced her tiny camera. "You're looking stunning this morning."

"Much obliged. How's this?" Tally placed her index finger to her lips and gave a sultry wink.

Click. Her face froze on the viewfinder, framed by the sunny square.

"Now take one of me," Alice commanded, fluffing out her hair and sucking in her cheeks. This was her favorite spot in Paris; it had been ever since Tristan had first shown it to her when they were thirteen and she'd come to stay in his family's town house over a long weekend. She felt a momentary pang, remembering why she and Tally had made this trip in the first place, but quickly cheered up as their waiter deposited a fresh, crusty *pain au chocolat* onto her plate.

Alice lifted it with both hands and opened her jaw as wide as she could.

"So, shall I ring Miguel?" she asked, spraying crumbs from the corners of her mouth. Miguel was her half-French, half-Spanish friend whom she'd met two summers ago in France's most celebrated nightclub, the Caves du Roy in St. Tropez. He was twenty, gay, drop-dead gorgeous, and knew everyone there was to know in Paris. Whenever Alice came here, she relied on him to organize their dinners and get them into the VIP rooms of the hottest clubs.

"Actually, I had a different idea," Tally said. She dropped

three sugars into her cappuccino, stirred them, and added a fourth. "I vote we don't call anyone at all while we're here."

"Why on earth would we do that?" Alice hungrily considered her *pain au chocolat* and went in for another bite.

"Don't you think it'd be fun just to have a girly weekend of shopping and doing our own thing? Miguel's an absolute sweetheart but his friends can get a bit much. Remember last time, when he took us to dinner with that bunch of random Italians? The one who liked me got so wasted that he threw up on my Proenza Schouler shoes."

Alice cackled, nearly spitting out her mouthful. "Fine, fine, but how are we going to know where to go? We can't just wait in line at places. That's like, *so* not done."

Now it was Tally's turn to laugh. "Let's throw ourselves to the winds," she gushed. "We'll roam round and *find* somewhere to go, some brilliant party somewhere. It'll be all our own. Go on, we've both got such a nose for that kind of thing. I'm dying to have an adventure!"

Alice broke into a grin. Tally's sense of fun was irresistible.

"All right, you win," she agreed. "But if you haven't found a party for us by suppertime, I'm calling Miguel. Now let's hit the shops. I'm in need of some serious retail therapy."

Plunging their way into the pristine streets of the Marais— the old area whose sandstone buildings and stylish boutiques made it a magnet for Paris's young, fashionable crowd—the two friends set to work. They rifled through the racks at A.P.C., Barbara Bui, Isabel Marant, and Zadig et Voltaire, picking out winter wardrobes of coats, dresses, skirts, shoes, and handbags. It wasn't until six o'clock, drained and stumbling under the weight of their haul, that they hailed a cab home. Alice stuffed her shopping bags in, then slid onto the seat next to them. Not that there was much room. Breathing a sigh of relief, she slipped off her ankle boots and rubbed her aching feet.

"Hurry up, I'm not waiting all night!" she called, as Tally stooped over something in the street. The girl was always pouncing on dirty things and bringing them back with her, like a cat dragging in its prey.

"You're gonna love me! Look what I found." Tally was clutching a scrap from a magazine.

"What, trash? Yeah, it's all over the pavement. I can pick some up too. Look, there's another bit."

"No, silly. Read the back."

Alice flipped the piece of paper over. On the other side was some kind of society column. The lead item was about the grand opening of a new club in Pigalle, once a red-light district, but now red-hot. The date was tonight, September 27.

"See?" Tally gushed. "I told you we'd find somewhere fabulous to party. This is going to be amazing! I can wear that silver sequin dress I just bought. Oh my god, I can't wait!"

"But we're not on the list," Alice pointed out. "It says it's a private event. How will we get in?"

Tally looked at her, a confident smile shining from her face. "Oh, we'll get in, darling," she proclaimed. "Have I ever been wrong?"

CHAPTER THIRTY-FOUR

*L*ater that evening, after feasting on oysters and champagne in the first *arrondissement*—smack in the center of Paris—Alice and Tally hopped into a cab and stepped out twenty minutes later down a narrow street in Pigalle. Amidst much complaining and swearing in French, their driver had dropped them straight in front of the club's red carpet, nudging his rickety white taxi between the lines of Bentleys and stretch limos and Smart cars.

"This is so insidery!" breathed Tally, taking in the locale's discreet, unvarnished exterior. Tonight of course, for its launch party, the place had been decked out with floodlights and velvet ropes and bouncers. But ordinarily, the only thing giving it away would have been the glowing red orb suspended outside.

"*Très chic*," Alice replied. "No wonder they called this place *Souterain*. You know, that's French for 'underground.'" She smiled to herself. She really was quite fluent.

"Whatever you say. How do you think we get in?" Tally

was crushed up against a lamppost; the pavement was so crowded that she and Alice could barely move. Nearby, a pen of flashing paparazzi roared every time some new TV personality, model, sports star, or fashion designer arrived and twirled for the cameras.

"There's the entrance." Alice pointed to a knot of wannabes clustered to one side of the red carpet. The line stretched about halfway down the street.

"Fuck me if I'm waiting behind that." Swaying over, Alice elbowed her way through the swarm and planted herself in front of the bouncer. She ran a hand through her long, brown hair. It was feeling particularly smooth tonight, thanks to the Kérastase masque she'd applied earlier on.

"*Nom?*" the bouncer demanded gruffly, barring her way through the velvet ropes.

"Pardon me?" Alice swallowed. She'd never blagged her way into a club before; she was used to obstacles like this melting away.

"Name?" the bouncer repeated in English with a heavy French accent.

"Umm . . ." Alice turned to Tally for a prompt.

But Tally wasn't there. Where the fuck had she gone?

"Oh yes, well, I'm a VIP," Alice babbled. "I think my father's already inside." She stopped. Her *father?* Did she want to sound like any more of a loser?

"And your fahzer's name eez?" the bouncer inquired, tapping his people-counter against his clipboard.

"Umm, it's Monsieur . . . Monsieur . . . François . . ."

"Sweetie!" Tally called, seizing Alice's hand from behind. "Sorry I lost you. I saw that pop singer Raphael going in and just had to stop and watch."

"Who?" Alice glared at her. Tally was always going on about obscure foreign singers, and now wasn't the time.

"Raphael." Tally insisted. "Oh my god, he is *sooo* beautiful."

"Ee is not zee only one," the bouncer uttered, staring at Tally as if he was a starving dog and she was a bone.

Alice narrowed her eyes. Didn't *she* look pretty too, in her new satin slip dress with matching black satin shoes? This was the part she always hated about going out with her best friend. Tally's new dress shimmered all over with silver sequins. Her stilettos were silver too, with long, tapering metal heels that looked like they could stab someone through the heart. Which, judging from the expression on the bouncer's face, they had.

"*Entrez,*" he said, unhooking the rope for them. "Be my guest."

"Thank you," Tally beamed.

"Whatever," Alice grumbled.

"'Ave a wonderfool night," the bouncer breathed as Tally passed. "But please do not forget I, poor Jean-Baptiste, outside and freezing weezout you."

"I hope you freeze to death," Alice muttered.

"Sorry?" Tally asked.

"Nothing. I wasn't talking to you." Alice ripped open her clutch and ferociously smeared on lip gloss. "Let's get drinks."

Souterrain's interior couldn't have been more different from its plain facade. The space had been tarted up to look like a lavish burlesque club, all plush fabrics and chandeliers and private alcoves. On the stage in the main arena, a mostly naked woman was doing some kind of magic trick involving a blow torch and a cage of doves. Revelers applauded from cabaret tables, while above them, three gallery levels spiraled toward the ceiling, each with its own dance lounge and floor show. The VIP area was a series of mock dressing rooms, where clusters of Paris's elite were knocking back bottles of Cristal. Alice and Tally slipped their way past stunning women dressed for the catwalk and angular men in skinny jeans to get to the bar.

"Excuse me, ladies, may I purchase you a beverage?" a man standing next to Alice inquired above the R&B music.

Alice looked him up and down. He was rake-thin with full lips and a black ponytail. His equally weird friend was already ordering drinks.

Alice shook her head.

"Yes, please! How lovely," Tally interrupted. "I'll have an Old Fashioned."

Alice nudged her. "Stop! Have you seen his hairdo? Freak. If he buys us anything, we'll have to talk to him."

"Of course we won't," Tally said into her ear. "Anyway, too late now."

"And you?" the man pouted at Alice.

"Ugh," Alice sighed. "I'll have a mojito, I suppose."

"How stylish. How festive," the man droned. "My name is Baffi. It means mustaches in Italian." He sounded utterly bored by everything that came out of his mouth. He stuck out his hand. It felt dry and limp.

"And I'm Nikita," Baffi's friend introduced himself. He was carrying all four of their drinks in his spidery hands. "Come, we'll sit over here."

Before Alice could stop him, Nikita had laid everything out on a low table and festooned himself over one of the ottomans round it. Baffi pulled out a seat for Alice, then positioned himself almost on top of her. He smelled like one of those people who don't shower very much, then douse themselves in cologne and think you won't be able to tell the difference. Alice rattled her mojito without taking a sip. There was no way she was trusting someone like that not to slip a roofie into her drink.

It would be so much better if they were with Miguel right now. Why had she listened to Tally?

"You seem like an ice queen but underneath I can smell it: You have passions of fire," Baffi whispered lazily in her ear.

Alice jumped. "What?"

"You have appetites," Baffi drawled. He fished the olive out of his martini and poked it slowly between his lips. "I can satisfy them."

Alice stared at him in horror.

"I think he's into you," Tally hissed, catching sight of Baffi's amorous expression. She'd finished her Old Fashioned and was chewing on one of the orange slices inside it. "Want me to leave you alone so you can hit on him?"

"Have you gone insane?" Alice said. "I need the bathroom. Are you coming?"

The ladies room, a welcome break from the noise by the bar, had been designed to look like a boudoir. Alice sat down on a pink pouf and checked out the selection of perfumes and moisturizers arranged on a vanity table. She spritzed some *Passage d'Enfer* from L'Artisan Parfumeur onto her wrist.

"I thought you had to pee," Tally said, tucking a loose hair into the pile pinned on top of her head.

"No. I just wanted to get away from those psychopaths."

"But your guy was hot. I thought if you kissed him it might help you forget about T."

"I don't want to forget about T," Alice said defensively. Tally was so thoughtless when she got drunk. Why would she mention Tristan at a time like this?

Tally's phone beeped. She grabbed it. "Oh." Her face fell. "It's a text from Rando."

"What does he want?"

"To see me next week." Tally threw her phone back into her bag.

"Well? Aren't you going to reply?"

"No. I mean, I wouldn't have given him my number except he looked so nervous asking for it the other night." A coy dimple appeared in Tally's cheek. "I'm in love with someone else."

Alice grimaced. Furiously, she pumped some L'Occitane hand cream out of its bottle and rubbed it into her cuticles. "You mean Mr. Logan, don't you?"

"Maybe," Tally giggled.

"I don't get it. What the hell do you see in him?"

"Everything! He's so manly and sexy and strong and kind and intelligent." Tally had gone dreamy. "Whenever we're in his class, all I can think about is ripping his clothes off and tracing my fingers round that tattoo."

"Tattoo?" Alice stiffened. Her mind started racing. She thought back to Mr. Logan in the Badger and Hounds. That woman she'd seen, the yellow scarf . . .

"Where's his tattoo?" she asked between her teeth.

"On his chest. Why?"

"How the hell do you know?"

Alice's voice was so dangerous that Tally looked up in alarm. "He told me. What's the matter?"

"Of couse he didn't fucking tell you."

"He did! Why would I lie?" Tally's voice was shaky. She hated confrontations.

"You're shagging Mr. Logan, aren't you?"

Alice shuddered. She hadn't known how irreversible those words would sound till she'd said them out loud. She had never accused Tally of anything serious, not once in their entire three-year friendship. But she couldn't take it back now.

"No!" Tally turned red. "What if I was, though—would it be so bad?"

"Of course it would. He's a *teacher*. And a sleaze."

"Well, I'm not." Tally paused, her eyes flashing. "But that doesn't mean I wouldn't."

"Fine." Alice stood up and straightened her skirt. She wasn't finished with her investigation yet. "Just so you know, someone else is."

"What—what do you mean?"

"I saw him in the Badger and Hounds the other day. He was coming down from those sordid upstairs bedrooms and there was a woman with him. I couldn't see her properly but they were definitely together. She looked just like you."

"I don't believe you. It can't have been him. It must have been someone else." Tally's face was heartbroken. Her eyes had become pools of tears.

Alice felt a stab of remorse. Maybe her guess had been wrong. But still, Tally needed to come to her senses. It was Alice's duty as a friend to protect her against herself.

"Look, I don't mean to sound like a bitch or anything," Alice said in a gentler tone of voice, "but you should really get over this little infatuation. It's making you look like a total fool in front of everyone. I'm your best friend, so I can tell you that."

She paused, remembering Tristan's wise insights about Tally the night they'd first kissed. Maybe that would help.

"Listen, Tals, in a way I totally get why you like Mr. Logan," she said sympathetically. "If my dad ignored me the way yours ignores you, I'd be looking for father figures too. I'd probably be far more messed up than you are."

"Thanks a lot. How charitable of you to even be friends with someone as *messed up* as me." Tally stalked toward the door. Then she wheeled round. "By the way, Ali, give me some credit. Do you honestly believe I would sleep with Mr. Logan in a fucking *pub?* I have better taste than that."

Alice watched the door slam behind her friend. Did she believe it? Nothing seemed certain anymore.

At precisely eleven o'clock the next morning, Alice was shocked out of her sleep by the sound of her cell. She scrambled blindly for it, reaching toward the spot where her bedside table would have been in Tudor House.

Ring ring. Ring ring.

Where was it?

Then she remembered. She was still in Paris. There was Tally, curled up like a snail at the very edge of the bed, as far from Alice as possible. That was an improvement from last night, at least. After they'd left the club, speaking to each other only in monosyllables, Tally had locked herself in the bathroom and started running water in the bath. Alice had figured she'd leave Tally alone for a while to calm down. She'd settled on their bed with *Grazia*, her favorite celebrity weekly, and listened to the faint splashing sounds emanating from the bathroom, waiting. And waiting.

Ring riiiing!

"For fuck's sake. Pick it *up*." Tally flung out her arm in desperation.

"I can't find it."

"Hang on. Here." Tally chucked the phone to Alice across the mountain of pillows that seemed to have sprung up between them since last night. Alice frowned. It looked like Tally had piled them there on purpose.

"Hello?"

"Al! It's Sonia. What took you so long?"

"You bloody woke us up. What kind of person rings at eleven o'clock on Sunday morning? It's practically the middle of the night."

"Sorry, babe." Sonia didn't sound sorry at all. "I couldn't wait. I have such brilliant news for you."

"What? Hold on, let me put you on speaker."

Alice pressed a button on her phone and laid it carefully on the pillow-barrier so Tally could hear, too. It was clearly meant as a peace offering. Hopefully, Tally would get the idea. "Go on."

"Okay, so, last night, while Dylan was in the bathroom, I saw this e-mail she'd left up on her screen. It was to her sister, I think—but I don't know. I mean, I'm not even sure Dylan has a sister."

Alice yawned. "Is this going anywhere?"

"Duh. Guess what it said? Dylan's not seeing Tristan at all anymore. Apparently she hasn't even heard from him since the party."

Alice's shoulders drooped in relief. "Nice one," she said. At least T had been telling the truth about something. "Good work, darling. What else did you find out?"

"That was it. She came back before I could read more. But here's some other news. You know how Bella Scott's dad is Lucian Scott, the famous director?"

"Obviously."

"Well, he's coming to *Pashminas to the Rescue*! I didn't think he'd bother, but Bella just told me he promised her. Oh my god, guys, do you know what this could mean for my film career?"

Oh my god, guys, Alice mouthed, pinching her nose. She caught Tally's eye. The two of them laughed silently.

"I'm having a credit inserted into the program," Sonia rattled on. "*Entire event conceived and directed by Sonia Khan.*"

Tally snorted. "But you *didn't* conceive it, Sone. It was Ali's idea."

"What? No, it wasn't. How can you say that?"

"Umm, because it's true?" Alice cut in. "We have witnesses. Anyway, we should really go."

"How's Paris?" Sonia's voice was sharp with jealousy.

Alice glanced at Tally. "Totally brilliant. We're having a wicked time. Fantastic. Oh, and Sone?"

"Yeah?"

"Thanks for that news about Dylan." There was a cheeky gleam in Alice's eye. "I thought you'd do some good snooping on this. Know why?"

"Why?"

"'Cause you're so *nosy*. Get it?"

Alice and Tally collapsed in hysterics on the bed.

"Oy, why are you being such a cow?" Sonia moaned. "I called you with good news, didn't I? Anyway, my cast came off yesterday. My face is back!"

"At long last. That means we won't have to listen to you complain," Alice giggled. She hung up.

"Hey, Tal." There was a solemn look on her face now. She had to sort things out with Tally or she'd be stuck with no one but Sonia, who was acting more like a lapdog than ever. "I didn't mean all that shit I said last night. I've been thinking, maybe it wasn't Mr. Logan I saw. He had his back to me and stuff. And I might have been a tad drunk that afternoon."

Tally chipped off a bit of her silver nail varnish. Then she smiled. "Drunk? What were you doing in the pub in the middle of a school day anyway?"

"Good question," Alice laughed, settling in for a fine old morning gossip. She was saved.

For now.

CHAPTER THIRTY-FIVE

Mimah stood on top of the very last toilet in Tudor House's second-floor bathroom, puffing on a cigarette and blowing smoke toward the air vent in the ceiling. There was a window on the other side of the stall door, out of which she was keeping watch. Streams of girls were flowing up to Quad and the dining hall to get their sustenance before another soporific Chapel address from Mrs. Traphorn. It was first thing Monday morning and the breakfast crush was on.

Hearing footsteps in the hallway, Mimah crouched on the toilet seat and frantically waved her hand to disperse the smoke. Getting nabbed might mean suspension, considering her previous offenses. But whoever it was passed by. Irritatedly, Mimah brushed her straight black fringe out of her eyes and stood up again. She should have been smoking in her room instead of balancing up here like an asshole. Her windows looked out onto the orchard, meaning it would have been easy to sneak a cig without being caught. The only thing stopping her was her roommate: Gabby fucking Bunter. Gabby was convinced she had asthma, and the last time Mimah had tried to light up in their room, she'd put on such an Oscar-worthy show of wheezing and gasping that Mimah had been afraid Sharko might hear. She'd decided not to risk it again.

Finally, down on the Great Lawn, a familiar figure appeared. It was Alice Rochester, swaying down the path in that imperious way of hers. Perfect. Mimah dropped her cig in the toilet, listened to its tiny sizzle, then watched as the water sucked it down.

"Sonia babe, you look fantastic," Alice cried over in the dining hall, grabbing a tray from the stack and pushing past a group of freshman students to get to her friend. She and Tally had arrived back from Paris late last night, creeping into Tudor long after lights out, and hadn't seen anyone yet.

"Thanks. Dr. Essex is a genius." Sonia stroked her newly liberated nose. "He made sure there weren't any bumps or scars. I trust him completely. If I ever get my boobs done, I'm definitely going to him."

"Why just your boobs?" Alice sniffed, shoveling scrambled eggs and sausages onto her plate. "Why not get a total body makeover? By the time you're twenty you could look like a waxwork."

"I see nothing wrong with a bit of surgical enhancement,"

225

Sonia said. "Everyone in Hollywood gets stuff tweaked all the time. It's the key to success."

"For *actresses*," Alice said. "Not directors. Directors need to have talent. Think Dr. Essex can help with *that*?" She slid her tray along to the end and fished out a knife and fork from the racks.

"Wait, sweetie." Sonia stopped her, as always ignoring Alice's barb. "That one has food crusted on it. See? Let me get you another."

She picked out a second, shiny utensil and checked it for dirt, hoping Alice was as thrilled to see her as Sonia was that Alice was finally back. It had been a dull, dull weekend at St. Cecilia's without her.

Alice popped up two pieces of toast and added them to her pile of food.

"How can you eat that crap after gorging on foie gras and salade niçoise all weekend?" Sonia asked. Her tone may have been scornful, but her expression was envious. Alice shrugged. Sonia had always hated her for being able to scoff whatever she wanted without putting on weight. Sonia was obsessed with dieting "to maintain my waistline" as she put it. She ate the same thing every day. Breakfast: non-fat yogurt with a fistful of berries. Lunch: a pile of lettuce leaves, four cherry tomatoes, a spoonful of crumbled feta, and a tangle of grated carrots—or, as Tally had dubbed them, orange pubes.

"Right, tell us where we are with PTTR," Alice said, setting her tray down next to Tally's at their usual table, dead in the center of the hall.

"Here we go." Sonia pulled a white file out of her tote and laid it on the table. "The rehearsals this weekend were smooth. Everyone came—except you two, of course—which is fine because you already know the routines and you're obviously amazing dancers." She smiled fawningly. "The Trap gave permission for a drinks reception for parents afterward. That means we can all get wasted without sneaking around. Oh, and we're sold out of tickets already. Umm, yes?" she said, catching sight of someone behind Tally and Alice. "Can we help you?"

"Hi," Mimah said.

Alice and Tally jerked their heads round.

"Mind if I sit?" Mimah eyed the empty spot next to Sonia.

"Whatever." Sonia didn't move her bag, so Mimah lifted it onto the table herself and took a seat.

All of a sudden, the cafeteria seemed to go quiet. Nearby, Flossy Norstrup-Fitzwilliam and Bella Scott stopped their conversation and stared.

"No way, are they actually friends again?" Flossy breathed.

"Shhh!" Bella Scott whipped out her phone.

"I was wondering," Mimah said, looking at Sonia, "if you've worked out the final order for *Pashminas to the Rescue*."

"Maybe I have. Maybe I haven't."

There was a silence.

"Okay . . ." Mimah rolled her eyes. "Mature. Would you mind sharing it with me?"

"That depends. Why do you want to know?"

Mimah glanced at Alice. *Throw me a lifeline,* her expression said.

"Just tell her, Sone," Alice ordered.

Sonia's jaw dropped.

"All I give a shit about is when my routine's going on," Mimah said. "The one I'm doing with Dylan. We both think we should perform it near the beginning. It's fantastically original. It'll give a kick-start to the show."

Sonia raised her eyebrows. "Oh really. A kick-start? Well, I haven't made my final decision yet but I'll bear that in mind. Thanks for putting in the request," she added coldly.

"No, thank *you*," Mimah said, pushing back from the table. She strolled off slowly, straining to eavesdrop on Sonia's reaction. The girl was so easy to manipulate that Mimah was certain her plan had worked—meaning that Stage One of her pashmina plot was in place.

Sure enough, Sonia snickered. "As if I'm going to let *them* go first," she whispered loudly. " *'Ooh, our routine's so impressive. The sun rises and sets out of our asses.'* Fuck that. I'm totally tacking them onto the end. Can you believe her nerve, Ali?"

But Alice had stopped listening. As she watched her ex-friend walk away, she noticed an unexpected bounce in her step. What was Mimah up to now?

CHAPTER THIRTY-SIX

Tristan chucked his acoustic guitar onto his bed and threw himself after it, stretching his arms above his head so that his biceps bulged out of his light pink polo shirt. The guitar bounced once and gave a toneless groan, which actually didn't sound much worse than the love songs he'd been trying, unsuccessfully, to crank out for the past hour. What the hell rhymed with *impotent* anyway? Tristan sighed. He'd never be able to start a band at this rate. But Seb and Rando were counting on him for the music. Maybe he should try his electric guitar instead. Or maybe he should just give up. He'd never be the next Thom Yorke.

A bell was ringing in the old stone chapel. Tristan crossed the bedroom and pressed his forehead against the window, staring out at the lawn. This time of day, when the light started to die and the air started to chill, was always the loneliest. The grass had been sunny before but now its patches of shadow were seeping into each other, and the younger boys who'd been playing football outside gathered their things and dispersed, scattering into different stone doorways around the school.

T ran his fingers through his quiff and turned toward the fields and woods, beyond which lay St. Cecilia's. He'd thought dumping Alice would be a relief. She'd made him feel trapped—like their relationship had to be *the one*; like she wanted to settle down and stop him from shagging anyone else, ever. But now he was confused. How was he meant to know whether or not he'd made a mistake? In frustration, he kicked the bit of wall beneath his window, then staggered back clutching his foot.

Damn. What kind of idiot forgets when they're not wearing shoes?

There was only one sensible option here: Facebook stalkage.

Alice had added a new photo album to her page. It was called *C'est La Vie: Babes Do Paris*. The cover picture showed her in the Place des Vosges with a group of street musicians strumming behind her. Tristan felt a twist of possessiveness. Paris was *his* city. He'd taken Alice to the Place des Vosges. She always told him if she was going there. Actually, she usually invited him. Fuck this.

There were more: Tally posing in front of Ladurée, the famous macaroon shop. Alice opening her mouth wide to pop in a pink macaroon, her lips glistening as red as the jam oozing out of it. Alice sipping from a mug in a pavement café.

Alice wearing a wispy black dress under a streetlight, looking stunningly beautiful. Alice, Alice, Alice.

Tristan leaped up and paced about the room, kicking aside the dirty rugby uniform that he'd shed after practice this morning. Maybe if he heard her voice he'd know what to think. Better dial from Skype though; if she saw it was him, she might not pick up.

With shaking fingers, he tapped out Alice's cell number on his keyboard. It rang once. Twice.

"Hello?"

Should he say something?

"Hello?"

Tristan's heart clanged in his ears. He hung up.

CHAPTER THIRTY-SEVEN

*T*wo miles across the countryside in the library at St. Cecilia's, Tally turned a page of *Othello* and squinted at the text through her forest of markings. Not wanting to miss a word that Mr. Logan said, she'd written all over the play in different colors and now could barely read a thing.

She tumbled her pen onto the desk in exasperation. This essay was going absolutely nowhere and it was due tomorrow afternoon. Disaster. If Tally handed in something bad, Mr. Logan's opinion of her would plummet. He might hate her as much as he hated Alice. But how was she meant to concentrate when Alice's words from Saturday night—"Just so you know, he's shagging *someone else*"—kept rolling round and round like marbles inside her head? It would have been enough to drive even Mother Teresa completely insane.

Tally cast a wistful glance at the poetry shelves across the aisle from her desk. She must have done that five thousand times over the past few days. She knew it was desperate, but the reason she'd planted herself exactly here, near the K section (K for Keats, of course), was the constant hope that Mr. Logan would materialize, just as he'd done that revelatory afternoon two weeks ago. Maybe he'd read her more romantic verses. Or praise her for being so diligent. Or make her tingle all over with one of his smiles. He might even ask her to dinner if he caught her when no one else was around. They could slip off to the new Thai place in town and stare into each other's candlelit eyes while rubbing chopsticks inside the vermicelli.

Just so you know, he's shagging someone else.

That was it. She had to find out.

Noisily, Tally piled her books on top of each other and snatched her gray school cardigan off the back of her chair. Zanna Balfour and Emilia Charles, sweating over French exercises together, looked up in curiosity, but Tally didn't stop to chat. She tramped over to the shelves where the girls had to leave their bags (in case they were tempted to nick any of the library's books) and headed off on her mission.

She knew exactly where Mr. Logan would be. Most of the St. Cecilia's teachers had small offices tacked onto their living suites, where they planned lessons, marked prep, and met with students. However, since Mr. Logan was a man surrounded by hot teenage girls, that arrangement was off-limits—he couldn't very well hold tutorials within striking distance of his bed. Instead, he'd been given a tiny room in Quad. Till this evening, Tally had been too nervous to disturb him there without a specific invitation, but often, passing by after supper, she'd seen a lone lamp burning up in his third-floor window. Now, as she climbed the narrow stairs, she thought how that light was like a beacon, symbolizing his dedication and passion as an intellectual.

The top floor of Quad was silent. The rooms weren't used all that often because of chronic problems with central heating and dampness. Her pulse racing, Tally stopped in front of Mr. Logan's wooden door. She took a deep breath, then knocked.

"Yes? Come in."

"It's Tally. Natalya."

Tally had no idea why she was still hovering out here when he'd clearly told her to enter. She pushed open the door. Warm, stuffy air rushed out to meet her. It smelled of books and coffee, and of something darker and masculine.

Maybe she shouldn't have come.

"Natalya." Mr. Logan swiped a hand through his hair.

"Yep, here I am." She forced a smile, feeling the butterflies in her tummy get worse.

"You're a welcome surprise. I caught a glimpse of you galloping off to gym this morning, but you didn't see me."

He was sitting in a cushy but dilapidated office chair, his feet up on the desk in front of him. A green reading lamp gave the oak-paneled room a cozy glow.

"I came to chat about my *Othello* essay," Tally said, trying not to catch Mr. Logan's eye in case he could tell she was lying.

For some reason she looked at his shoes instead, noticing that there were blades of grass crushed on the soles.

"Fine. Let's talk. As I told you, my door is always open to talented students." Mr. Logan flashed a smile. He didn't seem the least bit nervous. He grabbed a *Daily Mirror* off a battered armchair and chucked it onto his desk, then motioned for her to sit.

"So, what do you think of my kingdom?"

Tally drank in the dog-eared books scattered about the room, the Fulham FC scarf flung over the radiator, the bottle of John Varvatos cologne on a shelf. So that was Mr. Logan's scent. She shrugged as if she couldn't care less. "Not bad."

"Needs a woman's touch, doesn't it?" He winked. Then he looked at Tally for a moment. "I was just about to open some wine. It's seven o'clock. Refreshment time. What do you say?"

"Cool." Tally crossed her legs so Mr. Logan wouldn't see the ladder in her tights. Boozing with a teacher in the middle of the week was almost unheard of. Perhaps Mr. Logan considered her his equal. Would that be so impossible?

She watched as he brought down a bottle of red from the top shelf above his desk, unfolded a corkscrew, and sank its tip into the bottle's soft neck. The metal spiral bit in deeply. Then the cork came free with a ripe popping sound. Mr. Logan laid out two mismatched wine glasses and poured, the thick ruby liquid tumbling over itself.

"Here you go." He handed her one. "To you."

"Oh." Tally had no idea what to say. "No, to us!" She blushed. "I mean . . . not like *that.*"

Mr. Logan caught her eye. "Why not like that?" His voice had that same milky tone as when she'd first bumped into him in the library. Tally stared at him wide-eyed.

Mr. Logan laughed. "What's that look for? I'm only joking." Offhandedly, he jerked his chin toward the gold, dagger-shaped pendant she was wearing. "That's a pretty necklace. Don't think I've seen it before. Very unusual craftsmanship."

Tally put her hand to her throat and lifted the chain. It was long, plunging down between the buttons of her yellow school blouse.

"Thanks. I got it in Paris this weekend." She stopped abruptly. Idiot! Mr. Logan wasn't supposed to know that she and Alice had run off on the Eurostar. Playing truant was against all the most important school rules. She gulped a mouthful of wine.

But Mr. Logan didn't seem to have noticed. In fact, he wasn't even listening. He'd turned to his computer and was scrolling through iTunes.

"Right, what shall we listen to?" He chose Coldplay without waiting for a reply, and sipped from his glass as the first strains of "Yellow" started up.

"When I was younger, I wished that my parents could afford to send me to boarding school," Mr. Logan confided, leaning forward in his chair. It creaked under his manly weight. "But

now I'm here, I don't know how you girls survive. There's nothing for miles about. Don't you get bored out of your pretty little heads, trapped in the countryside?"

Tally straightened a pen and notepad on the coffee table next to her. She noticed that the title on the notepad's cover was *Jottings*. What a romantic word.

"Of course," she said. "Boarding school can be a total hassle. But then again, being around your friends day in, day out is such a laugh. It's like having a giant sleepover party every night." She winced. Great. That was the way to make Mr. Logan like her: talk like she was twelve years old.

"Anyway, my crew and I try to get to London as often as possible." She flicked a piece of hair over her head. "We've got good connections. Between us, we can get in pretty much anywhere."

"How about Hasted?"

"Hasted? There's nowhere worth getting in there. Not if you have any taste."

Mr. Logan laughed. "Come on, you can't fool me, I know what goes on with you girls. I know you sneak off to town whenever you can. Tell me, what are the good places?"

Tally ran her finger round the rim of her glass. If there was ever going to be a chance to hit him with the *other woman* question, it was now. She swallowed.

"Surely you must know. Haven't you been out anywhere yet? I thought I saw you the other day."

"Really? I've strolled round a couple of times. Only in the

afternoons though. Didn't find anything earth-shattering."

"There are some lovely *pubs*," Tally offered, observing him closely. "You must have been to one or two. Right?"

"Pubs?" Mr. Logan's face didn't twitch. "No, I've only seen them from the outside. You'll have to show me." He winked. "During half-term or something."

Was he serious? Tally wondered. Alice really must have been wrong about spotting him the other day. He was totally flirting with her. He *must* be interested.

"I'm sure the other teachers can take you," she said archly. "You and I might not like the same sort of place."

"Only one way to find out. And what would I want with the other teachers when I could have company like this?" Mr. Logan looked at his watch. "Anyway, enough messing about. Let's get to *Othello*."

Tally's mind started racing. She'd better think of something to ask him. But before she could say anything, Mr. Logan rolled his chair closer to hers.

"Listen, Natalya, I've been thinking. Can I pass an idea by you?"

Tally gripped her copy of the play, half ecstatic, half terrified. Could this be it?

"I love talking with you." Mr. Logan was gazing at her fixedly. "I think you have such talent. I'd like to nurture it." He wrapped his fingers round the other side of her book. "Why don't we start doing regular tutorials?"

Tally blinked. "What?"

"You come to me up here once or twice a week. We'll read things together, drink a bit of wine, talk about literature, immerse ourselves in poetry. I can't think of a better use of both our time. Will you think about it?"

Tally nodded, even though she didn't have to think about anything. She already knew the answer was yes.

CHAPTER THIRTY-EIGHT

*U*p in the room she shared with Tally, Alice was staring out of the window, wishing her friend was here—instead of in the library, where she'd inexplicably started doing her prep—to witness the ridiculous scene on the lawn. It was Sonia, of course. She was pretending to help the other members of the junior charity committee lug pieces of the set for *Pashminas to the Rescue* across the grass in the direction of the theater—but in reality, the only thing she was doing was issuing orders and chasing people about in her kitten heels. She was holding some sort of walking stick—fuck knows where she'd got it from—and kept pointing it at things and poking people to reinforce her instructions. Alice snickered. If Sonia's career as a director fell through, she could always be a dictator instead.

Back in the bedroom, stacks of History of Art worksheets lay untouched. A copy of *Candide* in French was sprawled across one of the chairs in the entertaining nook. Alice should have been working right now (thanks to the fact that her father had convinced her to do four Advanced Level subjects, she had an endless torrent of essays, exercises, and reading to do) but a few minutes ago, a mysterious phone call had interrupted her and completely thrown her off. She was still holding her cell in her hand. The culprit had rung from an unknown number and hung up almost straightaway.

Just then, Alice's phone lit up again. *Number withheld.* She shot out a manicured nail and clicked to answer.

"Hello? Who is this?"

"It's Mummy, darling. You sound terribly jumpy." Alice's mother, Beatrice Rochester, had a chilly way of speaking that intimidated anyone who didn't know her—as well as a lot of people who did.

"Oh hello, Mummy." Alice furrowed her forehead. This was bizarre; her mother hardly ever called. She and Alice's father didn't believe in coddling their children. "Can I ask you a question? Did you ring me just before and hang up?"

"Of course not." Beatrice's voice managed to express astonishment and boredom at exactly the same time. "Why on earth would I do that?"

"You wouldn't on purpose. I meant as a mistake. Never mind."

"Put them over there," Alice's mother said.

"Sorry?"

"Yes, there. No, on the table," Beatrice said. Alice sighed. Her mother wasn't talking to her at all. As usual, she was probably giving directions about flower arrangements or something to one of the household staff.

"Anyway, darling," Beatrice went on, "I wanted to let you know, we're driving up to St. Cecilia's for about one o'clock on Saturday. Your father and I are planning to take you to lunch in Hasted before your 'Pashminas Unite' spectacle, or whatever it's called."

"*Pashminas to the Rescue*," Alice said.

"Yes, that sounds right," her mother replied vaguely. "Can you arrange to be let out of school for a few hours?"

"Of course, Mummy. I'll reserve at Le Coq au Vin. You know, that French place in town."

"Good. I can't bear to listen to Daddy complain all the way through the meal like he did last time, when we went to that dreadful Thai restaurant. At least we know he likes Le Coq au Vin. I can't say I blame him for being choosy though. Honestly, for a town with two schools attached to it, Hasted is terribly shabby."

"It's not all *that* bad, Mummy," Alice protested. She rarely contradicted her mother, but for some reason she felt a twinge of defensiveness whenever people criticized St. Cecilia's. *She* was allowed to complain, of course, but that was different.

"Oh, and darling," Beatrice said, "make sure you tell the restaurant it's for five. We're collecting Hugo from Hasted House. And Tristan's coming as well."

"Tristan?" Alice gasped.

"That's right. I've asked him to join us."

"And he said *yes?*"

"Of course he said yes. Why wouldn't he? You are being awfully odd, Alice. Are you getting all your work done?"

"Yes, Mummy. Everything's fine. I'll see you Saturday."

Alice couldn't believe it. She was having palpitations. Her stomach was in a knot. What did it mean that T had agreed to come? It was possible that he was only being polite—he'd grown up with her family, and it wouldn't look right if he refused her mother's invitation. Still, he could easily have thought of some excuse. Could it be that he was having second thoughts?

Alice stared out of the window, taking deep breaths. Then she squinted. Coming down the path from Quad was Tally, carrying a pile of books and hugging herself with excitement. Surely the library couldn't have been *that* thrilling. Suddenly, Alice was distracted by her own reflection in the darkening glass. She looked pale and pasty, with bags under her eyes. There was no way Tristan could see her like this. She needed a facial. A waxing. A St. Tropez spray tan. And what the hell was she going to wear?

CHAPTER THIRTY-NINE

*A*fter art on Thursday, Dylan slung her powder blue quilted Marc Jacobs bag across her shoulder and skipped back to Tudor to meet Mimah for tea. It had been her best afternoon since she'd arrived at this posh prison. First, there had been tacos for lunch. Then Miss·Baskin had held up Dylan's male torsos collage to the rest of her class as an example of style and originality. And finally, Farah Assadi had asked to be Dylan's partner on the big plaster casts project after half-term.

"Knock, knock," Dylan said, pushing open the door to the room that Mimah shared with Gabby Bunter.

Mimah was sitting on her bed with a calculator, doing Physics equations at lightning speed. Her room was not one of Tudor's finest, to put it mildly. It was small and poky. It was also on the ground floor, which meant that anyone who walked by could peek through her windows unless she kept the curtains drawn. Even more inconveniently, it meant that Miss Sharkreve was far more likely to drop in at strange hours to check up on her. Sharko was abominably lazy and disliked climbing the stairs to the second and attic levels. Still, those risks hardly deterred Mimah from anything.

"You're looking chipper," Mimah observed. "Did your high school in New York win the national cheerleaders' championship or something?" She snickered.

Dylan rolled her eyes. Mimah never let up. "Whatever. Let's make tea."

"I'll make it," Mimah said. "You sort out the food. Just make sure you stay on my side of the room." She padded out. She was wearing her gray gym skirt layered over the school's gray tracksuit bottoms.

Dylan reached onto Mimah's shelf and grabbed hold of the Rich Tea biscuits. She peeled open the packet and started nibbling pensively at one. Just like the room she shared with Sonia, Mimah and Gabby's dorm was divided strictly down the middle. Mimah had insisted on that as soon as she'd moved in—it had been imperative to put a stop to any ideas Gabby might have had about them becoming friends. "You stay off my turf, and I'll keep off yours," she'd decreed.

The result, Dylan thought, was that the room looked like a clash of two worlds: freak world versus bleak world. Gabby's side was smothered in posters of dragons and fairies and landscapes out of fantasy novels like *Earthsea*. Her bedspread was covered by a giant tableau of a waterfall and a ghost ship.

Her fluffy slippers, laid out neatly nearby, were embroidered with characters from *The Lord of the Rings.*

Mimah's half, on the other hand, was a study in absence. She hadn't put up any photos or postcards. She hadn't unpacked any knick-knacks from home. She was still using the school's regulation blue duvet and pillowcase. It was as if she refused to admit that she was really living in this room—or as if she expected to be leaving it imminently.

"Are your parents coming on Saturday?" Dylan asked as Mimah returned with two mugs of Lapsang Souchong.

"What?" Mimah cracked a shortbread biscuit in half. "No. Fuck them. Obviously not." She fell silent.

Dylan guiltily sipped her tea, then sucked in her breath. It was way too hot. She hung out the tip of her tongue. How could she have asked such a dumb question? She should have known better than to bring up Mimah's family.

"If my dad ever tries to show his face here I'll send him packing," Mimah volunteered after a minute. She was staring at the empty bulletin board above her desk, and Dylan noticed that her face seemed pained.

"How about you?" Mimah asked. "Do you ever see your dad?"

"I wish," Dylan sighed. "He still lives in our old apartment in New York. I'm visiting him at half-term, though. I decided last night. Fuck my mom if she tries to stop me." She took a bite of her second biscuit, holding out her palm to stop crumbs spilling on the carpet. "You ever been to New York?"

"Yeah, once when I was ten, but that doesn't really count."

Mimah looked sharply at the dark, wet ring that Dylan's mug had left on her desk. "We all tend to prefer Europe, if you know what I mean."

Dylan wasn't sure who Mimah meant by "we all," but she could guess. Sometimes Mimah slipped up and talked like she and Alice and Tally and Sonia were still friends.

"Why don't you come with me?" Dylan managed a sympathetic-but-not-too-sympathetic voice. "We'll have a blast. I'll show you all the hottest bars and clubs. You'll need a fake ID though. I can help you get one."

"Yeah, maybe." Mimah set down her mug. "I'll think about it. Anyway, let's practice. We've got to get the Man Muncher perfect. If it's not the best thing in the show, it won't work."

She and Dylan cleared a space in the middle of the room and assumed their positions. Mimah clicked the music on and the floor began to shake as the girls pounded out their routine. At the end, breathing hard, they collapsed across the bed.

"Oh my god, we are so ready." Dylan grinned. She scraped back a clump of hair plastered to her forehead. "Do you think people will be surprised?"

"Oh, they'll be surprised all right." Mimah smiled to herself. "You have no idea."

CHAPTER FORTY

This one won't do," Sonia Khan tutted, tossing a black pashmina back into Farah Assadi's face. "Look, there's a hole in it."

"What hole?" Farah rifled through the luxurious material. Not that she really gave a toss. This was the only pashmina she owned, and she hardly ever wore it.

"Right here. How can you miss it?" Sonia demanded, pointing.

It was Saturday morning, and Sonia was sitting at a long table in Tudor House's common room, flanked by Tally and Alice, and taking the final inventory of costumes before tonight's show. She had a pad of paper in front of her, together with dozens of colored pencils, and was marking everything on a chart. It was essential that all the pashminas coordinated, that they didn't repeat any pastel shades too many times, and, above all, that the quality remained impeccable.

"But it's tiny." Farah was squinting at the five-pence-sized gap next to Sonia's curving, red-painted nail. "It's not like anyone'll see it from the audience."

Sonia glared at her. "This is a *fashion* show," she pronounced. "It's not Oxfam." She glanced at Alice with a smirk. "You'll have to borrow one from the general pile."

Farah snatched her wrap. "Power trip," she muttered to no one in particular, barging out the door.

Sonia nudged Alice. "Good riddance. Some people think they're too *alternative* to follow rules. I hate people who pretend they're poor when they've got more cash than the Pope."

"Sone, the Pope doesn't have cash," Tally pointed out.

"Whatever." Sonia had always distrusted Farah, who went out of her way to rebel against her wealthy Persian family—cutting her hair short, wearing loads of rocker-style makeup, and dating flagrantly inappropriate boys. Rumor had it she got one of the men who sold roses at the motorway junction out of London. "He gave me free flowers," she'd apparently told people. "I had to thank him *somehow*." Pretentious slag.

Alice picked up her Diet Coke can and sipped nervously, nodding at what Sonia was saying but hardly listening. She was practically shaking with nerves. Her parents and Tristan were due any minute now.

"Do you think I should have worn a skirt?" Alice leaned across Sonia to Tally, looking down at her drainpipe jeans. She'd paired them with Miu Miu peeptoes and a vintage silk blouse that she'd picked up at One Of A Kind Too in Portobello. "I don't know if this is sexy enough. Do you reckon I should show off my legs?"

"No way." Tally shook her head. "I mean, those Superfines make your ass look fab. Plus, you don't want to seem too available."

Alice nodded. Unavailable. Right. Reaching back, she checked that her crystal-studded hair clip was still holding her half ponytail in place. Her arms looked as tanned as if she'd just walked off the beach. Earlier this morning, she'd snuck out to an appointment at Hasted's one and only spa, where she'd let herself in for the works. Her skin was buffed and sprayed to a smooth honey color, her legs were totally hairless, and her face shone with adorable dewiness thanks to Marla the makeup artist's handiwork.

"Yeah, you look totally hot," Sonia chimed in, determined not to be outdone. "I love your teeth. Did you have them whitened?"

Alice recoiled. "Have you lost the plot? My teeth have looked like this for as long as I've known you."

"Oh." Sonia shrugged. "I guess I never noticed how sparkly they were before."

Tally stifled a guffaw.

"What?"

"*Suck up*," Tally coughed under her breath.

At that moment, Arabella Scott appeared, carrying an armload of bright pashminas, which she dumped onto the table with a grunt. "Here's my haul, girls. I don't care which ones you use."

Sonia perked up, tweaking a hot magenta one from the bottom of the pile. "Oh my god, isn't this the one you wore to the BAFTAs last year?"

Bella shrugged. "I s'pose."

"That. Is. So. Cool." Sonia shivered. "Maybe I should wear it for good luck, as I'm the compère. Hey, have you heard from your dad? Have you spoken to him today? Is he still coming tonight?"

"*Yes.*" Bella rolled her eyes in exasperation. "For the nine-hundredth time, yes. But please don't pester him all night. Sometimes he likes a few hours off."

Sonia looked wounded. She was about to make a retort, when Alice's phone rang.

"Shit. It's them." Alice went white.

"Oooh! Good luck." Tally kissed her on the cheek.

"I fucking need it."

"Be back at six!" Sonia called as Alice swayed on her heels out the door.

CHAPTER FORTY-ONE

There were three people standing under the portico in front of the main school building as Alice walked out, but none of them were her parents. Or her fourteen-year-old brother Hugo. Or Tristan, for that matter. As she approached, she saw a tall blond woman (wearing a skirt that was indecently short for her age) accompanied by a younger girl who seemed vaguely familiar. She also saw a man with graying brown hair swept back to make his already receding hairline look even more catastrophic. Alice stopped abruptly in the shadow of a column, realizing who it was: Victor Dalgleish, from *MindQuest*.

Hang on, that meant these people were . . .

"Hi, Mom," a voice said.

Alice wheeled round. She knew it. Dylan.

"Hi, Dill Pickle!" Dylan's mum was trotting forward on her outrageously high, not to mention outrageously red, stilettos. "You look fabulous. Oh, I wish it wasn't Saturday though, so we could see you in that darling school uniform. Victor was just saying on the way how attractive it is to see schoolgirls in their little skirts. Weren't you, Vic, honey?"

Alice raised her right eyebrow. Was this woman serious?

"I prefer wearing jeans, actually, Mom." Dylan cast a blank look in Victor's direction.

Her mother didn't seem to notice. "What a gorgeous day," she twittered on. "Shall we go straight to lunch, or do you want to give us the grand tour first? Let's do it that way, I'm dying to meet all your friends."

Alice smirked. Friends? She watched Dylan flounder.

Then, driven by some kind of insane impulse—the kind she usually only got when she was tipsy and seeking thrills—she glided out of the shadows and marched over to the group.

"Hello!" she exclaimed, switching on her most charming smile. "I'm Alice Rochester." She extended her hand to Dylan's mother. "It is so lovely to meet you. Dylan's told me all about you." Alice turned to the younger girl. "Are you Dylan's little sister? It's *such* a shame you're not at St. Cecilia's as well. We're like a big, happy family here."

"Well, isn't that delightful." Dylan's mother beamed. "What a polite young woman. I'm Piper." She shook Alice's hand. "And this is Lauren, and Victor."

Alice slipped her arm round Dylan, who was gaping at her in astonishment.

"Where are you taking the old fam for lunch, Dill? I'd suggest that new Thai place in town. It's called The Golden

Elephant, or something terribly exotic like that." She gave a conspiratorial laugh. The others laughed too. She was in her element.

"Uh, yeah, great idea." Dylan knew she should tell the bitch to shove it, but she couldn't help feeling flattered. So this was what it was like to be friends with Alice Rochester. It was intoxicating—even if it was fake.

Suddenly, Dylan's younger sister, Lauren, darted forward over the brick portico. "Hey, look who it is! Dylan told me you were at school near here."

Alice whipped around. Tristan Murray-Middleton was walking up the broad, shallow steps toward them. Her tummy swooped like a plane in turbulence. He was getting closer, his brown hair lifted by the breeze.

"Hey, Al," he said, touching the soft part of her waist as he grazed past. He smelled of warm soap and sunshine from jogging across the fields.

She watched him kiss Lauren and Dylan on both cheeks and then introduce himself, with that devastating poise of his, to Piper and Victor. Alice shivered. T, surrounded by the entire fucking Taylor family—had she just seen into the future?

"Tristan, we're late," she snapped. "We'd better leave."

The little party looked at her. It was like being some kind of outcast. She turned to go.

"Bye, Alice," Dylan said pointedly. "See you later, *sweetie.*"

Alice stopped in her tracks. "Bye," she said through clenched teeth.

254

"Rochester, eh?" Alice heard Victor Dalgleish murmur as she walked off. "Very powerful family. Giant trading firm. Good on you, Dill, you're obviously making the right chums."

"But how do you know that handsome boy?" Dylan's mother whispered loudly. "Who was he?"

"No one."

"Dilly, what are you talking about?" Lauren burst out. "You and Tristan are made for each other. I thought you were going to be together forever."

Alice's father peered at T over the top of his wine list in Le Coq au Vin. Richard Rochester's bushy gray hair and thick eyebrows made him look every bit the intimidating, successful businessman he was.

"Tell me, Tristan, how is that economics class treating you?" he asked in his Oxford-trained voice. "I'm pleased you followed my advice to take it."

T cleared his throat and finished chewing the escargot in his mouth. Alice noticed he had that earnest, slightly guilty look he got whenever he was talking to adults about his future.

She swirled her white-wine spritzer, pretending not to care how he answered.

"Er, yes, economics." Tristan pretended to straighten his napkin. "Actually, I have to say I'm not enjoying it. All those equations are such a slog. I'm thinking of dropping it and doing music instead."

Alice's father laid down his wine list and took a deliberate sip of water, as if to let Tristan's comment hover there for as long as possible, like a fly, before he swatted it. "Music?" Richard said *music* as if it was something stuck to the bottom of his shoe. "I can't see the merit in that. What good is *music* going to do you when you're out in the real world? Your father and I have both told you how important a good background in numbers is for a young man building his career."

"Yes, of course." Tristan nodded, looking down at his plate. He hadn't been hungry to start with, and now he wasn't sure he could face the steak frites he'd ordered as a main course. Plus, there was something else bothering him. Something to do with having seen Alice and Dylan looking so chummy back at St. Cecilia's . . .

Alice couldn't possibly have found out the truth about what had happened in the pub. Could she?

"Luckily for you," Richard Rochester boomed in again, brandishing a forkful of frisee lettuce, "*you* don't have to make a name for yourself. You've already got the Murray-Middleton name, so you're ninety-nine percent there. But do you think anyone's going to respect you if you gallivant about with a banjo?"

"But, Dad," Alice's brother Hugo butted in, "T is absolutely legend at music. You should hear him on guitar. He and a crew of older boys are always sitting round strumming, and some of them are starting a band. Even Mr. Burke says they're good. Isn't that right, T?"

"Really, darling," Alice's mother said reproachfully, "I

hardly think that was your father's point." But she smiled distractedly—Beatrice Rochester never smiled any other way—and brushed Hugo's hair with her ring-stacked fingers. Alice watched them jealously from across the table. Hugo was so obviously her mother's favorite child. Alice suspected it was because he was the only one who resembled her: pale, with yellow hair and brown almond-shaped eyes. He was the only one of the three Rochester offspring who dared to be cheeky in front of their parents.

Their two waiters served everyone's main courses, lifting the silver lids off the dishes. It was that kind of restaurant, which was why Alice's father liked it. Alice picked at her *sole meunière*, unable even to contemplate eating with T sitting next to her. From the moment he'd said hello under the portico until this very second, they hadn't spoken a word to each other. Hugo had done most of the talking in the Merc on the way here. He'd been rabbiting on about some prank he and his pal Rattles had played on their GCSE Chemistry master, and had kept poking Alice with his bony elbow in his excitement.

She glanced at T out of the corner of her eye, across the vast no-man's-land between them. Had it meant something that he'd touched her waist back at school? It must have. Everything people did had a meaning. Maybe it was a signal. Maybe he was trying to show her that he cared more about her than he'd ever care about Dylan and her vulgar family. He'd better. *Together forever*, Dylan's sister had said. Fuck that. She shoved a whole green bean into her mouth.

"Alice," her father said.

"Yes, Daddy?" Alice looked at him innocently.

"How's your A-level English coming along? I read in the *St. Cecilia's Quarterly* that they'd hired in some youngblood to teach. Have you encountered the man?"

"Yes, Daddy, Mr. Logan. Tally and I both have him. He's quite clever. And it's always constructive to have a male perspective in literature, don't you think?"

Richard regarded her proudly. That was his girl, sharp as a tack. "You see," he said, addressing Tristan again, "subjects like English and French and music are all right for women. They're feminine topics, and no one's going to think girls are poofs if they take them. But for men it's quite another thing. *You* can't exactly leave university and get a job in an art gallery, now can you?"

Tristan kept his mouth shut. There was nothing else for it when Alice's father went off on one of his sexist rants. He sneaked a look at Alice—she was jabbing her knife into the pile of fish bones on her plate.

"Well, that was an adequate meal." Richard Rochester said finally, and dabbed his mouth with his linen napkin and smoothed his tie. "I think Beatrice and I will wander round Hasted now; I expect Bea is itching to ogle the shops. God knows why—they have the same crap in London." He chuckled indulgently at his wife.

"Hugo, T, why don't you two walk Alice back to school?

She must have a lot to do if tonight's going to be worth our trip here."

"Sure, Dad." Hugo shoved back his chair.

For the first time during lunch, Alice dared to look fully at Tristan.

"You don't have to come, if you don't want to," she informed him. "I'm perfectly capable of walking back alone."

He turned his chestnut eyes on hers. "Of course I want to," he said.

CHAPTER FORTY-TWO

*T*ristan! Watch this," Hugo yelled. He was pointing toward an impressive-looking haybale in the field that he, Tristan, and Alice were crossing on their way back toward St. Cecilia's. They'd chosen this route to make the most of the mild, sunny afternoon. The sky was only slightly hazy, with a few stubborn streaks of cloud clinging to the top of the dome.

Making sure the others were paying suitable attention, Hugo sprinted toward the hay and, taking a flying leap, sailed over it. He skidded onto his ass.

"He soars, he clears it!" T cheered, breaking into applause. "Nicely done, Roach."

Hugo flung his arms into the air in the shape of a victory V. Nearby, a grazing horse bobbed up its head, mid-chewing, to stare at the commotion.

Normally, Alice would have thrown herself into the action. She'd always loved spending time with Hugo and T, ever since they were toddlers and used to chase each other round the Rochesters' garden in Kensington. It was so endearing, the way Hugo emulated Tristan, and the way T treated Hugo as his equal despite the fact that they were two years apart at Hasted House. Even that nickname, Roach—T had given it to Hugo last year, when Hugo had been so determined to learn to roll perfect joints. These days, he signed all his e-mails that way.

Right now though, all Alice could think about was getting rid of her little brother—a problem, since Hugo wasn't exactly a master of subtlety. He'd never been known to take a hint.

But, with every step they took, they drew nearer to St. Cecilia's—and then Alice's window with Tristan would be shut. She had to do something.

"Hugo!"

Her brother glanced up from the cigarette that he'd begged off of T. "Yeah?"

"Would you do me a favor?" Alice cooed in her most wheedling voice.

"What is it?" Hugo looked at his sister suspiciously. Al had probably forgotten something in the restaurant and wanted him to run back and get it. She was always sweet-talking him into doing annoying stuff like that.

"See those wildflowers over there? I'd so love to have some for my room but I'm afraid of the stinging nettles. Would you pick some for me? Pretty please?"

"No! You're such a *girl*. Get them yourself."

Alice's heart sank.

Then her brother perked up. "Nettles . . . ," he repeated. "Actually, that's a wicked idea. I'm going to collect some for Rattles." He shoved the cigarette back at Tristan.

"Rattles?" T raised his eybrow. "What does *he* want with stinging nettles?"

"Nothing," Hugo said. "That's the whole point. I've got to get even with him for that prank he played last week. Don't wait for me, you two—I'll catch up."

T grinned as Hugo took off for the far side of the field. "I'm fucking glad I'm not fourteen anymore. The lower years at Hasted are so vicious. It's like dog-eat-dog."

"It's worse for girls," Alice said. "They're so much meaner to each other than boys."

"Oh, go on. Look at what Hugo's doing. Can you imagine waking up with a bed full of stinging nettles?"

Alice shrugged. "Some people would probably prefer that," she said.

Playfully, Tristan caught her eye. Then he looked away, suddenly realizing that they were alone for the first time since . . .

Shit. He cast a glance at Hugo, who was now a small dot at least 100 meters away. How the hell had he got into this situation? He was silent for a few steps. Then he cleared his throat. He had to find out if Alice knew.

"So," he said, "I noticed you and Dylan were looking quite pally when I arrived at St. Cecilia's before lunch."

Alice stared straight ahead. Dylan, Dylan, Dylan. Couldn't T ever talk about anything else?

"Are you two friends now?" he asked.

There was something funny about Tristan's tone. Alice bent down to rip a clover from the grass. Maybe he knew this was a stupid conversation.

"Oh, I wouldn't call it *friends* exactly," she said. "I never talk to her. I just felt sorry for her—she was looking so desperate." Alice glanced at T, twisting the clover in her fingers. "It's such a shame that no one's really warmed to her. Though, quite frankly, I can see why. How come you care?"

"Me?" It was all T could do to hide his relief. "I don't care in the slightest. I was just interested in how *you've* been, that's all."

"Oh, I've been brilliant. Totally. Tals and I went to Paris, you know. It was so amazing. Hang on a minute." Alice halted and tossed away her flower. "Do you mind if I lean on you while I take off my shoes? They're such a pain on this grass."

Tristan hesitated. "Er, yeah. Sure." Stiffly, he took a step closer. Alice laid a hand on his taut shoulder, and with the other reached behind herself and slipped off one of her platforms. She did the same with the other.

"Thanks." Without her three-inch heels, her head barely came up to T's chin. But she didn't care. It might mean he could smell her grapefruit-scented shampoo. He'd told her he liked it once, while they were kissing—he'd taken a handful of her hair and let it fall across his face.

The blades of grass felt smooth and clean under Alice's bare feet as she walked. She craned her neck toward the sun, savoring the coolness of the ground and the warmth of the sky.

When she looked down again, Tristan was gazing at her, his face lit by a half smile.

"I forgot how much you like the countryside," he said.

Alice shook her head. "How could you forget? We've been messing about in the country together since we were, like, four years old."

She brushed her toes, their nails sparkling with silver paint, over a cluster of late daisies. "Remember when we used to make chains of these and wear them round the garden as crowns? You were King and I was Queen. I had that pink silk nightgown. And Hugo used to serve us plates of worms he'd dug up." She crouched on the grass and started picking the blossoms.

T laughed, tumbling to the earth next to her. "Now, that I *do* remember." He nodded across the field, to where Hugo was still huddled over a snarl of nettles, stuffing his plastic bag. "Not much has changed."

He observed Alice in profile as she threaded together the flowers: the dark curve of her lips, her thin, rather severe nose, her deep-set eyes charcoaled in by long, delicate lashes. She'd slipped her hair out of its clip and was letting it flow freely about her shoulders. Its luxuriance framed her face.

They sat in silence for what seemed like years. T couldn't think of a word to say.

What did he want?

To do it or not to do it?

Suddenly, Alice turned to him and draped her circle of daisies over his head. "There. King again." Lightly, she touched his chest, straightening the chain.

"Al."

She lifted her eyes, her face right next to his. "Yes?"

"I . . . I wanted to tell you . . ." He leaned in closer.

"T!" Footsteps pounded up next to them. "Why are you wearing that silly daisy chain? You look like a complete dick-head."

Tristan sprang to his feet as if the ground had turned boiling hot.

Hugo was next to them, clutching his nettle collection in one hand and Alice's wildflowers in the other. "Here, Al." He thrust them at her. "Don't let them die."

"It's about *time* you got back," Tristan teased. "We were starting to bed down for the night."

He lifted the daisies over his head and handed them back to Alice. "Keep it."

She watched the two boys walk ahead together, the strand dangling from her fingers.

CHAPTER FORTY-THREE

*M*y god, look at all this," Seb Ogilvy remarked later that evening as he sauntered, wide-eyed, into the theater at St. Cecilia's School. "Someone's made a bloody effort, haven't they?"

"Yeah," George Demetrios chortled. "You!" He pointed at the slim navy suit and skinny striped tie that his friend had put on especially for tonight's event. It was pretty comical. Seb looked like he was at a different party from George, Jasper, Rando, and T, who had all stuck to their habitual uniform of baggy jeans, blazer, and half-tucked button-down shirt.

"Fuck you too," Seb said. He slipped his tiny whisky flask out of his pocket and took a covert sip. The flask had been a present from his father for his sixteenth birthday, and it was engraved with his initials: *SWPO.* Sebastian Winston Patrick Ogilvy. He carried it with him everywhere.

He checked the time on his phone. It was six thirty—half

an hour before the show was due to start—and the theater foyer was packed. Everywhere were chicly dressed parents, somewhat less chicly dressed teachers, freshly scrubbed Hasted House boys, and the St. Cecilia's girls who'd been lucky enough to get tickets in the crush before they sold out. The place looked almost unrecognizable, thanks to Sonia's rather zealous decorating job. Seb pinched the corner of a pashmina that was coiled round a pillar, along with several others. Above it, dozens more pashminas were tacked to the ceiling in waves (or *undulations*, as Sonia referred to them) so that the whole room looked like the inside of a Bedouin tent. Vases of pastel-colored flowers sat atop white tables, which were stacked with fine cheeses and skewered sausages and pâtés and crudités, not to mention champagne and wine, for the reception.

Seb furrowed his forehead. Wasn't this soirée meant to be for charity? Good thing they'd spent so much on the refreshments . . .

Something slapped his hand lightly from behind.

"Naughty boy! Don't touch." Sonia flashed a grin—even though she wasn't joking. *Hic!* she hiccuped. She'd knocked back a couple of vodka tonics with Alice and Tally backstage to combat her nerves, and it had worked.

"Seb, you look gorgeous." She stared at him. He totally did. The navy of his suit complemented his deep blue eyes, and his skinny tie was *so* London cool. It was exactly the kind that stylishly emaciated indie rockers wore. Sonia just knew that the band he and Tristan were launching next month was going to take off. Big time.

"You look . . . beautiful too," Seb said nervously.

"Thanks, Sebby. I have to. It's my night. You know, this whole thing was my idea. I conceived it. The program never lies." Sonia waved hers in his face.

He nodded, drinking her in. She was wearing a thin, shimmery, floor-length gown (she'd bought it at The Cross in Holland Park), that scooped way low at the back—almost to her ass crack—which meant, Seb realized with a tremor, that she wasn't wearing a bra. Her hair, half-pinned up, reminded him of a waterfall. She seemed taller than usual. He looked down. She was wearing the most gigantic shoes he'd ever seen. If they'd been any higher they would have been stilts.

"Sone!" Jasper squeezed her bare shoulders, rocking up with T and Rando. "Not bad, not bad. Like what you've done with the place."

George Demetrios lumbered over and swept in for a kiss on each cheek. "Hot, darling. *Love* the costume."

Sonia narrowed her eyes as she felt his stubble against her skin. Couldn't people even shave when they came to such an elegant event? She cast a disapproving look at the boys' outfits. She'd badly wanted to make the evening black tie, but Miss Sharkreve had insisted that no one would come if she did. "The guests are doing us enough of a favor as it is, traveling all the way here," Sharko had said in that sappy-but-firm voice she liked to use when she was bossing people around.

Favor my ass, Sonia had thought. But she'd settled for smart-casual.

"So," Rando cleared his throat. His eyes were searching the room. "Where are the others?"

"What others?"

"You know, like Alice and . . . people."

His friends snickered.

"They're backstage beautifying themselves, of course," Sonia said. "You can't see the models before the show. It's like not seeing the bride before the wedding. God." She rolled her eyes.

"Okay," Rando said, "no need to—"

"Ooh, I've just seen someone I absolutely must talk to," Sonia cut him off. She pecked Seb's cheek. "Enjoy the pashminas, boys. See you after!"

T elbowed Seb. "*Now* we know why you got so dressed up."

"Aw, is Sebby blushing?" George pinched his cheek.

"No! It's just hot in here." Seb yanked his face away and took another sip of whisky. Why couldn't anyone ever leave him alone? He put the flask back in his pocket, but kept his hand on the lid just in case.

On the other side of the room, Sonia darted through the double doors into the auditorium, trailing her target.

"Hello," she announced, thrusting herself in front of Bella's father, Lucian Scott. He jumped.

"Christ, you scared me. Hello there."

"You probably don't remember me. I'm Sonia Khan, a

friend of Arabella's? I came to your Christmas party last year?"

"Oh, er, yes, of course," the director said. "How lovely to see you."

He clearly hadn't a clue who she was, but Sonia was undeterred. When she was a famous director, she wouldn't remember people either—they'd remember *her*. That was the whole point. There was no way she'd be as fat as Lucian Scott though, she thought, stretching over his stomach to kiss him hello. The man probably hadn't seen his feet in years.

"I was *such* a fan of your last film," she told him. "*Gagging for Love* is really just phenomenal."

"That's very kind. Now, why aren't you backstage with my daughter and the rest of them, preparing for your big performance?"

"Actually," Sonia began, "that's what I wanted to talk to you about. I don't need to be preparing. See, I'm not strictly *in* the show. I *am* the show."

Lucian Scott raised his eyebrows.

"I mean, like, in the sense that I created it," she rushed on. "Directed it. You know, like a director. Duh, what am I saying, of course you know. You are one!" She gave a high-pitched giggle. The director frowned and glanced at his watch.

Sonia nearly slapped herself. This was not coming out right. How was she ever going to launch her career if she couldn't even speak to a fellow auteur?

"Anyway, Lucian, sir, I'm so glad you came." She hoped the

desperation wasn't coming through in her voice. "The thing is, I wanted to ask you . . . Since I'm just starting out and everything, it'd be so helpful to have a professional comment on my work. Would you mind terribly telling me what you think of the show?"

Scott's face softened. "Now, there's initiative," he declared. "I appreciate that in young people. Listen, er, Sarah, why don't we have a talk afterward. If everything goes smoothly, perhaps I can arrange work experience for you on one of my sets."

"Oh, yes!" Sonia nearly hugged him in excitement. She didn't even care that he'd forgotten her name. "Thank you, Lucian. It *will* go smoothly. I know it."

The lights dipped to dim and then back again. The five-minute signal. "Shit!" Sonia squeaked, stiff with fear. "I've got to get to the dressing rooms for my pep talk."

By now, most people were sitting in their seats, waiting, and the mood was anticipatory. Boys and girls were giggling. Parents were double-checking that their cameras worked. Up near the front, Tristan and his crew were staring at the closed curtains, underneath which they could see girls' feet scampering about in a panic.

"Reckon this'll be any good?" Jasper asked T, kicking back.

"Of course. It'll be legend." George leaned across. "Half-naked totty parading about for an hour—how could it not be?"

Someone's mother, sitting in front of him, turned round and cleared her throat disapprovingly.

"I *am* sorry, madam!" Jasper exclaimed, shaking his head. "Please let me apologize for my friend. Language like that is totally unacceptable."

"Precisely, young man. At least someone realizes it."

"I wonder what Dylan will be wearing," Jas continued, dropping his voice. "I meant to tell you, T, I think she's hot. That rack? My god."

"Er, thanks. I think."

Just then, the lights dimmed all the way.

"Woohoo!" someone squealed, followed by laughter.

The first strains of *Vogue* serenaded the auditorium—"Christ, not Madonna," T buried his face in his hands—and slowly, the curtain rose. Thirty girls stood on stage, each frozen in a dramatic pose. They were wearing pashminas in every color of the rainbow, all tied in exactly the same way: knotted at the back and hanging straight like shift dresses at the front. Each girl changed poses sharply in time with the music. Behind them, a video of pashminas waving artistically in the wind was being projected onto the wall. The effect was impressive.

From the audience, the Hasted House boys and St. Cecilia's girls threw out a few catcalls, and the cheering escalated as the dance started in earnest. All the losers and horrible dancers had been banished to the back two rows, thank god, where they were bobbing from side to side and jigging their arms up and down. One of them was actually snapping her fingers, despite Sonia's vehement instructions not to.

The cool girls dominated the front of the stage, twirling and swaying their hips and kicking their legs in the air.

"Phwoar," breathed Jasper, getting several glimpses of underwear.

"I bloody hope they get skimpier than this," George said.

Tally let herself scan the audience as she went in for a shimmy. Fucking terrifying, those 250 expectant faces, their energy rushing up to her. Neither of her parents was here, but she didn't care. Only one person mattered. She was dancing her heart out for him.

Next to her, Alice was staring at the light in the projection box at the back of the theater, forcing herself not to look down. She had to concentrate on the routine. She had to ignore the fact that Tristan was in the audience. If she fucked up, not only would *he* think she was a total fool, but her father would never let it go. Richard Rochester did not condone mistakes.

At the other end of the line, Dylan was throwing in a few flashy moves wherever she could—a superhigh kick, an extra-fast pirouette. This dance was just a warm-up, a piece of cake compared to the Man Muncher. She couldn't wait.

The song ended. Each girl held her position, panting.

So far so good.

CHAPTER FORTY-FOUR

ackstage, Mimah was staking out a corner of the dressing room so that she and Dylan could get their costumes on in private, away from prying eyes. She'd already dragged together three racks of costumes left over from old school plays, and was now positioning them against one wall to form a sort of cubicle. Around her, the dressing room was bustling. In front of the floor-length mirrors, six girls were crisscrossing pashminas over their bras as elegant halter tops, while Farah Assadi, wearing a bright orange pashmina wound round her body, was spraying herself with gold glitter.

Over the speaker system by the door, Mimah could hear The Kills' song "Cheap and Cheerful" playing from the stage, which meant that Alice Rochester, Tally Abbott, Bella Scott, and Zanna Balfour were out there performing their bit. It was just over halfway through the show, and for the past forty minutes, the junior class had been parading along the catwalk in revealing pashmina getups, showing off the dance routines they'd practiced over the past three weeks.

Judging by the applause, the spectacle was going down a treat.

"We did it!" shrieked Bella Scott, bursting into the room hand in hand with Tally, seconds after the music stopped. "I can't believe it."

Alice and Zanna ran in after them. All four were wearing pashminas in various shades of blue and purple, tied as skimpy togas.

"I totally messed up." Tally laughed. "Did you notice?"

"So did I!"

"Obviously! You bloody well nearly knocked me over."

"Quick!" Alice cried. "Where's my peach pashmina? I need to wear it in three songs' time."

"Fuck, fuck, fuck." Zanna giggled. "All I can concentrate on are those Hasted boys in the audience. It's crawling with them." She reached under their pile of clothes and dug up a bottle of Absolut that was by no means full. She screwed off the lid. "This is the only way I'm going out there again."

"Oh yes, please, hand over some of that." Tally swiped the vodka and took a glug. "Hey, Ali." She spilled a bit down her chin. "I spotted your parents. They're right near the front."

"Fantastic, just what I need to hear. *Not*. What was the expression on Daddy's face? Shit!" Alice stumbled over a Marc Jacobs bag that was lying on the floor and nearly fell flat on her face. "What muppet left this lying around? Is it yours, Zanna? It's actually quite nice."

"Umm, that's mine," Dylan spoke, above the clamor. Everyone fell silent as she looked up from the mirror where she'd been tarting herself up. One of her eyelids was covered in sparkly silver eyeshadow.

"Oh really? Yours?" Alice asked, clearly chagrined that she'd paid Dylan a compliment. "Are you trying to sabotage other people so you can be the star of the evening?"

Dylan glared at her. *Are you trying to make up for your little "fake friends" show earlier on?* she wanted to ask.

Instead, she smiled. "I can be the star of the evening without sabotaging anyone," she remarked, "I think you'll find." She felt a small swell of triumph at her wit.

Alice said nothing. She looked surprised that Dylan had dared to talk back.

"Hey, Dill, come on," Mimah called just in time, beckoning toward her lair. "We'll get ready over here." She dropped her voice to a whisper as Dylan squeezed inside. "No need to show those bitches our costumes in advance."

"Damn right. So, did you bring them?"

Mimah winked. She slipped two tiny items of clothing from her gym bag, one red and one white. Dylan unfolded the red one.

"Oh my god! This is too perfect." She held up a minuscule ruffle skirt—so minuscule it would barely cover her ass—and shook it between her fingers. Its layers bounced.

Next, Mimah took out a red pashmina, which she handed to Dylan, and a white one, which she kept for herself. "Let's get ready!"

Dylan shook her head. "I literally can't believe we're doing this dance in front of everyone's parents. And The Trap. Are we totally mental?"

"Yes, but in a good way," Mimah proclaimed. "They're going to adore it."

Over the speaker, the opening hum of Massive Attack's "Hymn of the Big Wheel" started up. Streams of girls pushed out of the dressing room. Clothes-wise, this was the creative climax of the show, with twenty people parading on stage in pashminas tied every conceivable way.

Mimah practically started jumping up and down. "Two songs! We're on in two songs! And 'Big Wheel' doesn't even have a dance in it. It's like the quiet before the storm!"

Dylan grinned. She'd never seen her friend get this excited about anything.

"Okay, chill out and pin this for me." She offered her back to Mimah. Dylan had wound her red pashmina round her boobs and, on the bottom, was wearing only the teeny skirt.

"Hang on," Mimah pointed out. "You've still got your bra on."

"I know." Dylan folded her arms, turning pink. "I don't feel like taking it off."

"But you have to, it looks absurd. Our costume's a boob tube. It's not meant to have bloody straps."

"But I hate not wearing a bra." Dylan gestured at her breasts. "They fly around everywhere. It's so embarrassing."

"Don't be a loser. I'll pin it tight. They won't even move." Dylan looked doubtful.

"The boys'll love it," Mimah prompted. "Tristan's here, isn't he? I thought I saw him."

"I don't care about Tristan anymore."

Mimah dropped her arms at her sides in exasperation. "Look, either we do this properly or we don't do it at all," she snapped. "What was the point in practicing so much if you're going to chicken out now?"

Dylan looked at her. Mimah was already wearing her costume, having somehow managed to pin it without Dylan's help. No straps were sticking out of her tube top.

"Fine," Dylan sighed. "Wait a sec." She squeezed herself between one of the clothes racks and the wall so no one could see, and unhooked her bra. She clutched it in her hand for a second, feeling exposed. Once she dropped it, there was no going back.

The next second, Mimah saw Dylan's Calvin Klein double-D cups hit the floor, and Dylan emerged with the pashmina wrapped round her again.

Good.

"Much better," she said.

"I guess. Make sure you fasten it right."

"Obviously, darling." She felt Mimah messing about with the material. "There."

Dylan reached back and tugged. The pin held firm.

Mimah took a deep breath and put her hands on Dylan's shoulders. "Right, ready?"

"Ready." Dylan's teeth were chattering. She hadn't realized she'd be this nervous.

"Wait a sec," Mimah said, "I've fixed your pin a bit sloppily. Let me just hide it." She fiddled behind Dylan's back for a minute. "All done. Gorgeous."

They walked into the wings, where crowds of juniors were peeping over one another to see onto the stage. "Milkshake" by Kelis was playing. The girls performing were wearing metallic-pink bikini tops from American Apparel, with hot-pink pashminas on the bottom, tied like sarongs. Mimah could hear the boys whooping.

The song was winding up. She and Dylan and Mimah were on next. They pushed their way through the crowd.

"Oh, hang on, sweetie," Mimah said. "I forgot something."

"What did you forget? Want me to come with you?"

"No, it's nothing important. Be right back."

Mimah took a few steps toward the dressing room. Then, as soon as she was out of Dylan's sight, she stopped. She darted over to the group where Alice was standing and pulled a small, folded bit of paper out of her skirt.

"Here." She slipped it into Alice's hands.

"What on *earth* is this?"

"You'll find it interesting, I promise."

Alice cast a suspicious glance at the note, which had her initials on the front. She raised her eyebrows but said nothing.

"Look, I'm going on next," Mimah told her. "Don't open it till we're on stage. *Please.*"

She ran back to Dylan just as the lights went dark.

The audience was roaring. The previous dancers scampered offstage and Mimah and Dylan ran on, assuming their positions. Mimah heard the first notes of their song, "Sexyback," and the lights came up.

"Yeah! Hurrah!" the audience screamed when they saw the girls' costumes. They'd been well warmed up by now, and besides, they knew that the show was almost over, that it was just the finale after this.

In time with each other and with the rapid beats, Dylan and Mimah started gyrating, their bodies fluid yet tense. They took a 360-degree jump in unison, then did a high scissor-kick and slithered all the way down to the floor. Impressed cheers and whistles flew up at them. Their dancing really was a cut above everything else in the show.

"Dylan! Dylan!" Jasper chanted. His friends laughed.

From the wings, Alice glared. She'd momentarily forgotten the note in her hands but now, in a rush, she unfolded it. Her eyes widened.

"From Mimah." She nudged Tally. "Look."

Tally started reading and quickly covered her mouth. "Oh fuck! No way. Do you really think . . . ? Would she actually *do* that to Dylan?" They glued their eyes to the stage, in suspense.

Just then, the spotlight shone onto Dylan. She was obviously about to do a special move.

Preparing to turn three cartwheels down the runway toward the audience, Dylan ran, skipped up onto one foot, and raised her arms in the air. She cast her hands to the ground and kicked her legs above her head—but as she did so, the red pashmina around her boobs started to unravel. Its ends flew out. Dylan didn't notice; the concentration and momentum of the cartwheels kept her going.

Landing at the tip of the catwalk after the third one, she threw her arms above her head in a gymnastic finish.

But something was wrong. The faces nearest to her were gasping and laughing. She flicked her eyes past them. So were all the other faces in the audience. Suddenly, Dylan felt something drop from her waist to the floor. Looking down, she saw what they saw: She was completely topless, her breasts ballooning out for every single person to see. "Fuck!" she screamed, covering her chest with her arms.

At that moment, a torrent of expletives flooded Dylan's ears from backstage.

"Lights!" Sonia was wailing. "Lights, you fucking cretins, lights!"

The theater went black. There would be no finale.

CHAPTER FORTY-FIVE

*T*en minutes later, in the theater foyer, Sonia fought her way through the mob of parents, teachers, and students toward the packed refreshments tables. She kept her head low, trying to attract as little attention as possible—no easy task, in her sparkly evening gown and six-inch stilettos. Passing a stack of unused programs, she cringed. *Entire event conceived and directed by Sonia Khan*: The words sprang out at her from the cover in bold, size-sixteen font. Why, *why* had she put them there? Whose stupid idea had it been? She was about to seize the whole pile and hide them under a stray pashmina when she heard an indignant voice next to her.

"I simply cannot believe you condoned this display of teenage flesh," a woman was saying. "I mean really. Near-nudity and racy dances in front of hundreds of people? Surely it was an accident waiting to happen."

Sonia stole a glance at the speaker. It was someone's mother.

Around her, a group of stony-faced parents were glaring at Mrs. Traphorn.

"Bloody right. Not what I call 'family entertainment,'" chimed in a red-faced man.

"No need to panic," the headmistress responded soothingly. "In our opinion, students learn valuable lessons from experiences like this. But don't worry, action will be taken. I intend to see to it personally."

Sonia ducked past, hoping The Trap wouldn't see her. The shit was clearly going to hit the fan. But that was later. For now, she was only worried about one thing.

"Hey, Bella," she said, joining a group near the food.

"Oh hey, Sone." Arabella Scott twirled a loose strand of hair and went back to drinking her champagne.

Sonia looked round hopefully. "Umm, did your dad enjoy the show?"

Flossy Norstrup-Fitzwilliam and Emilia Charles, who were flanking Bella, cracked up.

"Are you implying Lucian Scott's into topless teenagers?" Emilia snickered.

"Yeah, like he's some kind of pervert?" Flossy added, throwing a sausage into her mouth.

Sonia shot daggers at them. "No, I'm implying that maybe *some* people can see through a tiny mistake and appreciate other things. Like talent. And dedication."

Bella shrugged. "Daddy doesn't have time for that sort of thing. He left five minutes ago."

Sonia's heart sank. "Did he say anything about me? We were talking before the show . . ."

"He didn't say anything about anyone. That's probably the last time he'll come to a school event. He hates amateur nights."

Sonia reddened.

"Hey, Sone," Emilia Charles broke in, nibbling on a piece of Stilton, "do you think you'll be forced to resign as Charity Rep?"

"Ooh, maybe you should resign anyway," Flossy said. "You know, like an apology."

"Don't be ridiculous. I have absolutely nothing to apologize for." Sonia swiped a glass of Pinot off the table and swirled it round, hating Dylan and Mimah more than ever.

Thanks to them, her film career might be over before it had even begun. If they thought she was going to forget about this, they could think again.

"I have never, ever in my life seen anything so hilarious," George Demetrios chuckled, knotting his cashmere scarf round his neck against the brisk air. On the patio outside the theater, he, Alice, Tally, Jasper, and Seb had taken refuge from the throng of parents and were sharing a bottle of wine that they'd finagled from one of the caterers.

"Mate," Jasper said, "seeing those puppies made the whole show worthwhile. That girl's hot. I reckon she needs some loving."

George chortled. "And I suppose you're the love doctor, are you?"

Jasper grinned.

"You boys are repulsive," Alice whined, even though she was secretly reveling in the gossip. "Hey listen, want to hear something even more hilarious?" She left a dramatic pause. "It was no accident that Dylan's top fell off."

"What?" George was so overexcited that flecks of his spit landed on Jasper's blazer.

"Yeah. Mimah rigged it. She did it on purpose."

"No way."

"Want to bet?" Alice dug her fingertips into her jeans pocket—the trousers were too tight for her to fit any more of her hand in there—and produced the note. "See? I mean, *what* a bitch. It's just brilliant."

"Christ," George said. "Genius. Seb, take a look."

But Seb kept quiet.

"Oy. What's your problem?"

"Dunno. Just don't find it funny, I suppose."

Alice glanced at Seb uncomfortably. Something bothered her about his silence, but she wasn't sure what.

"Go on, mate," George protested. "What's not funny about seeing two giant tits on stage?"

"Fine, as long as it was an *accident*," Seb said. "But on purpose? What kind of shit thing is that to do to someone in front of all their family and friends?"

"Dylan doesn't have any friends," Tally snickered. "So it

doesn't matter." She passed the wine to Alice. "Hey, Ali, as if we didn't see enough of Dylan's boobs when they were plastered all over the common room. Right, babe?"

"Totally." But Alice was hardly listening anymore. She pulled her jacket tightly round herself. There was something she needed to do.

"Mom, take me with you. Please, *please*," Dylan begged Piper Taylor. They were standing in St. Cecilia's parking lot next to Victor's red Jag, with its flashy *VIC1* license plate. Dylan hated that stupid thing. Didn't he realize it basically said "Vicki"? Not that now was the time to worry about what a loser her mother's boyfriend was.

"How can I face another day here?" she moaned, tugging on her mom's Chanel suit. "Let me switch schools. Please, let me come back to London."

"Oh, honey, now that's out of the question." Piper shook her head, grasping her black clutch in front of her as if to fend Dylan off. "You just started here three weeks ago. Since when are we a family of quitters?"

Oh, I don't know—since you quit on Dad? Dylan felt like hurling back. She didn't, though. If she said that, her mom might not want her around. She just stared at Piper with tears in her eyes.

"Now come on, sweetie, don't cry," Piper relented. "The people in the audience must have seen it all before." She glanced at Dylan's chest. "I don't know how yours got so huge though, and I ended up with these."

"Mom! Exactly how is that supposed to help?"

The car beeped. Inside, Victor tapped his Rolex and rested his head on his hands like they were a pillow.

What was this, charades?

"Coming, baby," Piper said. She ducked into the leather seat and waved her fingers at Dylan. "Bye bye, Dilly. It was great seeing you. Now cheer up. Go back in there and show them."

The door slammed.

"I already did 'show them,'" Dylan mumbled to herself, striding away as the Jag's red backlights faded like glowing embers into the misty dark. "That's the whole fucking problem."

She walked toward the lit-up theater, but as she drew near, a feeling of dread mired her feet in the grass.

Suddenly, a voice shot out of the darkness. "Dill, is that you?"

"Oh my god. Who's there?"

Jasper von Holstadt was strolling toward her with his hands in his pockets. He cocked his head. "Chill out. So it is you. I hardly recognized you with your clothes on."

"Fuck off," Dylan snapped. "How dare you come out here to laugh at me? Why don't you run off back to your friends? You can all be popular together."

"Hang on a minute, I was only joking." Jasper leaped between Dylan and the path to the Great Lawn. "I barely saw anything at all. No one did. Anyway," he added, "you've got nothing to be ashamed of. Believe me."

Dylan strained to see his face in the moonlight. He wasn't mocking her, as far as she could tell.

"And by the way, I didn't come out here to find you. I was actually wandering off for a smoke. Will you do me the honor?" Like a true English gentleman, Jasper offered her his arm. He was wearing a soft blue blazer that flawlessly suited his tall, well-built frame.

Dylan thought of her room in Tudor, dismal and lonely and stuffed with Sonia's things. Sure, she could go back there to ride out the night in bitterness and rage. Or . . .

"Okay." Tentatively, she rested her hand on Jasper's sleeve.

Maybe, just maybe, her luck was turning.

Alice creaked open a heavy steel door at the back of the theater and ventured outside, careful not to let the overgrown thistles sink their teeth into her jeans. She was standing in a scrubby lot, which was hidden behind shrubs and over-shadowed by the building's fire escape. A line of trash cans lurked nearby.

"Hey," she spoke into the darkness.

"Hey." The figure in front of her, perched on a brick ledge, didn't budge.

Alice felt her way forward. Not having been out here for a while, she couldn't remember where the potholes were.

"Can I bum a cig?" she asked.

Silently, Mimah held out her pack of cigarettes. Alice sprang up next to her and struck a match, listening to the babble of voices inside the theater rise and fall like waves. It was only the girls and teachers left now; the boys had already been escorted back to school. She knew she and Mimah were safe out here, smoking. No one ever came this way except the janitor, as the two of them had discovered to their infinite convenience during GCSE Drama last year.

"So," Alice said at last, looking straight ahead, "that was quite a prank."

"Glad you approve."

There was a pause.

"Did you do it because of me?"

Mimah shrugged. "I didn't do it *because* of you. But I thought you might think it was funny. The juniors needed some spicing up."

"Too right." Alice took a drag. "Anyhow, thanks, babe." She paused. "Go on though, you must have been planning it for ages. How long? And how the hell did you pull it off?"

Mimah winked and tapped the side of her nose. *Wouldn't you like to know.*

They smoked in silence for a minute, getting close to the ends of their cigarettes.

"Hey, Mime," Alice broke in, "are you coming to my cousin Coco's engagement party at half-term?"

"I don't know. Is that the one in Rome?"

"Yep."

"I didn't get the invitation." Mimah's voice was even.

"How weird, it must have been an oversight." Alice picked a dried leaf off her jeans and inspected it between her finger-nails. "Never mind, you're invited now."

Mimah flicked away her cig and hopped down from the ledge. "Then I'll be there," she said.

She turned her back to Alice and headed inside, secretly letting her mouth curl into the same smug shape as the new moon.

Not that Alice would have caught the smile anyway. She was thinking of other things by now.

She sat on the cold bricks for a long time, gazing across the lawn toward Hasted House and stroking, on her wrist, the dried blossoms of the daisy chain that she'd saved from this afternoon. Whatever T had meant to say to her in the fields would have to wait.

But for once Alice could deal with that.

She knew the two of them weren't over yet.

The scandal continues...

TURN THE PAGE FOR
A SNEAK PEEK AT THE NEXT
YOUNG, LOADED, AND FABULOUS NOVEL:

EVERYTHING BUT THE TRUTH
by Kate Kingsley

"Darling!" squealed Sonia Khan as Alice's tall, thorough-bred figure appeared in the viewfinder of her £10,000 digital camcorder. Sonia had been filming the crowd, waiting for her friends to arrive, and now her tiny ski-jump nose—recently redesigned and sculpted by the Khans' celebrated plastic surgeon—crinkled in delight. She'd only seen Alice and Tally a few hours earlier at school, but that didn't count. When their crowd was out partying, the social clock was automatically reset.

"Where *were* you?" Sonia demanded petulantly. "I've been fighting for the past half hour to save our spots." She gestured at the ocean of club-goers that was tossing and heaving her like a dinghy on the waves.

Alice shrugged and inspected their surroundings. Formica's interior more than made up for its lame facade. A cavernous former coffee warehouse, the place had been recently refurbished to look like a party house for hippies with trust funds. The main room had lofty ceilings, giant skylights, and concrete floors spread with woven rugs. Off to the sides, comfy lounging areas were furnished with restored vintage couches and coffee tables. Candles flickered on every surface. Tangled fairy lights and a spidery antique chandelier illuminated a low stage at the back. And, true to the venue's name, a long Formica bar dominated the section of the room nearest the entrance. The place was clearly beneath police radar, too—a few people were daring to smoke indoors, and Tally could definitely smell weed.

In answer to Sonia's question, Tally twirled and shook her butt. "Wardrobe malfunction."

"Oh my god," Sonia tittered, covering her small, heart-shaped mouth with her hand. "I would not go out like that if I were you."

"Well, you're *not* me. Thank god."

"Whatever. Hold my drink, I've got to interview Alice for my music-video-documentary special." Sonia thrust out her cocktail, which was pale green and stuffed to the brim with some kind of vegetable.

"Umm, what the hell is that?" Alice pointed. "A ritual Indian concoction? Did you bring it especially from home? Mummy's favorite recipe?"

"No, it's a cucumber gimlet." Sonia was training her lens on Alice's face, ignoring her friend's barb, as always. "House speciality. Have that one, Ali. I'll buy another. I don't mind."

"Well, I do. Keep that thing away from me."

Sonia peered harder through the lens, trying to hide her hurt expression. Doing favors for Alice Rochester was one of her most cherished hobbies. In fact, it was her only hobby—besides shooting artistic documentaries, and anyway, that was more of a career. Back when Sonia and Alice had both joined St. Cecilia's at age eleven (three years before Tally had been shipped over from Russia), Sonia used to follow her idol round, lugging her satchel to lessons and buying things for her from the cafeteria and agreeing with everything she said. The reason Sonia had done those things wasn't that Alice was the cleverest, or the funniest, or even the most stunning girl at school. It was that Alice was the coolest. And years later, now that they were sixteen, she still was. There was something about her that made everyone crave her approval. Whenever she entered a room, people shut up and listened.

"Right." Sonia put on her professional director's voice. "Action! Hello, I'm here with Alice Rochester. Tell me, Alice, how do you feel about the debut performance of the Paper Bandits? After all, you've known the boys longer than any of us."

"Well, Sonia," Alice said, batting her eyelids at the camera, "I'm very proud of my boys, and I'd like to wish the entire band the absolute best of luck. All my love, Paper Bandits!" She blew a kiss.

"Ooh, Ali, do that again so I can zoom in! It'll be my closing shot."

Tally rolled her eyes. "I hate to butt in, Sone, but aren't documentaries meant to be, like, unposed?" She took a sip of Sonia's gimlet and made a face.

"For your information, there's a difference between *posed* and *refined*." Sonia glared. "Not that you'd know." She swung her camera round to face the stage. "Oh. My. God."

Through her lens, Seb Ogilvy had appeared. He was tuning his bass guitar, his skinny jeans and skinny white cord jacket clinging to his lanky frame. "Fuck. Fuck." Sonia was practically drooling. "He is So. Incredibly. Hot."

"I see you've got over your crush then." Alice snorted.

"Shut up! He might hear. Have you ever seen anyone more gorgeous?"

"Um, yeah—like, every other guy in this room. Come on, it's Seb. How can you fancy him?"

"Al, keep it down," Tally hissed. "He's less than a meter away from us." She shook her head. "I cannot believe the boys are in a band. I mean, what if they turn out to be famous?"

"We'll be their groupies."

"I'll be Seb's groupie anyway," Sonia sighed.

"If you can run fast enough." Tally smirked.

Sonia ignored her. "Hey, Ali, where's Mimah, by the way? She's about to miss everything."

It was true. Jemimah Calthorpe de Vyle-Hanswicke, their other best friend and the fourth member of their crew, hadn't shown up all evening.

Alice shrugged. "She's not coming. Said she had to go to dinner or something."

"Dinner? With who? Everybody's *here*."

"I know. She was being totally cagey."

The lights dimmed.

Seb leapt into place. Tom Randall-Stubbs materialized and perched at the drum kit.

Tally pinched Alice's arm. "Doesn't Rando look professional? *Rando!*" she squealed. Tom Randall-Stubbs jerked up his head, caught sight of Tally, turned bright pink, and dropped his drumsticks.

But Alice didn't notice. She was staring straight ahead, holding her breath.

Where was the one person she'd come to see?

A split second later, her heart went wild. There he was: Tristan Murray-Middleton. His arms were strong and suntanned from captaining the Hasted House rugby team. His face was nervous yet determined beneath his unruly quiff. Tristan looked smoldering at the worst of times, but now that he was onstage Alice hadn't a hope in hell. She traced one of her white peep-toes over the scuffed floor, suddenly back in the Easter holidays last year, when T had first decided to start a band. He'd hauled his guitar to her house one night, and the two of them had stayed up till the sunrise, drinking red wine and making up ridiculous song lyrics and falling over each other with laughter, the way they used to do when Tristan had been nothing more than her oldest, closest friend in the world.

Alice sighed. Things were different now. They'd been different for over a month, ever since the beginning of the term—ever since the night that Tristan had kissed her in secret in the fields between their two schools. The two of them had smoked a joint together and rolled in the grass for ages, breathing in the smell of pot and earth and each other. Alice had fallen for him, harder than she ever had for anyone. But things had quickly gone wrong—and now she was dying to get him back.

Tristan cradled his guitar in his hands.

"Hello, everybody." He spoke tentatively into the microphone. "Thanks for coming. We're the Paper Bandits."

"Woohoo!" someone cheered. Tristan chuckled.

"I'd like to sing a song." He flushed nervously. "Actually, I mean, I'd like to sing a few."

The audience laughed.

"Cute!" Tally mouthed to Alice.

Sonia was staring at Seb, her mouth hanging open.

"It's called," Tristan cleared his throat, "'If This Is Love.'"

Alice stiffened almost imperceptibly between her friends. That title! *She* was the only girl T had ever been in love with—she knew it. He must have written this song for her.

Tristan struck a chord on his guitar and Alice waited, hardly breathing.

> *"Your kisses thawed*
> *My hibernation,*

Your love's beyond
Imagination."

As the lyrics filled the room, a smile broke over Alice's face. Yes. It was true—*beyond imagination*. No one could love Tristan like she did. She'd known him her whole life. They shared everything—all their secrets. All their ambitions. All their insecurities. Everything.

"But you take so much
I don't want to give.
Why can't you just
Live and let live?"

Wait a second . . . that wasn't right. Alice's eyes narrowed as the drums kicked in for the chorus. Tristan rocked his head to the beat.

"If this is love
I'll do without it.
If this is love
I think I'll pass.
I don't want love
No doubt about it.
Thought love was slow
But you're moving too fast.

"No, I don't want love.
I'll do without it.
Your love's iron.
Mine breaks like glass."

The room spun. Alice reached out to steady herself but there was nothing to hold. "You take so much I don't want to give"? "If this is love I think I'll pass"? What the hell were those lyrics supposed to mean? Was this how T felt about her?

"Need some air," Alice muttered to Sonia, swinging on her heel.

There was only one thing for it: to get drunk and forget about everything. But before she could even start, things went downhill. Toward the back of the crowd, Alice's gaze was arrested by a familiar figure. A few meters away, a girl was gyrating to the music, hips undulating, blond hair shining under the spotlights. Alice stared.

What the fuck did Dylan Taylor think she was doing here? That American bitch had a talent for cropping up in inconvenient places. Dylan had burst into Tristan's life over the summer holidays, seducing him while he'd been visiting his uncle in New York. Then she'd followed him back to London, barged into Alice's year at St. Cecilia's, and insisted on flaunting her balloon-sized boobs to anyone who'd look. Thank goodness, Tristan had dumped her. Fine, he'd subsequently dumped Alice, too, but that wasn't the point. The point was, what would it take to make Dylan go away for good?

A swarm of girls was blocking the last few meters to the bar, and Alice began to shove her way through.

"This band is bloody hot," a leggy redhead was squawking in a ridiculous faux-cockney accent.

"Oy, hands off," ordered her mate—a snaggle-toothed blonde. "The lead singer's mine. Ten quid says I can seduce him before midnight. I swear he just winked at me from the stage."

"You lucky bitch, Lulu. Did he really?"

"Yeah. He wanted me. Badly. Ouch!" Lulu yelped, rubbing her rib cage as Alice's elbow landed a particularly good blow.

Just then, a hand seized Alice's shoulder.

"Excuse me!" demanded a posh male voice. "You there! Where do you think you're going? Haven't you ever heard of a queue?"

"Haven't you ever heard of a loser?" Alice wheeled round. Oh shit. The boy she'd just insulted was film-star hot. His deep green eyes flashed from under his cropped brown hair. Sexy stubble softened his manly jaw.

"I didn't mean—," she mumbled.

"Shhh." The boy pressed a finger to his lips. "What's your poison? My treat."

Alice gaped at him. Then she melted into a smile. This might turn out to be her lucky night after all.

KATE KINGSLEY has lived on both sides of the Atlantic, spending time in New York, London, Paris, and Rome— so she's more than qualified to chronicle the jet-set lives of the Young, Loaded, and Fabulous girls.

Kate also writes for magazines such as *GQ* in New York, where she's had the enviable task of interviewing fashion designers like Paul Smith and celebrities like James McAvoy. This is Kate's first novel. She's currently hard at work on her next book about the YL&F crew.

Need a distraction?

Lauren Strasnick

Serena Robar

Amy Belasen & Jacob Osborn

Charity Tahmaseb & Darcy Vance

Teri Brown

Eileen Cook

Niço Medina & Billy Merrell

From Simon Pulse

Published by Simon & Schuster

Even the tabloids
won't tell you the full story. . . .

A new trilogy by Ed Decter

From Simon Pulse
Published by Simon & Schuster

Nothing can stand in their way . . . except their own dark secrets.

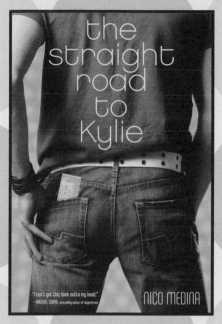
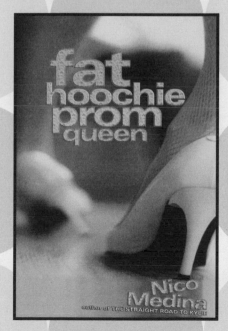

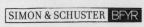

  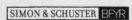